LURED BY LIGHT

ALSO BY BETH BARANY

LURED BY LIGHT

A JANEY MCCALLISTER MYSTERY, BOOK 2

BETH BARANY

FIREWOLF
BOOKS

FIREWOLF BOOKS
771 Kingston Ave., #108
Piedmont, California, 94611
www.firewolfbooks.com

SIGN UP HERE FOR NEW RELEASE NEWS:

http://bethb.net/luredfr

PUBLISHER'S NOTE: This is a work of fiction. Names, characters, places, and incidents are a product of the author's imagination. Locales and public names are sometimes used for atmospheric purposes. Any resemblance to actual people, living or dead, or to businesses, companies, events, institutions, or locales is completely coincidental.

COVER DESIGN by Nada Orlic
BOOK DESIGN by Beth Barany

ISBN: 9781944841287 (ebook)
ISBN: 9781944841317 (print)

To all who yearn to light up the sky like a star.

ONE

Janey McCallister sipped the vermouth she'd been nursing the last hour and pondered the stars in the SkyBar screen viewer. She was lead criminal investigator at Bijoux de L'Étoile, the planet's most luxurious space station hotel-casino, and was off duty. She worried her lip. Mom's new experimental treatment was holding, but for how long? Then her thoughts drifted to *him*. She shut them down.

From where she sat, the view was outstanding. The last guest to use the screen viewer had left it at high magnification centered on the luminous star Rigel—the big, beautiful one at the foot of the Orion constellation. The Orion constellation was actually a nebula—a nursery where stars were born. The most brilliant star in the constellation, Rigel shone achingly bright in the rainbow-speckled starfield, its stark and perfect beauty calling to her. There was no atmosphere between the station's high-powered scopes and the star to mar its brilliance. A perk of being in high Earth orbit, in the fanciest, most exclusive space station turned famous hotel-casino.

Scientists said there was a massive black hole at the center of the Orion Nebula where all matter near it had disappeared.

Just like her love life.

Normally at 10 p.m., she'd be in her quarters, getting ready for bed and chatting with Orlando, flirting while he was on his lunch break in New York, but he'd dropped out of touch about two weeks previous. So there wasn't any point in hanging out in her teeny space waiting on him.

What the Venus hells had happened?

She thought they'd had a pretty good thing going—vid calls nearly every day for two months, sharing stories about their workday—it was almost like he was there with her. He'd made her laugh. He'd listened to her.

They'd met on a case on L'Étoile. An intense, rocky beginning, but then they connected. And how! Like two stars colliding and making something new. Then he was gone. And she didn't know what this new thing between them was… or had been.

Was he okay? Or was he just being a jerk, playing her like she'd thought when they first met? Even though he'd come clean. The subterfuge had been for the case, he'd said. Yet there were layers she didn't know about Orlando Valdez, Sol Unified Planets undercover cop.

Why was she pining after him? She had her friends. She had her mom. She had her interesting job that kept her on her toes. She had the amazing starfield views. If he wasn't reaching out to her, he wasn't worth her time or energy.

The stars held no answers.

Didn't matter. Her life was here at Bijoux de L'Étoile, the hotel-casino space station, the premier experience for those chasing the latest glamorous thrill. And she was paid—and paid well—to preserve the guests' safety, jewels, and reputations. So that's what she'd focus on.

"Take my mind off pointless black holes," she said to Faizah, the bartender on shift. "Let's talk about Kim's surprise party. Help me plan it." Janey was dressed in her casual-chic off-duty outfit—stylish jeans, a faux leather jacket, and a sea-blue silky blouse—preferring those to the jewels, gown, and heels she most often wore when she was on the job watching for card sharks and pickpockets.

Kim Iona's birthday was in three days, and Janey wanted to give her friend something to smile about. She'd seemed down since she'd returned from her quarterly break Earthside but wouldn't tell Janey what was bothering her.

Kim Iona was the security staff office manager. Ten weeks ago, she'd helped Janey out with a challenging murder case. That was when she'd met and clashed with Orlando.

Faizah smiled and gestured for her to hold one moment while she served a guest at the other end of the bar. The elegant older woman she served wore diamond studs in her ears, and if Janey wasn't mistaken, tiny diamonds even decorated the woman's silver hair, which was done up in a coiffed, fancy bun. Her neck was adorned with a diamond choker. Her jewels must be worth at least the value of a major corporation zone. Such wealth could be better used to help those who needed it, not ornamenting some rich maven on a pleasure stay. There were lots of foundations in corporate zones feeding the hungry, and yet people still were hungry. Then again, maybe the woman donated twice that amount to help people in need. Janey tried not to judge.

The silver-haired woman looked familiar, but Jane was off-duty and had no reason to slip into facial rec mode. The woman snagged her cocktail, and at a quick pace, she crossed the bustling casino floor and headed toward the viewing area, where guests clustered to watch the acrobats in their nightly Zero-G show. In her off-the-shoulder silver shimmery evening gown, fit for a ballroom, the woman sat gracefully in a grouping of couches facing the floor-to-ceiling window and applauded dancers in jetpacks and sequined slim-fitting spacesuits. The show was finishing up. In the background, the starscape sparkled through the thick viewscreen windows.

Just another evening living it up in high Earth orbit.

Bijoux de L'Étoile, or L'Étoile for short, shared its orbit with weather satellites, spy satellites, and the space junk robo collectors, and it was anchored to the Earth by StarEl, the staff space elevator, turning as the planet turned.

Faizah came back to Janey's end of the bar, a laugh in her voice. "You're here to bug me because I didn't reply to your comm?" Janey had left her a message a few hours ago.

Janey swiveled back to her friend, who tried to hide her mirth behind a lifted elegant eyebrow.

"You know it." Janey gave her a mock-stern eye. "I want to get this party planned by tomorrow night—not so last-minute. Never know what I might be dealing with." Odd cases pulled her away at all hours.

"Relax a little, *Shigetu*." *Beautiful* in Oromo, the predominant dialect in the Independent Empire of Ethiopia. "You could be dealing with a *who*!" Faizah winked and twirled one of her rainbow ribbons entwined in her braids. A tall Ethiopian beauty, Faizah was dressed as a flamboyant hippie tonight with her faux-leather jumpsuit and colorful ribbons.

"None of that." Janey's heart fluttered. "Haven't heard from him in over two weeks. Thought we had a good vid-pal thing going." Constant contact for eight weeks, almost every night since he left. Her end of the day wrap-up, and his start of the day check-in. That was a relationship. Right?

"You've been brooding here for an hour. Why don't you call him?"

"Did. No answer. Not even a way to leave a message. His comm channel is offline." Janey lifted the glass of clear liquid to Rigel and its nearby supposed black hole. "Here's to my non-existent love life. Not sure why I bother."

"He could be working…"

"I know." Janey finished her drink and sighed. "He could have at least told me he was going undercover. What if …"

"You want another?" Faizah asked sympathetically.

"Want? No. Need? Maybe. But no, that's enough of a nightcap. I have an early start tomorrow." As usual. She stifled a yawn and stared up at Rigel.

Maybe she didn't know Orlando as well as she thought she did. Maybe they weren't colliding stars after all. Just one big black hole.

She rattled her empty drink, ice cubes clinking. Rehashing how he ghosted her wasn't going to solve anything.

Faizah headed down the bar to serve more patrons. The casino was busy as usual during these late evening hours, but it was close to her bedtime. She wanted to be up for an 8 a.m. vid call with Mom to check in on how the doctor's visit went the previous day. Several years ago, Dana McCallister had been diagnosed with Myasthenia Gravis, a rare neuromuscular degenerative illness, and she was on a new round of experimental drugs Janey had high hopes for. But she wasn't getting better.

If this new cocktail of drugs didn't work… She didn't want to go there. She focused back on work. After the morning cal with Dana, she had to prepare for the morning team briefing to get her security team up and running for the day's work.

Except for that murder a couple of months ago, se and her team mostly handled petty theft, cheating at cards and the other casino games, and sorting out staff altercations. She yawned again.

Faizah came back down to her end of the bar. "*Shigetu* —investigations, you're great at, but parties are my domain. Let me plan the party. I'll let Kim know, and we're good to go."

"Don't tell Kim. It's supposed to be a surprise party."

Faizah frowned and rinsed a glass. "Stop with the surprise party approach. Kim hates surprises."

"But she handles them at work so well."

"Which is why she doesn't need any in her private life."

"Makes sense. So what shall we do?"

"How about a picnic in the arboretum?" Faizah asked.

"How about a potluck? Kim loves my mom's cherry pie."

"Perfect! You round up the friends and menu, and I'll clear it with Madge. I was going to check out the teff starters she set up for me."

Madge was chief gardener and managed the wondrous arboretum on the upper levels.

"Does that mean you'll bring your yummy bayenetu?"

Faizah's vegetarian sampler plate on injera bread was delish.

"Absolutely!" Then Faizah headed back to the thirsty guests clamoring for refills and to fill orders from the waitstaff serving the raucous high stakes gambling tables, crowded three people deep.

Janey sipped the last drops of her watery drink and surveyed the busy casino from SkyBar one last time. The swirl of movement around the huge room was like eddies and waves and currents, as random and complex as any natural phenomenon. Men in tuxes or long jackets and women in elegant gowns or chic pantsuits drank as they gambled, laughing and chattering.

She said good-night to Faizah and stood up to go. Just then, from deeper in the casino, a young woman in a short, rainbow-sequined, barely-anything-there dress dashed past the bar. Fear tightened the young woman's mouth, her olive skin splotched red. Her short brown hair flopped in her bloodshot eyes as she pushed through the crowd, saying something Janey couldn't hear above the clamor of the huge room.

The young woman made barely a ripple in the boisterous, game-playing crowd, but Janey noticed her. She was trained to notice anything out of the ordinary, but this was more than different. This was startling. The young woman bore an uncanny resemblance to her best friend, Christine, who'd been dead for over four years now.

Time to intercept and find out why the young woman was in such a hurry and so distressed.

Janey rushed to interrupt the woman's trajectory toward the casino exit.

She strode through the crowd while her ocular implant ran a facial rec and delivered her the woman's name and hotel registration: Amelia Gain. Her check-in date was seven days ago, and her hotel registration and premium room service were paid for by the Eshe Kamal Coffee, a corporate city-state inside of the Independent Empire of Ethiopia. She looked young, no more than twenty-three, but corporate often sent their staff to L'Étoile as a corporate perk or for bonus vacations. And five to ten percent of L'Étoile's guests came from Eshe Kamal Coffee.

Amelia's heart rate accelerated, and her breathing shortened—all details Janey registered in a flash on her ocular implant in her right eye, which scrolled data continuously across the top of her visual field. The young woman was afraid or stressed.

Janey was two arm lengths behind her, then one. Close enough to hear what the young woman was saying under her breath.

"Oh my god, no! No more. I can't... He can't... I won't..." Amelia's words burst out between sobs.

Near the slot machines at the casino entrance, Janey reached out to touch Amelia's shoulder to slow her progress and get her attention. "Can I help you?"

Had this woman been accosted or worse?

Amelia flinched from Janey's outstretched hand and shook her head. Tears streaked her cheeks. "No!" Her strident voice carried above the whine and buzz of jangling slot machines.

Casino guests glanced in their direction, shock and even disapproval on some of their faces.

"I'm security." She showed Amelia the holo of her badge, flashing up from her wrist communicator. "Is something wrong?"

Amelia shook like a leaf in a strong gale and gazed at her as if not comprehending. She glanced over her shoulder, back toward the bar, the poker tables, and the restaurant. Her gaze darted up toward the mezzanine level, where the hotel allowed private and secure meetings in lavishly appointed suites.

Janey didn't see any movement out of the ordinary. No one was on the stairs between the mezzanine and the casino floor.

"Is someone pursuing you?" Janey tried again.

Amelia's lips quivered. The young woman had the same brown-hazel eyes as Christine had, the same lean frame, the same deep sadness in her eyes, and the same yearning for help. It was like Christine was begging for her help. No, that had never actually happened. Janey blinked. In front of her, Amelia Gain pleaded with her eyes, her quivering lip, and heart-aching misery.

In the next moment, apparently no longer able to hold herself up, the young woman collapsed in Janey's arms, babbling hysterically. Janey caught the words, "Hate him. Monster. No more. Can't take it anymore. Got to get away."

Janey wrapped an arm around the young woman's slender shoulders, helped her stand, and hustled her past the noisy, bright slot machines and into the elegant hotel lobby, styled in white and blue-greens to feel like a Mediterranean piazza. Refreshing warm salt air and the calming sounds of waves pulsed through the high-ceilinged space. The space had no effect on the young woman as Amelia sobbed quietly into her shoulder.

Janey was thankful that the round lobby held no other guests. At the welcome desk, Peter Redstone, one of the hotel managers, was on duty. Concerned, he glanced at her.

Janey mouthed, "Back door."

Peter nodded and pressed a button under his counter.

Eight feet ahead and beside the end of the long counter a door was hidden. Seamless to the wall and invisible unless you knew what to look for, a door cracked open in front of Janey. It led directly to a service elevator that would take them three levels down to the security wing. Saved time.

In over three months that Janey had been on the station, she'd found all the shortcuts and secret passages she could. The station maps for the guests didn't show these secret passages, and neither did the station maps for new employees. They were helpful in a pinch, like this one. She wanted to slip away from the front of the house as quickly as possible, in case this woman was in danger. Even if she wasn't, Janey would get to the bottom of this—whatever was happening here. She always did.

"This way," she said, leading Amelia into the secret passage and onto the elevator. Amelia didn't resist. She didn't even seem to pay attention to where she was, as engrossed in her anguish as she was.

Thirty seconds later, Janey guided the young woman out of the elevator and down the gently curving grey corridors of the security wing. Amelia's sobs slowed a little. Her bio-readings were a bit wonky, fluctuating on Janey's readout screen faster than most people's. Understandable given her circumstances.

Then Amelia seemed to come out of her frozen state and wriggled in an attempt to slip out of Janey's arms. "Let go of me!"

Janey let go of the young woman and lifted her hands, palms out.

"Where-where are you taking me?" Amelia gazed about at the grey corridor walls that curved toward what was, for her, a distant unknown.

"It's okay. I won't hurt you. I'm Investigator McCallister, with station security. Remember?" Janey flashed her badge via her wrist holo again.

Amelia peered at her with wide eyes, an unusual violet, her pupils dilated. Could she be on a synth? Drugs flowed freely on L'Étoile.

"Security? Then you-you can help me, right?" Amelia covered her mouth, holding back a sob. "I just-just had to get out of there! He-he... no more. I can't take it anymore." Janey's readings for the young woman flickered for a moment and then showed a slowing and more normal heart rate.

"I can help you if you're in danger." Janey slipped out of her sheep-wool lined leather jacket and wrapped it over the young woman's bare shoulders.

Amelia shivered and drew the jacket closer around her. Janey wrapped an arm around Amelia's shoulders again. "Come on. I'm taking you to a safe place, so we can talk and sort this out. And we'll warm you up."

"Where?"

"To the conference room a few doors down."

"Who's we?"

"Just me and a friend, my colleague, Kim." Janey led Amelia to the conference room around the next curve and palmed the door pad. It unlocked and snicked open with barely a whisper.

"You'll be safe here. It's the security staff wing." Janey led the woman to a cushiony chair at the wide table, near the coffee maker.

Amelia sat and stared at the wall screen, set to a wide expanse of stars, currently highlighting Saturn on one side. The granules of the outer rings sparkled at high magnification. Someone had set the view to Saturn's rings because Janey had her own office and didn't use the conference room much anymore. It had probably been Kim. She knew Janey loved Saturn. All those rings and moons.

Janey sat beside Amelia and asked, "Do you have someplace safe to go?"

Amelia just shivered and rocked in her seat—typically, a self-soothing gesture.

"Water? Coffee? Tea? Something to eat?" Janey popped up and busied herself with getting a glass of water for the young woman.

No response from Amelia. Shock could be setting in or a high was melting off.

Into her wrist comm, Janey waved to medical, requesting a staff member for a full workup. Possible rape victim. She needed to cover all bases.

"I could use some coffee," Janey said quietly. It looked like it would be a long night.

She'd been helpless when Christine went missing. She'd been untrained and hadn't seen any of the signs to indicate her best friend wanted out of their wonderful life. She'd been powerless to do anything to help Christine.

She wasn't powerless anymore.

She had the authority of her lead investigator position and the full support of her investigative team. She'd prevent anything worse from happening to this young woman.

The best thing she'd done for Christine was to find her body when the police couldn't. Though that act was the start of closure, her friend's murder had broken her heart. There was no way in Venus hell she'd ignore the signs and let anything befall this woman in front of her.

TWO

"Here." Janey set the glass of water in front of Amelia. The young woman sipped it without making eye contact. At least she wasn't shivering anymore.

Janey took a seat beside her, the starfield and Saturn over her shoulder, so the young woman could peer into the vastness of space if she needed to. Seeing the stars and planets always helped Janey find her way back to herself. Maybe the view would help the young woman too—whether or not she was a believer.

From the stars, we were born, and to the stars, we shall return.

Janey started with a simple question, even though she had the answer. "What's your name?"

Amelia gazed past her at the viewscreen wall. She wasn't wearing a bracelet identity communicator that served as an all-around computer and holo screen. Some people had embedded identity chips under the skin, instead of bracelets. That must be Amelia's case.

"Then can I take your scan?"

Amelia shook her head, no, and focused on Janey, her pupils back to normal. She spoke, her voice soft and high-pitched like a little girl's. "Amelia Jones." She blinked, looking small, helpless. But her next words belied the childish act. "I'm sure you have access to my hotel registration, if you are really hotel security."

"I am, and I have. Nice to meet you, Amelia. I'm Investigator Janey McCallister. You can call me Janey, okay?" She said *Amelia Jones*, not Amelia Gain as her hotel recorded stated. She'd ask her about that, once the young woman was warmed up a bit more.

Amelia nodded, her hand white-knuckled around the glass of water.

"Can you tell me what happened? Did someone hurt you?"

Amelia glanced at Janey, tears in her eyes. "Can I have that coffee you offered?" Her high voice wobbled. She downed the eight-ounce water in one gulp like it was a shot.

"Sure." Janey got up and busied herself with the coffee. At least the young woman was relaxing and capable of interaction.

She waved a message on her wrist comm to Kim to join her in the conference room. Kim was part of the on-call team tonight and was probably in her quarters taking care of her orchids or designing a new dress—two of her hobbies. It had been a quiet night, until now.

`Delicate case; a woman in distress. Status: unknown. Possible 10-18.`

A 10-18 was an urgent matter. She didn't know if this was one or only a sensitive personal matter. Better to err on the side of urgency.

The coffee percolated, permeating the room with its rich aroma. Mom always started difficult conversations with a fresh cup of coffee with Janey, so that was Janey's habit too.

Janey sat and spoke in a gentle tone. "Do you mind if I record our conversation?"

Amelia shrugged and gripped her hands in her lap.

Janey waved on for the recording device embedded in the conference table and stated her name and rank, then added. "Interviewing Amelia Jones." She turned to the young woman. "Please state your consent, Amelia, for the record."

Amelia sighed as if it was a great effort to speak. "You have my consent to record, Investigator."

"Thank you." She didn't want to rely on her implant. It always recorded everything but was for private use only. Not for court use. If there was even a case here. That was what she needed to find out. "Amelia, did someone hurt you physically?"

The young woman blanched and wouldn't meet her gaze.

"Who? Amelia, if someone here hurt you, we can arrest and hold them."

No reply.

"Okay, we'll start with something easier. Where are you from?"

"Granton SF," Amelia said in a small voice.

Granton SF was one of the many Granton zones on, around, and off-planet. This one was in the San Francisco area on the North American Pacific coast. One of the forms of self-governance in the Sol, Grantons were universal basic income zones, where all your needs were met, and you only worked if you wanted to—for fun, fulfillment, and the extra income. Janey knew the Granton SF well.

"I lived there for ten years. In the Marina District.

How about you?" Janey smiled at Amelia, but the kindness was lost on her. Amelia was staring at the viewscreen again. Janey gave her a minute, allowing a chance to respond and tell her which neighborhood she was from. A chance to reminisce.

Granton San Francisco was where she had met Christine during her first semester of college. They were both studying to be high school teachers—Janey in science and engineering, and Christine in English and communications. They'd both been so optimistic at the innocent age of eighteen, the whole world open before them like an orchard of ripe fruit.

And that was where Christine died when they were both twenty-eight. Their whole lives still in front of them. That was four years ago. Then Janey's life had taken an abrupt left turn, and she'd left the Granton and hadn't been back since.

Amelia didn't speak, didn't share any kinship with her about the vibrant, shining city by the bay where life had been fun and breezy, just like the weather. So Janey dove in. "Your hotel record says your last name is Gain, not Jones. Why is there a difference?"

The young woman's eyes widened in fear. Her vitals fluctuated for a moment into panic, then leveled out. She shook her head. "I don't know. A mistake, I guess."

"I can check the records, but why don't you start from the beginning? Tell me when you arrived on the station."

"A week ago." Amelia hugged herself.

"Good. That's what our records say. At least that jives." Janey smiled.

Amelia did not.

"Amelia, I'd like to scan your identity chip for a complete ID and bring medical here to examine you.

Make sure everything is okay. All right? I need your permission for both."

Every guest knew their personal privacy was guarded on L'Étoile—not shared with the rest of the Sol-wide 'net —so Janey needed Amelia's official consent to dig into her personal records and run a medical scan. But the young woman hadn't expressly given it, yet. Either she was too much in shock, or she was more calculating than she led Janey to believe.

"Is that coffee ready?" Amelia didn't break her gaze from the view of the stars on the screen.

"It is." A pause in the interview was in order to give the young woman more time. There was no need to pressure her, and the hot beverage would warm them both up.

Janey bustled to the counter to serve them steaming cups of java, the best the station had to offer, straight from Chef Gina Gutierrez's six-star restaurant.

Janey carried a small tray to the table. "Cream?"

"Yes, please." Amelia gripped the cup as Janey poured in cream.

Janey took hers black at this hour. She wanted to feel the jolt of caffeine more directly. She sat. The young woman sipped the hot coffee, head down, looking small in Janey's jacket.

The door beeped, and then her comm vibrated against her skin, signaling a staff request. It was from Chef Medical Officer Tseng announcing herself. Janey unlocked the door from the table screen.

The doctor entered with one assistant, Alison Horsely, trailing her. Janey held up a hand to halt their approach. They stood at a respectful distance by the end of the table.

"Amelia, the doctor is here to check you out, make sure everything is okay. Is that all right with you?"

Amelia said nothing and peered into her coffee.

"We could go to medical, through the staff lift. Or stay here. We have a small break room just behind that wall." Janey pointed to the wall opposite and then glanced at Tseng. Tseng nodded assent. "Either way, I'll be with you if you want."

"Yes, please. Here's fine." Amelia stood.

Janey led them to the break room. A sliding door embedded in the conference room wall slid open without a sound to reveal a small area, outfitted with a bed against one wall, a couch long enough to sleep on, and a washroom opposite that. The room was for cat naps when one of the security team didn't want to use their quarters, or for the occasional guest who wouldn't or couldn't go to medical or a holding cell. The wall screen had been left to a melodic piano lullaby with an abstract holo vid in blues and greens, undulating like waves in time to the soothing music.

Janey held Amelia's hand while the doctor performed a medical exam and took a sexual assault forensic exam, also known as a rape kit. The young woman was quiet and cooperative. With her specialized handheld scanner, Alison unobtrusively inspected Amelia's clothing and body.

After telling Amelia she was done, the doctor stepped out to confer with her assistant. Janey helped Amelia to her feet, gave her a moment of privacy in the washroom to get dressed, and led her back into the conference room. Though the young woman had more color to her cheeks and looked less glassy-eyed, she was quiet, subdued as if curled up into herself like a young fern.

"Why don't you sit again?" Janey said.

Amelia did, her back to the doctors and the rest of the room, and faced the viewscreen of stars again.

Kim entered the conference room.

Tseng approached Janey, a quizzical look on her face, and said, "Can I talk to you privately?"

Janey glanced at Kim. Kim nodded, understanding that Janey wanted her to keep an eye on the young woman. Janey stepped away to confer with the doctor.

"There's no evidence of a rape," the doctor said. "But there has been recent sexual activity, though there's no trace of anyone else's DNA on her. She probably—"

"Washed."

"Or had protected sex." The doctor nodded. "Other than that, she's in good health. No evidence of physical abuse. I'd like to run a full tox panel. She shows some signs of recent drug use. Did you get her official okay on that?"

"Not yet." Janey eyed Amelia seated at the table, hunched over the coffee.

"I'll wait," Tseng said.

"Thank you," Janey said and returned to the young woman.

Kim was sitting in Janey's seat, but she stood as Janey approached.

"Has she said anything?" Janey asked softly.

Kim shook her head, concerned.

The physical exam yielded no evidence of the rape Amelia alluded to. There was no good reason to protect her. But Janey couldn't let this young woman back out there where something bad could happen to her, irrational though it was. There had to be a legal way to house her for at least a day until she found out what was going on.

"Amelia, do you know what the doctor found?" Janey asked.

Amelia said nothing.

"I want to help you, I do, but…"

Amelia sighed, world-weary, and glanced at Janey. "But what?"

"There's no evidence that you were sexually assaulted. Can you tell me what happened tonight?"

Amelia went back to looking at the stars, but not before Janey caught a glimpse of tears.

"If you tell us who hurt you, maybe I can get some evidence."

Amelia shook her head and wiped her cheeks.

"No, you can't tell us, or no one hurt you?"

Amelia didn't move.

Janey stood, a heaviness on her chest.

Amelia turned back to her. "I was hurt. By him."

"Him, who?"

Amelia gazed up with mournful, wet eyes and shook her head. For a second, it was as if Christine peered at her through Janey's haunted dreams.

Janey sat down, heavily. "There may be a way I can protect you, for a little while. I need your express permission, verbal and palm, to access your complete personal records."

"Why?" the young woman's voice squeaked.

"I told you. To find a way to protect you. Find out what's going on." On the table screen, she called up the form for Amelia to impress her palm print upon. "Your consent will also allow the doctor to test you for drugs with a small blood sample."

Amelia sighed again, brushed one last tear from her cheek, and glanced at the screen on the table, a look of resignation in her eyes. After a beat, Amelia pressed her palm to the form.

"For the voice consent, please say you agree."

Amelia sighed, shrugged, then nodded.

"Out loud, please," Janey prompted.

"I agree," the young woman said in that small voice.

The doctor's assistant, Alison, efficiently drew blood from Amelia's arm. Then the doctor waved good-bye and stepped out of the room, her assistant right behind her.

Kim set steamy cups down in front of them, a generous amount of cream in Amelia's cup. Then she pulled up another chair and sat with them, completing the triangle, a quiet, calm presence as if they were all in this together.

Amelia sipped her coffee, head down.

"You mention a 'him,'" Janey said. "Can you tell us who he is?"

Amelia's vitals flip-flopped—heart rate up, respiration shortened, and blood rushing to her center mass—all signs of fear or anger.

Janey needed to try something else.

"Amelia, where were you in the casino before I caught up to you?"

Amelia stared at her coffee.

"One of the private suites on the mezzanine?" Janey guessed.

Amelia darted her gaze up at Janey, breathing short, her heart rate still elevated.

Bingo.

"Which one?"

Amelia shook her head. "I don't know."

"Describe it to me."

She shrugged. "Rugs and lots of pillows, reds and blues."

Each suite was designed in a theme, but house-keeping remodeled the suites often, and Janey didn't keep up with their latest décor changes. But it was a lead. Better than nothing.

Amelia shoved her cup aside, spilling coffee on the table, and reached out with both hands to Janey's arm, squeezing hard. "Please, you have to give me sanctuary. You have to. I can't stand it anymore."

"You want to disappear? Change your identity? Leave your life?" Jane asked. Receiving sanctuary was a big deal in a world where everyone was tracked for taxation, health, and profit, depending on where you lived. Amelia wanted to become untrackable from her corporate-state. Not an easy thing to do without resources and help.

Kim nodded as if knowing where the conversation was going.

"Yes," Amelia said in her small voice.

"From who, Amelia? What happened? Who do you want to get away from? You need to give us a name. Someone from work, from Eshe Kamal Coffee, perhaps?" Janey glanced over at Kim, who got the message.

Kim waved in rapid gestures into her comm. Data appeared on Janey's. With a flick of her wrist, like brushing aside an errant bug, Janey waved open her comm's holo screen and read. No one else from Eshe Kamal Coffee was currently onboard L'Étoile. So no one to easily talk to without making a vid call. Kim also sent over the quick and dirty details on the company.

Eshe Kamal Coffee was an agricultural corporate city-state based inside the Independent Empire of Ethiopia. The corporate entity controlled a massive vertical chain of coffee growers, distributors, and sellers across the Sol, with over five hundred million citizens. They were one of the biggest players of this coveted, expensive, and high-demand commodity. It wouldn't be easy to disappear from their bottomless resources and controlling long arm. Coffee conglomerates were almost as wealthy and influential as the asteroid mining groups.

"Who?" Janey prompted. "Who do you want to disappear from?"

"From the ones who kidnapped me." Amelia's vitals flickered on and off on Janey's screen as if there was a malfunction, then they snapped back in place, clearly on the scared spectrum. The young woman tightened her grip on Janey's arm. "I need sanctuary. Now. Please." Then she sat back as if exhausted. "Or they will kill me."

THREE

"Who, Amelia? *Who* is trying to kill you?" Janey asked. "You need to tell us if you want us to help you apply for sanctuary."

Amelia paled and shook her head.

"I can't promise you sanctuary, not until we have substantial cause. You need to tell us more," Janey said. "Who kidnapped you? Who is trying to kill you?"

Amelia's lip quivered, and tears formed at the corner of her eyes. "What do you mean substantial cause? I just thought I could request sanctuary and it was done. Doesn't the law—"

"We can only act with just cause. I need more information, Amelia," Janey said. She wanted to take this woman's word for it, but she still needed to do her job.

Amelia slipped down in her seat, shrinking inside Janey's coat as if she wanted to disappear.

"Amelia, any detail will help. We can protect you, but we need to know more," Janey said.

"The sooner you tell us, the sooner you can start your new life," Kim said earnestly, hopefully, as if she knew what was entailed in the process. Maybe she did. One of the first employees on board when the hotel opened almost ten years ago, Kim never talked about her past before working on L'Étoile.

Amelia peered up at her, imploring, haunted, and Janey's heart's clenched.

Christine's unseeing eyes—the way Janey had found her.

She had a chance to protect this young woman in a way she'd never been able to with Christine. She hadn't even seen the signs with Christine. Maybe if she had, she could have done something—helped her friend, got her help. Something. Anything.

"It's late. Maybe after some rest..." Janey said to Amelia, then she turned to Kim, who radiated hope with her steady, calming presence. "Can you find a room for her?"

Kim nodded. "Of course. It's done." Then she turned and said to Amelia. "Amelia, come with me. I'll take care of you. I'm Kim Iona, the office manager and back-of-the-house mom. Let's get you into some cozy clothes and settled in bed." Janey suppressed a yawn. It was nearly midnight.

Amelia eyed Kim and then Janey, unsure, withdrawn, and suspicious.

"Kim is my friend," Janey said. "I trust her with my life. Plus, she makes sure I get paid." Her joke didn't get a reaction. Sometimes humor could break the ice, warm up a suspect, create a human connection, but not tonight.

Amelia loosened her grip on Janey's arm, tentative. "Okay," she said in her high little-girl voice.

When Kim came around the table, Amelia stood and handed the jacket back to Janey. "Thank you."

Her voice was firmer as if she was coming back to herself.

Janey took her coat back without a word. Her shoulders hunched and her gaze downward, Amelia let Kim lead her out of the conference room. Janey cleaned up the coffee cups, giving her a chance to sift through what she knew and settle on her next steps, even though housekeeping would pass through the room in a few hours. When she was done with the cleaning, she sat at the end of the table, tipped her chair back to kick up the footrest, and admired Saturn on the wall screen.

She'd seen a lot of petty crime on the station since arriving three-plus months previous, but she'd never caught a rape case, supposed rape case, or a kidnapping. She didn't want to doubt Amelia's word, yet there was no DNA evidence, no names, and no one to arrest. She couldn't dismiss her claim though. Everyone deserved a chance at happiness.

She'd gotten Amelia's permission to push past the privacy firewall, so she tapped into the young woman's records and couldn't find anything beyond what Kim had sent her. She indeed had come aboard the station seven days ago, her full passage—hotel, food, and round-trip transportation aboard the daily space jetliner—paid for by Eshe Kamal Coffee.

Amelia was listed as a sales associate at Eshe Kamal Coffee, was twenty-three years old, and was the only one in her party. She was a citizen of Eshe Kamal Coffee, based in Addis Ababa, and had been for four years. No mention of her prior citizenship of the San Francisco Granton—if that story was even true. That was odd. Perhaps a clerical error, as people's citizenship back to birth was usually in their record. She could call the records department at the SF Granton, but that wouldn't help with Amelia's current situation. Plus, the records office could only confirm or not. They never noted why someone left the Granton. Not helpful in Janey's current line of inquiry.

What brought Amelia to L'Étoile? Had she hooked up with someone here, and had that led her to her current troubles? Or perhaps she'd gotten into trouble before she arrived?

Since her room and board was paid for, she could have come on board as a reward or a bonus for excellent sales. Amelia seemed young for a sales associate position, but some people found that kind of life exciting and pursued the ambitious global corporate life. Yet, Amelia hadn't seemed full of ambition. She'd been scared, cowed, and cagey.

To double-check Kim's initial quick search, Janey searched the guest list for anyone with the same company but found no one. In her time on L'Étoile, she'd observed that guests came to the station for a few primary reasons: to party, to relax with their friends, to drink and gamble, and to go back home and brag about their exploits. Amelia may have come to party and things went horribly sideways.

Maybe Amelia had arrived with other young people. Janey next called up the list of all the guests who'd arrived around the same time as Amelia. Space jets arrived once or twice a day—usually, one in the morning and one in the evening—and each carried anywhere from one hundred to two hundred passengers. But she didn't find other twenty-somethings on the list of arrivals on Amelia's jet that departed out of Spaceport Tokyo or from the one out of Spaceport Las Cruces, Janey's hometown.

She'd grown up in the spaceport's shadow, but she

had dreamed not just of travel but of exploration. She'd dreamed of working at Titan station and studying the rings of Saturn, up close and personal. But all that changed when she'd had her eye accident at thirteen, and her whole life had upended.

Janey turned her thoughts back to the case. Amelia indicated she'd been in one of the private suites above the casino and restaurant. Janey called up the bookings for those suites.

Some of the suites were booked, but the reservation identities were masked—as was protocol. Without knowing who she was looking for, she couldn't snoop past the firewalls without earning the wrath and demerits on her record from the chief—and probably a report to the big boss. She couldn't afford that. In her first month here, she'd earned two demerits and had been facing a three-strikes-and-you're-out scenario. Even though she'd righted that almost wreck by solving a tricky theft and subsequent high profile murder, she couldn't afford to get on the bad side of her employer. Mom relied on her paycheck for the expensive new experimental treatment. That seemed to be working for now, thank the stars.

She *could* cull through hallway vid feeds around the time Amelia fled that area, but again, without knowing who she was looking for—needle in the proverbial haystack.

Still, it was worth a try. She called up the vid feed and reviewed it for the hour before she met Amelia at four times the speed. Amelia burst out of one of the mezzanine suites a few minutes before Janey had spotted her racing past the blackjack tables. Confirmed. She ran the vid forward at the increased speed but no movements stood out.

Next, to establish a timeline for Amelia, Janey sped up to eight times the speed to review the previous two hours before that. A lot of people zipped by on the mezzanine hallway and went up and down the stairs that flickered all colors of the rainbow. Servers entered and left the suite.

But still no arrival of Amelia or anyone else into the suite. When did Amelia arrive, and who else was in there? She reviewed the previous two hours and still no movement. She'd just spent forty-five minutes and was none the wiser. Time to go for the straightforward approach to find who Amelia was running from. She needed some help though.

She commed Soren Stinson, the lab and crime scene tech she worked with most often. Good thing he was on call.

Like firefighters, security staff worked twenty-four hours on call, then forty-eight hours off, then regular hours, which were rarely regular, with odd days off in between the long and the short shifts. Good thing leave was every six months for a month at a time. She was looking forward to spending some quality time with Mom.

"Janey, good starlight to ya," he greeted her with his usual chipper self.

"Good starlight to you, too," Janey said in a sober tone. "I have a room sweep job for you. It's a new case. A delicate one."

"Oh boy!"

"Soren, this is a possible rape case."

"Oh, I'm sorry. That sucks. What and where?"

"I need you to sweep the unoccupied mezzanine suites for any biosignatures, traces, and anything along the electrical and visual spectrum. As broad a sweep as you can, but I'm especially interested in one person's DNA. I'll send it to you along with the rooms I want you to search."

"And the occupied suites?"

"I'm going in as room service."

"Okay. Do I have time to wrap up a game in the commissary? I just need ten minutes."

"No. Duty calls."

"Yes, ma'am. Oh, Janey—" Then Soren's voice dropped out as if the call was cut.

"What's that, Soren? Say again," Janey said impatiently.

"Someone said they saw Orlando in the casino tonight."

What the Venus hells?

"Who said that?" Janey clenched her jaw. Why, that low down—he was on L'Étoile and didn't even tell her. And she'd been at SkyBar for an hour. Had he seen her and not even said hello?

"Not sure when. Ed was fixing one of the roulette tables. Forget I said anything. Sorry. On my way. Soren out." He commed off before she could say anything else.

Eduard Kou was one of the security team and on duty as a table mechanic since he loved to tinker. When had he spotted Orlando? If Orlando was here on a job, he'd be under an alias and undercover. He'd be impossible to ferret out until she was standing right in front of him. *Venus hells!* Work and love were too complicated to exist together in her life, clearly. She was better off without him.

She left the conference room and headed for her quarters. Time to follow up on this lead before whoever was in the booked suites left—if indeed someone was still in there. It was 12:45 a.m. The casino would be full and in rowdy mode. She'd hardly be noticed. Perfect.

Five minutes later, Janey entered the casino, dressed in a low-cut black top and short skirt, white apron, black tights that showed off her long legs, and black heels with wide soles. Sexy enough to call attention to her assets, yet sensible enough to maneuver through the kitchen, the poker and craps tables, and private casino suites. Heavy makeup completed the ensemble, thick red lipstick, dramatic eye shadow heavy on the sparkles as was the latest fashion, and eyelash extensions also lightly sparkled. She sported her favorite brunette bob-cut wig that hid her shoulder-length blonde hair.

The big boss, Frederick Schoeneman, wanted the security team to either be dressed down as serving staff or dressed up as guests when they worked the casino floor and in other guest areas of the hotel. He wanted L'Étoile guests to feel like they were in a paradise amongst the stars, not in a guarded enclave.

Janey carried a tray and a towel on her wrist as if she'd just come from dropping off food in a client's suite. She entered the casino, made a beeline for SkyBar, and set her tray at the end.

Faizah was still on duty and came over with a few drinks. Janey had commed her when she was getting dressed and had placed an order, in preparation for her undercover op.

Janey expertly set the drinks in the center of the tray, nodded at Faizah, and headed for the stairs. A twenty-foot-high wall of live succulents cascaded from the mezzanine to the floor and hid the stairs from view, unless you knew they were there.

A tinkling laugh rang out from near the poker tables. Janey glanced over and saw the silver-haired diamond-adorned older woman from earlier in the evening, smiling coquettishly and making eyes at a man. The man had a thick, curly mane of dark brown hair and broad shoulders. Just like Orlando's. Even though she could only see the back of the man's head and shoulders, she faltered in her first step on the stairs, spilling the alcohol a bit onto the tray. Couldn't be him, could it?

Mind on the job, McCallister.

She took the stairs in quick steps and spilled no more of the drinks.

She had three suites to check. Time to get to work.

At the first suite at the end of the walkway, a bald skinny man answered the door dressed in blue flower-patterned kimono, a confused look on his face. "Yes?"

"Oh, hi." Janey flipped her short bob out her eyes. "An order's come in for Amelia. Rob Roy and a Christmas martini." The man's hotel record blipped onto the corner of her implant screen, but she didn't read it. It was his reaction she wanted.

The man gave her the once over, frowned as if she was found wanting, and didn't show any recognition at Amelia's name. "I didn't place the order."

"Sorry."

"Not me. No thanks." He stepped back and let the door slide shut in her face.

At the second door, a woman of indeterminate age answered, sparkles all over her long black face, round hair, and pink princess ball gown.

"Ooh, more! Only two?" She reached for the drinks.

"Did you order these, miss?" Janey hauled the tray out of reach. "Amelia ordered them."

The woman giggled. "No. We don't know an Amelia, do we, girls?" She called over her shoulder at her friends to see if anyone had ordered the drinks. The women laughed and denied it, but said they'd take them anyway if she was offering.

"I need to get these to the rightful owners," Janey said and moved away from the door, with drinks still perched on the tray. The door glided shut soundlessly. More idents populated her implant screen for her to review later if she needed to. She didn't need to right now.

She had one more door to check. Where was Soren? Hopefully, he'd come up via the service elevator at the end of the mezzanine walkway, hidden behind a mini screen of banana plants, and was sweeping for trace in one of the three empty suites as she'd ordered. She just couldn't comm him and get an update without breaking cover. She wasn't about to do that. Not when she had one more door to check.

She tracked in front of the door of the third occupied suite. Though she couldn't hear it, the entry chimed automatically, so the occupants inside would know she was there.

A fit middle-aged man opened the door, dressed in a marine blue button-down silk shirt and grey slacks. The two top buttons were unbuttoned. "Yes?" He was fit and tanned, with a full head of blond-brown short-cropped hair.

The ident popped. She ignored it to focus on the man in front of her.

"Room service. Did you order a Rob Roy and a Christmas martini?" She pitched her voice higher than her usual alto.

"I didn't, but maybe"—he scanned her short skirt and low-cut top—"you're just what I ordered. Such service." He winked at her.

Janey wanted to slap him, but not until she got inside

the room and drew her badge. No, she wouldn't slap him. She was a professional. First, she needed to confirm she was in the right place.

"Actually, Amelia ordered these, and I was told to make sure she got these personally."

The man made a sad face that seemed a bit fake but also confused. "Amelia was here, but she left in a huff hours ago."

"Maybe she'll come back, and I can leave these for her." Janey gave the man a small smile and glanced at him under her lashes.

The man grinned and waved her in. He returned to sit on the plush couch with red and blue tasseled cushions atop a velvet brown couch. Amelia had mentioned the red and blue cushions.

Janey placed the tray on a low table, bending over to be sure to give the man a good look-see of her assets.

She straightened and smiled sweetly. "May I get your ident for room service?"

"Of course." He showed her the inside of his wrist for her to scan, letting her debit his account.

"Thank you." Janey waved her holo screen over his embedded identity chip, pulling credits like any waitress, then adjusted her device to scan on all spectrums. Unlike a normal waitress. She was looking for any and all heat signatures over the last few hours. She made a show out of reading her holo, then said in a high voice, "Mr. Haverhill?"

Residual heat signatures of at least two bodies over the last six hours. The ident and her ocular screen readout confirmed his name.

"It's Jonas Haverhill, the Third. Mr. Haverhill was my father." He stared at her legs. "But you can call me Jonas."

"What happened to Amelia? She's missing her drink." Janey kept her eyes wide and hopefully innocent. She glanced around the lavishly appointed suite, done up in an elaborate Turkish style, red and blue rug weavings interspersed on the walls, thick rug on the floor that you could sink into, low true-leather chairs, and lots of ruby red and royal dark blue cushions and wide brown velour couches. Nothing looked disrupted. The suite contained a bathroom and small kitchen, but there was no bedroom. The suites were mainly used for private meetings and parties.

Haverhill waved a hand. "My girlfriend has a flair for the dramatic. She just got some upsetting news from back home. She'll be fine." He ogled at her cleavage. "If you want to wait, I'm sure she'll be happy to join us."

"On duty. Sorry." She hustled to the door; it door slid open. She'd had enough and gathered what she needed.

"Miss?"

She glanced over her shoulder.

"If you want to earn some extra credits…"

Janey laughed and stepped out of the suite. No thanks, buster.

Fraternizing with the guests was against the rules. All guests and staff knew that, but he certainly didn't act like he knew. Or he didn't care about the rules. The extremely wealthy often acted with impunity. Media reports were full of such behavior. Whether or not Haverhill was the one who abused Amelia, Janey disliked him already. Time to discover who this Haverhill was and get an angle on him before bringing him in for questioning.

FOUR

Janey hustled down the mezzanine hall, considering her next move. She needed to look into Haverhill and uncover his connections to Amelia. The man clearly knew the young woman. Was he the one involved in her kidnapping? She had nothing to go on.

She'd have Soren check her room scans because nothing unusual popped. His lab instruments were more refined than what she programmed into her wrist comm. Where was Soren anyway? She waved into her comm, requesting an update. He didn't pick up. He must be in the middle of his scans in one of the three empty mezzanine-level rooms.

Something wasn't sitting right about Haverhill, other than him being an objectifier of women and that he made her skin crawl.

She hadn't notified Chief Milano about Amelia's case. Milano wouldn't want to be woken up after midnight for a young woman's unsubstantiated kidnapping.

So far, though, Janey had no evidence to corroborate the young woman's story. She needed hard evidence to safeguard the young woman, go after whoever was responsible, and to start the sanctuary process.

Janey had never handled an alleged kidnapping case before. She clipped down the stairs to the casino floor, the tray left behind in the room with the drink. A raucous roar came from deeper in the casino from one of the high-stakes tables. She should check it out…or hand it off to either Edward Kou or Mandlenkosi Dube.

She yawned, considering. Kou tinkered at a poker table in his handyman undercover garb. He gave her a hand wave when she glanced in his direction. His partner on shift, Dube, played blackjack undercover on the other side of the casino to keep an eye on things. He was dressed in a deep-blue dashiki suit with gold embroidered trim on the V-neck and cuffs. He'd barely glanced at her as she passed by earlier on her way to the mezzanine, but he'd noticed her.

Dube was a decent enough card counter himself to spot it in others. But he didn't have her ability to read micro-expressions, not having opted for any ocular enhancements when he was younger—and when it was still legal—as she'd been able to. But his math and analytical skills served him well in his card-watching capacity. He'd caught his fair share of card counters over the years, she'd heard.

She could wake up one of the on-call security agents, Meilani Shawhan or Antonia Lane, to check out the commotion.

No, it was most likely a small matter, and she was here, had clocked herself back on duty, and was dressed appropriately for undercover work in her waitress get-up. She could check out the loud players at the high roller tables before she dug up what she could on Haverhill.

She headed deeper into the packed casino, squeezing past crowds at the craps and roulette tables.

People, mostly men, cheered and shouted at one of the pai gow tables—a fast-paced Chinese gambling version of dominos. Janey approached the boisterous game but not too close. She didn't want to interrupt, only get a feel for the potential for escalating fights, so she paused behind the outer circle to get a sense of the mood.

Twenty men surrounded an inner circle of fifteen or so men pressed around the green felted table, intent on the game, all shouting in Chinese—Mandarin to be more specific. She understood some words and could say the basics. It sounded like they were hurling insults at each other, depending on whether they were winning or losing.

The mood was raucous but not overly so. The dealer or pit boss hadn't flagged security about any betting or playing irregularities, so Janey didn't feel she needed to insert one of her team to monitor the action, though Kou would be the natural choice as he'd blend in. His heritage was Chinese-Dutch, and he spoke several dialects of Chinese, as well as Dutch.

She broke away from the group and backtracked toward the casino exit. She was three paces away when something registered. There was a Caucasian man amongst the group. Just one, among over thirty Chinese men. A dark-haired man dressed in a red velvet embroidered matador jacket.

Maybe it was Orlando Valdez. Maybe Ed was right that Orlando was here. But gambling? Maybe Orlando was undercover on a case. Anger heated her chest. He could have told her he was on L'Étoile. Then she tamped down the heat. He had a right to go where he pleased.

He had a job to do after all—as did she. But she had to know. A gut instinct tugged her, so she reversed directions and made for the table. She wanted to see what was going on. That was all.

"Can I get you gentlemen anything? Coffee? Anything else?" she asked first in New Standard and then in Updated Mandarin.

When they gambled, the Chinese mostly asked for coffee. Their North American and European counterparts, mostly men, sucked down their hard liquor. No matter where they were from in the Sol, women seemed to love all kinds of sweetly flavored martinis and other mixed drinks. Unexpected factoids she'd picked up in her job.

Ten men held up a finger. She nodded and was about to turn toward the kitchen again to fulfill the order, when a man called out from deep in the crowd.

He spoke in a New Standard with a clear French accent, all guttural r's and nasal vowels. His voice was pitched high enough to be heard over the rowdy Chinese gamblers. "I'll take a double menthe digestif on the rocks *et un* Perrier."

There were always exceptions.

"Right away, sir," Janey said, loud enough to be heard and clipped to the kitchen, a heaviness in her chest. Maybe it wasn't Orlando, though he was masterful at being undercover. If it was him, she had half a mind to slap him. No, that wouldn't be professional.

On her way to the kitchen, on her right side, she passed the last high roller tables of baccarat and blackjack. They had a prime spot nearest the enormous window viewscreens and were treated to an enormous view of the Pinwheel spiral galaxy—actually twenty-one million light-years away—piped in due to the powerful telescopes mounted on the station's exterior. It was as if L'Étoile hovered at the edge of this massive phenomena and could plunge into it at any moment.

On her left was the renowned six-star Phoenix Restaurant, run by the formidable and talented Chef Gina Gutierrez. Guests nestled behind bushes and tall plants, hidden from prying eyes in peace, to eat luxurious and exotic dishes.

On second thought, it couldn't be Valdez, not with that higher register voice. Valdez's voice was a deep bass that had rumbled through her chest.

Sadness washed through her like a riptide, then was replaced by heat crawling up her neck, anger at her foolishness. Why was she still pining after him when he'd cut off all communication? He obviously couldn't let her know he was working. If that was what it was. He could have let her know. What else could it be?

She needed to let her schoolgirl crush go. But if she did see him or hear from again, she'd rip into him so hard he'd wished he'd never set foot on L'Étoile.

The voice of reason shouted at her. *That wasn't fair. Trust, but verify.*

Trust, my patootie. She pushed out a breath but kept her spine tall. No need to telegraph her inner turmoil.

Focus on the job, chica.

Janey nodded to Tomika who guarded the swinging kitchen door against hapless or hungry guests. Tomika Te Mutu understood her role now and her need to enter the kitchen from time to time undercover. Actually, it was Chef Gina who'd granted her the exception and informed her entire private kitchen security staff she ran like her own gang to allow Janey into her precious kitchen whenever Janey needed to.

She bustled past the swinging doors and called out—

as any server would—for ten black coffees pronto. She wanted to deliver the French man's drinks personally, so she waved the order into her comm to SkyBar. Her next stop.

"Wesley," Janey called to one of the sous chefs. "I need these delivered to the pai gow table number three. Can you handle it? I have another order to grab from the bar."

Wesley nodded. "Not to worry. I'll even beat you to the table." He grinned at her, showing off his perfect white teeth. He was a short, trim man, about twenty-five, efficient in his movements as he hustled to fill the cups from tanks always full of the premium coffee. Only the best for their guests.

"Not if I don't get to the table first."

"Bet?" Wesley lifted an eyebrow.

"Name it."

"A match at the firing range. You and me and those moving targets. Best two out of three."

Wesley liked to imagine he was a gunslinger from the Old West, but he had little experience compared to Janey's. He was improving, though.

"Glutton for punishment," Janey said. "Beating you last week wasn't enough, eh? Sure. And if I win, you make me your famous country fried chicken with collard greens."

"Deal." Wesley assembled the coffees with efficiency.

Janey smiled and headed out of the kitchen. Wesley had been top of his class when Chef Gina had recruited him right out of culinary school—before he had a chance to open his own Southern restaurant in Paris and take that city by storm he liked to joke.

She wove through the humming crowd to SkyBar and picked up the potent dark green digestif and the Perrier.

She arrived at the pai gow table a foot ahead of Wesley and another kitchen server. Wesley flashed her a grin as if to say, "I'll beat you next time."

At the table, the noise level had risen to near ear-splitting.

"Digestif for the gentleman!" she shouted over the fracas.

The crowd parted a little. Janey managed to slip in between the male bodies, way more focused on the table than on her. She pushed her way through and stood behind a man with wavy shoulder-length brown hair.

"Sir, your drinks!" she yelled above the swearing and laughing.

He glanced at her over his shoulder, mischief in his big brown eyes, framed by long dark lashes. He winked at her. "Put the drink here, lovely lady, and watch me win this hand." He patted the green felt table ledge. "I need lady luck."

Janey's breathing hitched. Orlando. Orlando Valdez, Sol Unified Planets special investigator, specializing in undercover work and charming women on all of Earth's continents and its space stations. Facial rec in her implant flashed his ident as Jacques Laval, residence Luxembourg, and he'd traveled alone and paid his own way.

"Lady luck!" men shouted in English and Mandarin. Some men shouted racial slurs at Valdez about being the pale-faced ghost who was going to lose and go to Diyu, a version of the underworld in Chinese culture.

Valdez laughed and shouted back his own slurs in Mandarin. Something about a Chinese man's hell having no women.

Without replying, Janey clenched her jaw and set the drinks down at the edge of the table. She swallowed the angry retort threatening to spill out about where he could shove his drinks and pivoted away.

There was no good reason to break her cover, no matter how much she wanted to space him. She shoved out a breath. She was a professional and she'd act like one. And he was undercover. Must be serious if he couldn't even breathe word of it to her. Fine and good-bye.

She'd barely made it a step away from the table when Valdez snaked out an arm around her waist and tugged her into the side of his warm body. Men laughed but barely glanced at her.

"What are you doing?" she said in his ear through gritted teeth. But, stars alive, it felt good to be so close to him. His woodsy aftershave, at odds with his cosmopolitan demeanor, hinted at something wild and mysterious. She wanted him despite her anger.

"I missed you," he whispered, eyeing the table. And then louder he said, "You're my lady luck!"

More cheers went up.

"I thought I was more than that," Janey said under her breath. "What's going on?"

"You are," he said as quietly. "And, a lot."

"Where have you been? A job?"

"One sec. It's my turn." With a flick of his wrist, Valdez revealed his two pair of dominoes. A great roar went up. "I won!" he crowed. He hugged Janey. It felt real, not just for show. "My Lady Luck!" She hugged him back.

Pandemonium ensued with more racial slurs, congratulations, and groans.

Janey placed one hand on his silky shirt, his muscled chest firm beneath her palm. She was about to push against him when a shout rose above the rest, chilling her blood—something no one who worked at the casino wanted to hear.

"He cheated!"

Highly unlikely in pai gow.

She scanned the crowd around the table, high-res vision, taking in the crowd in a sweep. Some of the pai gow gamblers were reaching inside their coats. Weapons of any kind weren't allowed on board, except by staff, but anyone could stow a steak knife once on board—or make one from food-crafters, if they were handy and desperate. She had to be sure, so ran her x-ray scan for a split-second. Too dangerous to her to run it longer. Yep, some were packing knives and daggers.

On this impromptu undercover assignment, she wasn't packing. She'd gotten used to the quiet nature of her work. But now she wished she had her laser-sighted gun, snug in her room safe.

In half a breath, Valdez wrapped an arm around her neck and held something pointy to it. Only the tip. She was guessing a dagger. The bastard. Up to his old tricks of lying to get what he wanted. She was right not to trust him.

"They're armed. Knives." She spoke past the mild pressure on her throat and glared at Valdez. Normally she'd flip him, but she was pinned from moving by the Chinese gamblers who pressed in behind and beside her.

"I know," he whispered in her ear. To the others, he shouted, "I'll kill her, I will. Back off!" He stepped backward, dragging her with him.

The crowd cleared behind her.

"Get me off the station!" Valdez shouted at her. "Please," he whispered, desperation pitching his voice higher.

She raised her hands. "Don't hurt me," she said to

play the part of the frightened waitress. At a whisper, she said, "What is going on?"

Was he in too deep? Or had he orchestrated this chaos? Could this be a cover for something else entirely?

"Get me off the station." He tightened his grip around her neck.

She jumped, more surprised than scared, but it sold the part. "I can't, sir," she squeaked. "Don't have clearance."

They passed the blackjack tables, and she caught Dube's eye. He was about to stand. What rash move might he try? Janey shook her head. The man hadn't been field-rated for combat. Neither was Kou, but both men were good in a brawl and were making progress in street fight training.

Dube sat, a relieved look on his face. He needed more confidence, though he had good instincts. Why hadn't she insisted all the agents get trained sooner or accelerated the training? She needed back-up against a crazy ex-whatever Valdez was. Kou trailed them, behind the mob of gamblers. Good, he was keeping an eye on her.

"Call your boss. Call the hangar chief on duty. Whoever. Do it!" Valdez kept the French accent. Impressive.

"He's asleep," Janey said, breathless.

"Wake him." Valdez backed them up past SkyBar and past the jangling, musical slot machines that never slept. The Chinese gamblers followed them, circling to cut them off at the open wide exit to the lobby.

Janey glanced behind them and mouthed "door" to Peter, still on duty at the front desk. Pale-faced, Peter nodded.

Janey said under her breath, "Door at one-eighty. Run on my mark."

Five Chinese men dashed around the slot machines. Janey screamed, wriggling out of Valdez's grip, which hadn't been that tight anyway. She sprinted for the wood-paneled wall, where a thin black vertical seam was the only indication that there was anything different from the rest of the wall. She pushed the panel. Second time tonight. First Amelia. Now Valdez.

The door swung inward, Valdez a half a pace behind her. The panel would shut on its own. She dashed to the service elevator, clicked the down button, and jumped in. Maybe Valdez wouldn't keep up. That was a mean thought.

But he was right there, a half a step behind. He glided in as the elevator door skimmed almost shut.

"What the Venus hell, man!" She glared at him, catching her breath.

"My case has gone sideways. I swear I didn't cheat."

FIVE

THE LIFT DOOR OPENED ON THE SECURITY
service level, but Janey didn't step out, crossed her arms.
"What's going on?"

Valdez sheathed his knife back into his belt and
covered it with his red velvet embroidered matador
jacket. He was wearing fitted black slacks and a white
silk privateer shirt. He was eyeing her cleavage, a little
smile on his lips, his damn dimple showing.

"Eyes forward, buster."

"You're right." He schooled his expression and met
her gaze, serious and earnest. "What is the matter,
Janey? I thought we—"

"You thought wrong. I haven't heard from you in two
weeks. And how the hell did you get that knife on
board?" She crossed her arms on her skimpy waitress
outfit. If only she had on a long-sleeved turtleneck,
instead of her waitress get-up of a sleeveless low-cut top.
Pants would be nice, while she was wishing, instead of
the short skirt and tights.

He straightened, sobered. "I'm sorry. I really am."

"The knife?"

"I know my way around a food crafter."

"You mean how to subvert one."

He shrugged.

"Where the Venus hells have you been?"

"Working. I'm sorry about before, back at the pai gow table."

"What would you have done if I hadn't come along?" She wasn't ready to forgive him.

"Improvised." He shrugged again and peeked out to check the empty grey utility corridor. No one was about.

"You're incorrigible." She left the elevator. But he didn't.

"Wait, Janey—I wanted to call, but—" He had his hand in the way of the closing door.

"You disappeared."

"I had to. Work." He pleaded with his gaze. "I couldn't contact you."

"Whatever." But she heaved a breath, then narrowed her eyes at him. "Couldn't?"

"Not even a coded message. My case. It's a sensitive one." He glanced at the grey recyclo flooring, his eyes haunted. "And now, it's blown. Why would they—"

"What?" she asked when he stopped.

He shook his head.

"I was worried about you," she finally said and sighed. She wanted to lean into him—to not have his case between them. She stayed on her side of the half-closed elevator door.

"Me too," he said just as quietly.

"What are you going to do?"

"I don't know. I don't know why they turned on me. I need to see the gameplay," Valdez said as if to himself.

"You're going to hack into the L'Étoile system."

"What? No. I have a personal cam here." He pointed to a button on his high collar—the only button on the collar.

"You aren't going to tell me what's going on."

"Can't." He looked pained. "Not by choice."

"So you're following the rules on this one."

"Stakes are *gros*." He said that last word in French, back of the throat R.

There was a short low whirr, and Orlando glanced at his wrist comm. Then at her. "Janey, I have to take this." He reached for her hand. "I'm really sorry about back there." She let him take it, rubbing his palm with her fingers.

"Go."

"I'll contact you as soon as I can," he said and let the door close.

"*Gros*?" she asked, but he only gazed back and the door shut. Then all was quiet. *Gros* as in high, she bet. Stakes were high. He was a Sol Unified Planets under-cover agent after all. They policed regional governments on Earth, around Earth, on Luna, in the Asteroid Belt, Mars, and the science stations around the outer planets.

Just as she was forgetting all about Orlando Valdez, he had to show up on her station and ruin her night. He wasn't having such a good night himself. Were all his cases so messy? Probably.

She stormed down the corridor to her quarters, madder at herself than him. She really had to get out of her waitress get-up and back into her work attire. It was going to be a longer night than she expected. She had to be prepared to take reports from the Chinese on the handsome white devil who stole from them.

She sped through a shower and dressed in black slacks, blue lightweight long sleeve shirt, and her favorite cobalt blue silk long coat. Five minutes later, she was back in her office digging through Haverhill's records with a fresh cup of coffee—the real stuff, not the extruded liquid her room or office food crafter made.

Twenty minutes later, she hadn't been pinged by the night security desk with a complaint from the gamblers. Odd. Kou and Dube had checked in with an all-clear and went back to their activities—Kou to his table repairs, and Dube back to a blackjack game. She was back to Amelia and her complaint.

Haverhill—Jonas Haverhill, the Third, to be exact— was a big gambler. Hotel records showed that he'd arrived ten days ago. He'd racked up a healthy tab at roulette, up some days and down others. More down than up. He'd spent in total two million credits—enough to feed, house, and clothe a village for a year. He'd booked the mezzanine suite a few times and credited lots of drinks to his room, easily more than enough for one person—more like drinks for three or four people. She continued to scan his records to see meals every day at the Phoenix, some room service meals, several sets of clothes from the maker booths, and several fitting sessions with the clothing concierge. Multiple daily deep tissue massages at the spa and a handful of line items marked *private* concluded the charges.

Janey had seen that before. Those expenses were usually tips, food crafter services, and special concierge requests. If her investigation warranted it, she'd need to run the details down with housekeeping.

Jonas's hotel bill was invoiced to Haverhill Industrials. Named after him, she supposed, or another family member. No one else was listed in his party. Who else was he feeding and clothing? Or was that all for him?

She ran a search on his company and discovered it

was a multinational conglomerate in the minerals domain, with mining operations in partnership with others in the deserts and dry mountainous regions around Earth and on a few asteroids. Haverhill was the CEO of Haverhill Industrials. The company made core components for every computer both on the planet and off, especially with the rare Rhodium, essential to the nano- and micro-tech community, including planet-exploring probes. Haverhill Industrials was valued at multi-billions and traded high on the stock exchange.

All told, he was a very rich and probably politically connected man. No one got into the asteroid mining business without connections.

Janey ran a search through all the media channels, and not so surprisingly, she came up with little. Just an official bio attached to his corporate trading portfolio. Nothing on his personal life, his naughty or illegal habits, or his enemies. His identity had likely been managed and polished—a common tactic with C-suite executives. Most wealthy and politically connected people curated their 'net footprint and made sure to make themselves as invisible as possible from any potential hackers and to stay far out of reach from backlash from disgruntled workers or attacks from enemies.

How did Amelia fit into Haverhill's sphere? She was a sales associate based in Addis Ababa in Africa. He was an industrialist jetting both around the planet and off, headquartered in the Arizona-New Mexico Assessment Region in North America. There the region's privacy laws protected corporate executives and management. Corporations benefited from the best tax laws on Earth. And land near the Las Cruces spaceport was protected from rising sea levels, making it prime real estate. Industrialists could jet off the planet at a moment's notice to meetings on the other side of the planet or to one of the space stations in orbit.

Haverhill's company headquarters were in a corporate protectionist zone where corporations had more rights than people did. She should know. She grew up in within the zone, in Las Cruces, in the shadow of a major spaceport and Space Wing base. Life had been tough. Mom had worked two jobs. Since middle school, Janey had run herself hard to qualify for as many scholarships as she could so she could get into a Granton-region university, far away from the corporate zone. Literally. By the time she left home for the San Francisco Granton, she'd won several track awards and was at the top of her class academically.

She turned her attention back to Haverhill, but there wasn't any more digging she could do until she got privacy clearance from him. She didn't want to ask the man. Not until she had to. The Bijoux de L'Étoile guests came for the privacy and the cachet. She didn't want to disturb either if she could help it. He was no doubt good buddies with Schoeneman, and she couldn't afford to piss off the owner. Her paycheck depended on her not rocking the boat, flying under her boss's radar, and keeping trouble to zero—or, at least, out of view of Chief Milano.

Yet she'd never had a woman claim someone was trying to kill her and ask for sanctuary before.

Haverhill's flippant behavior and lack of concern for Amelia clashed with the young woman's distress.

She checked the time and yawned. Still no complaints from the Chinese about Valdez's alleged cheating. One less thing to handle.

She sent a silent ping to Kou. She didn't expect him to get back to her—he was probably finishing up his repairs before the new shift started—so she was surprised when she got a ping back right away. She opened the live audio comm.

"Boss, I'm on my way back. Ferreira arrived early. Want my report now or in a few, when I get to you?"

The newest security agent to the team and the youngest at eighteen, Larissa Ferreira split her time between the casino and the hangar as she learned the ropes.

"Anything to report?" Janey stifled another yawn.

"Just that the Chinese gamblers dispersed as soon as you left, like mice when the cat appears. No further complaints surfaced."

"Okay, thanks, Kou. I'll look at your report in the morning. No need to sitrep directly." She needed some shut-eye. She hadn't planned to work night shift. But then Amelia showed up.

"On it, boss. Whatever you want."

Kou was a good guy, but he deferred to her too much. She needed to toughen him up, give him some command jobs, and get him field-rated. It wasn't the first time she wondered why the older man hadn't pushed for those things, and why Chief Milano never had pushed for those things for him either.

She cleared the wall screen and saved the data in her private files. Though Kim was likely asleep by now, she sent her a message to not let Amelia wander the station unaccompanied and to start the administrative prelimi-naries for Amelia's sanctuary application.

Janey then started the security research section for the sanctuary application. According to Amelia's personal file, she was a former citizen of Granton San Francisco and had been born there. Former because she'd left the zone and hadn't bothered or known to file to maintain her citizen rights while she was out of the Granton.

Since Amelia worked for Eshe Kamal Coffee, an Ethiopian global corporate entity, she was its corporate citizen now. Eshe Kamal Coffee was a powerful coffee corporate city-state, one of a handful on that existed. This corporate city-state controlled twenty percent of the planet's growers, distributors, and sellers or this coveted, expensive, and high-demand commodity. For Amelia to relinquish her citizenship rights from Eshe wasn't the hard part. The hard part would be disappearing from those after her.

But that was a matter for tomorrow. The young woman was safe for now.

Had her friend Christine reached out for help? Is that what got her killed? Or had she needed help when her plans went sideways and there was no one to call on? Why hadn't she reached out to Janey?

She yawned again. "Lights off," Janey commanded to her office AI assistant, left, and then took the staff lift one level down to her quarters. As she entered her one-room studio space, her comm pinged. She gritted her teeth. Really? He was calling her now.

"I owe you an explanation," Valdez started.

"You owe me nothing." She commed off. Maybe she was still pissed. She was also tired.

She got ready for bed and slipped under her covers. She switched her wrist comm to silent mode. It would buzz if there was any kind of emergency.

As a backup, she commanded Rhea, her personal AI wired into the room, "Rhea, set night view and close all personal comms, except urgent ones from Mom."

"On it, Janey," a natural female voice said and switched off the lights. On the ceiling screen, wispy clouds shifted sedately across a field of dark blue as if blown by a calm summer wind.

That was mean of her to cut Valdez off like that.

"Rhea, open audio only for recording."

"Sure thing. Go ahead."

"Valdez, you totally owe me an explanation," she dictated. "I don't hear from you for two weeks, then you pull that crap on me. I don't know if I can trust you ever again. Damn it."

Did she even want to re-engage with him?

"Archive this one too?" Rhea asked.

"Yup." She closed her eyes, commanding her body to relax.

The message would be stored along with the thirty-plus other messages she hadn't sent since he'd ghosted her.

What was the point of all her messages? She was like a lovesick puppy, mooning over him. It was over, wasn't it? He'd ghosted her. Okay, it was for a job. Then he attacked her, expecting her to be his cover in an op he couldn't or wouldn't talk about. What the Venus hell?

Valdez was an undercover agent for Sol Unified Planets, the world government that included all human habitats extending out to the Saturn stations—and oversaw all Grantons, corporate states, empires, and kingdoms. He bopped all around homeworld space stations and planet-side, and maybe even beyond, for all she knew, going where his cases took him. She, on the other hand, was stationed on L'Étoile for another three years and nine months, minus vacation leave every six months. She had to stay put.

Her mom depended on her for her entire livelihood and medical treatments. Janey was not going to throw that away for the most exciting man she'd ever met—and one so far off her list of what a potential mate could be. As if she would ever have room in her life for such a thing.

"Rhea, play Pacific coast surf off the Sonoma coast."

Waves crashed softly, lulling her under.

He'd been working and couldn't tell her anything. Need to know and all that. Maybe she could forgive him.

"Rhea, wake me at oh-seven-hundred."

"You got it, Janey," Rhea said. "But there's a non-urgent message from your mom. It just came in. Would you like me to play it?"

"Color?" They color-coded their audio messages for fun and variety.

"Pink and labeled 'silly.'"

Her mother was always sending her funny and cute cat and puppy videos.

"Then no. It can wait."

"Okay, Janey. Good night."

The surf pounded on the rocks and pulled her under.

Then the nightmare returned.

SIX

I<small>N HER NIGHTMARE, HER HEART POUNDED IN</small> her ears. Wet bark stuck to her boots. The frigid early morning ocean wind bit into her cheeks and whooshed down her coat collar and across her back. She shivered. On a narrow deer path, she struggled through the pine branches that slapped her face. She followed the path deeper into the fog-shrouded forest, called by a knowing beyond words. Or maybe there had been words but she'd forgotten them.

Blackness filled her field of view. The darkness of space. The void. She was falling, then floating, then staring into a dark hole in the ground. Dirt, dank forest smells, and rotting. Her gut clenched. There it was. A shallow grave. Her friend's body dumped like trash, arms and legs akimbo, covered by dirt and underbrush, her eyes opened and unseeing, and her skin sallow and a marbly white. She knelt, her knees soaked by the damp ground, and scrabbled in the dirt, clawing to rescue her friend. Christine shouldn't be in the ground.

"Out of the way, Ms. McCallister." A uniformed police

officer tugged on her arm. "This is a crime scene. Off-limits to civilians."

"Christine! What have they done to you?" Janey cried, her throat raw and torn.

In the drizzle, a police officer in a red windbreaker took Janey by the arm and led her to the back of a black van. Someone put a blanket around her.

Janey rocked and cried in grief, consumed by chills and sweat.

Her own crying woke her up, and she bolted out of bed, cold feet on the floor. Sweating. Awake. Not in a forest. In her quarters. With her abrupt movement, the room lights in her quarters shifted on—too bright. Her cheeks were wet, her fists up.

"It's oh-four, Janey," Rhea said. "Would you like me to start the coffee?"

"No. Lights off," Janey ordered, and she crashed back into bed and flung an arm across her eyes.

"As you wish," the room AI whispered, and the lights shut off.

Oh, Christine. Why hadn't she solved her murder? Janey had been the one to find her in the woods a week after her friend never showed for their weekly running date along the marina seawall.

Guilt tugged at her heart. If only she had arrived earlier to meet her. If only she'd known that something was wrong. But she hadn't on both accounts.

She hadn't had that nightmare in years. Amelia's case was kicking it up—the way Amelia looked like Christine. Amelia's fragility. Those haunted eyes. And something else. Her dream mind saw a connection, but her awakened state snuffed it. The connection drifted away like a whiff of smoke.

Janey shivered and felt for her blanket. It wasn't on

the bed but on the floor, where it must have fallen some-
time during the night. She retrieved it and stared at the
ceiling. The clouds were gone, replaced by the stars—her
favorite constellations. The W of Cassiopeia, the hump
of Camelopardalis, and the house of Cepheus hung over
the horizon, all constellations she could see growing up
in the summer months a few hours after the sun set, if
she was out if the city proper. Longing for home and
hearing Mom's voice washed over her.

"Rhea, time."

"5 a.m. local. Would you like your coffee now?"

She'd slept another hour. That was good, but she
wasn't normally up for another two hours. "Yes. Lights,
low. Play Mom's last message."

In Las Cruces, Mom should be getting up for her day
and Janey didn't want to trouble her by interrupting her
routine. They usually talked before Janey went to work
and before her mom started lunch. Maybe her mom
would need to sleep in. She'd been doing that a lot. The
new treatment was wiping her out, though doctors said
the neurotransmitter counts were stable. Janey didn't
know whether to be worried or not, but, of course, she
worried.

While she dressed for a run at the gym in a blue
sports bra, blue tank top, blue long leggings, and
running shoes, she listened to Dana tell jokes in her
raspy voice and share news about how the aunties
and uncle-moms were doing and what their kids
were doing lately, all grown now like her. And like
all the kids she grew up around, she was an IVF-er
—her mom's genes mixed with anonymous male
genes. They were a close-knit group. She'd grown up
scrabbling on the wrong side of the tracks in the
shadow of the spaceport and lots of factories,

constantly in and out of each other's houses and yards.

She downed her first cup of coffee of the day and headed to the staff gym. At 5:15 a.m., the place was mostly empty. She waved to her compatriots caught up in their own routines. The sooner she ran the dream out of her system the better. She stretched, hopped on the treadmill, and warmed up with a mellow jog. Her thoughts strayed to Christine anyway and the circumstances surrounding her disappearance. Details had been sparse, and Christine's murder was still unsolved.

The police had suspected Christine's fiancé, but they couldn't prove anything and had cleared him quickly. Janey had been the one to insist to the police that Christine hadn't left Granton San Francisco like they thought she had. Even Christine's fiancé thought she'd left and didn't want to report her missing, thinking she'd just gone to her parents up north. Janey had felt in her gut something horrible had happened to her best friend. She hated that she'd been right.

The police never replied to her insistent questions about how specifically Christine had been killed or why. They repeatedly shooed her away from what was initially a missing person case, but it was her snooping in Christine's personal documents that eventually led her, and the police, to Christine's body.

Since she'd become an investigator, first with Space Wing and then with L'Étoile, she hadn't had the time to investigate Christine's case. No, scratch that. She hadn't wanted the heartache of opening the wound. She hadn't had the courage to face the pain.

It was time to change that. On the treadmill, she slowed her jog to a walk, set up privacy mode so no one around her could hear her call, and placed the call anonymously. It was morning in San Francisco. She could probably catch the detective as she arrived for the day.

She spoke into her comm. "Call the San Francisco Granton PD and connect me to Detective Aziz."

Detective Manoush Aziz had been in charge of Christine's case.

Then Janey came to her senses. What would she say to the detective? Janey had no new evidence to open Christine's case, and her badge gave her no jurisdiction outside of her locale. But then it was too late to back out because the operator was speaking in a cool, calm voice.

"Granton San Francisco Police Department, how may I direct your call?"

"May I speak to Detective Manoush Aziz?"

"There is no one here by that name."

"Maybe she's retired. She worked there four years ago."

"Checking, please hold." The operator switched her over to the hold music—a Bach number she recognized but couldn't name.

A minute later the operator came back on. "That detective is no longer with us."

"Where did she go? Did she leave a forwarding address?"

"No, ma'am. I mean—" The operator's voice was cut off and another person came on the line asking for Janey's ident and then tried to open a video feed with her.

She hit deny on the video request. "This is Investigator—" Janey was about to announce herself, but a warning flashed on her ocular implant—tampering on the comm line. From whose end she didn't know yet. Venus hells. What had she stirred up?

Heart pounding, Janey closed the comm and jumped off the treadmill. "What the—"

She didn't need to kick up trouble from the past. She already had a case, here, now.

Maybe she wasn't ready to dive into Christine's case. Maybe she lacked the courage after all.

Venus hells.

Time to put her mind back on things she could control. She had a job to do here on L'Étoile. People she was in charge of. People she cared about. She could do nothing for Christine now.

She jumped back on the treadmill, clicked it to a run pace and an eight percent slope, and pounded out her frustration with long, loping strides. At mile one, her mind calmed. At mile three, her thoughts drifted to Amelia and the young woman's history. The past didn't have to define your future, but clues to Amelia's motivation for her current choices were most likely in her past. And if Janey understood Amelia's choices and what led her to her current problems, then maybe Janey could protect her better.

Most adults didn't move away from their Granton as Janey had. Those like Janey who worked hard to get in very rarely left. So why had Amelia? Though the rate of Granton-born leaving was probably higher than in imports like her who still had ties outside the Granton. And Amelia was born there.

So was Christine.

She had to talk to Amelia and get her side of the story on why she left the San Francisco Granton. Had she experienced a tragedy like Janey had, or had she wanted to leave for other reasons?

Whether you were born there or moved there, all Grantons supported their residents with universal basic

income, free housing, healthcare, education, and professional training. It wasn't a free ride; it was an exchange
for access to any and all medical data. Like millions of
others, Janey had readily given up that privacy right in
order to live with full support. These multi-county
regions dotted Earth and included a few space stations,
working together in trade as a kind of autonomous
confederation. The total population of all the Grantons
was around eighty-million, and for the most part, they
functioned smoothly and peacefully. Crime was low.
People could pursue work they loved—as Janey had and
as Christine had until tragedy struck.

Yet Amelia had left.

Christine hadn't wanted to leave. At least, as far as
Janey knew.

By the time she finished her three-mile run, she felt
more settled. Back in her quarters, she took a shower
and then changed into black slacks, a blue blouse, and
her favorite long, flowing matching silk duster jacket.
Under her clothes, she wore protective body gear, as she
did every day—a habit from Space Wing. The lightweight
gear was a full-body thin layer. The fabric was made of a
weave of liquid ceramic, made out of nanoparticles. Into
her belt holster, under her coat, she slid her favorite gun,
a laser-sighted pistol. Into her boot went a backup gun—
a small ladies' ceramic-graphene handgun. For the other
boot, she shoved a sheathed four-inch blade, black
carbon steel and crafted by hand. All weapons she'd
carried as an investigator in the Space Wing. Now, she
felt ready for just about anything.

She was back in her office by six-fifteen, much earlier
than the day shift and before the night shift was due to
report back. Her scalding coffee the way she liked it from
the conference room was perched on her desk. She

turned one of her wallscreens to a live broadcast of the sun, so the light in her office looked like the warm morning sun over the Mediterranean. Buttery soft light filtered in. By the time she finished her hot brew, she knew how to get more information on Amelia and Christine, possibly in one call.

She got the number from the Granton's registry and called Records. Someone should be in by now as it was 9:30 a.m. local there. The person who answered was courteous yet firm in needing to see Janey's credentials before she waved over Amelia's Granton residency file. Then Janey asked to be patched through to the Cold Cases division at the San Francisco police department. The person hesitated, then did as Janey asked. Not many people liked to be reminded that there were cold cases in an area of relatively low crime.

A gruff voice answered the comm. "Cold Cases."

"I'm looking for the files on Christine Baptista from four years ago."

"Ident? I don't recognize your calling code."

"I'm calling from the Investigative Service on Bijoux de L'Étoile."

"Ooh, L'Étoile! I've always wanted to go there. So exotic. I'd probably have to cash out my whole UBI for one night, but it'd be worth it if the mister okayed it. What's it like?"

In the Grantons, everyone was allotted a number of credits for their entire life, mostly in the form of allotments for housing, education, health care, and food—a type of Universal Basic Income. It was quite generous, but you could cash out, provided you agreed to the consequences.

"They keep us on our toes here, ma'am. I was hoping you could help me—about the files."

"Oh sure. Hold on. I'll pull them. Send ident verification while I do that." The officer put her on hold, and melodic piano music filled Janey's ear.

And just like that, Janey was going to get to look at Christine's cold case file. She sent in her ident, which would get logged. Someone would maybe kick up a fuss in the detective's bureau, if they cared to review cold cases. But she was betting on the detectives being too busy with whatever was on their desks to have the time. She'd been a pest four years ago, but maybe everyone was gone who'd known her then. Besides, she had a badge now. So what if someone at SF Granton PD knew she had Christine's file?

"Investigator McCallister?" the cold case officer said, worry in her voice.

"Yes?"

"The file is thin." The officer sounded apologetic as if it was her doing the file was sparse.

"That's okay. Send it."

"You have new evidence? Are you going to reopen the case?"

"Possibly. I have a related case. I don't know where it will lead."

"You call me anytime. Maybe I can help. Maybe I can earn some extra creds and earn me another night on the Bijoux. Or take the fancy space jet instead."

"Thanks, Officer? ..."

"Detective Juanita Verde."

"You've been with the department long?"

"Is that your way of asking if I remember the case?"

"You don't miss a thing."

"I may be semi-retired and a good ol' gal, but I still got it." Detective Verde chuckled. "Mister wanted to get out the rain but didn't like so much sun, so we left the

Seattle Granton and I got us bunked here when the former cold case lieutenant left for warmer climes."

"The fog isn't for everyone," Janey agreed. "Thank you so much for the files." She reviewed the digital files and saw audio, video, and text.

"Will you be needing the evidence?" the detective asked.

"Not just yet. I need to review the files first."

"Very well, Investigator McCallister. Best of luck to you. And if I can be of any assistance—boots on the ground—"

"Thank you so much." Janey closed the comm.

That had gone better than expected. She had some reading to do.

She sat at her desk, called up her widescreen, and opened Amelia's file. That was easier than starting with Christine's. Amelia's Granton residency file was essentially a series of lines—not that many. Detailed there was her birthdate and location, her schooling, club activities, and birth name. It was Amelia Jones, not Amelia Gain as the hotel records had it. Maybe Amelia had changed her name when she left Granton SF. Janey read further.

When Amelia was nineteen, in April of that year, four years ago, she was reported missing from Granton SF. The date listed was a week before Christine disappeared. The next line item in Amelia's record was "Found employment outside Granton SF. Taken off rolls."

Amelia had gotten out alive.

But Christine hadn't. Were the two women connected in some way? She had to find out.

Her stomach churned, and her body heated. She wasn't ready to talk about her old friend to anyone just yet. Not even Kim. She had to find a private place to open Christine's file.

SEVEN

Back in her tiny quarters, Janey washed her overly warm face in the bathroom and glanced at her reflection in the mirror. She looked haggard. She didn't know if she could plunge back into Christine's murder, but she had to do it. She had no more excuses.

"Rhea, close all comms except for urgent calls."

"And except for Mom's?"

"Of course. Open private files on main wallscreen."

Janey had moved Christine's file onto her private server as soon as she'd received it from Detective Juanita Verde. Janey wasn't acting in any kind of official capacity on Christine's case and didn't need the hotel records to have any trace of her work on it. Not until she had something, if anything, that connected Amelia's situation to Christine's. Even then she wasn't sure if she'd enter Christine's case into her work files or reports. She wasn't sure there would ever be any more official records on Amelia, either, if her sanctuary went through. It was better not to leave any breadcrumbs, in case someone really was after the young woman.

Janey straightened things in her studio, though there wasn't much. Her bed was already made, her clothes were put away, and her tools were squared away in a toolbox. She couldn't put it off any longer.

She opened the vid file labeled "crime scene."

She blinked back tears as she stared at the crime scene footage where Christine's body had been found, by her, on an April dawn morning, at the edge of the San Francisco Bay. Her body had been moved from the crime scene. Must have been transported to the morgue. The area was a small clearing amongst a copse of pine trees. Fog shrouded the scene and the two people around a dark hole, a barely disguised grave. Just like in her dream.

The impossible had happened. Her idyllic life shattered; her best friend murdered.

She wiped her cheeks and focused in on the audio. The crime scene tech was saying that the scene was staged.

What? No one had told her that.

No one had told her anything. They'd shut her out of the case. She'd been a civilian.

Well, she wasn't a civilian anymore.

She replayed that moment again.

"Look here," a male voice said and gestured to the body. He was covered in full protective gear to not bring in or carry out any traces of evidence, no matter how small. "The earth has been disturbed and patted down as if with a gloved hand or a piece of wood. No shoe prints. But there are wild boar hoof and wolf prints. The crime scene was probably staged."

Janey couldn't immediately see what he was referring to until he moved to one side and waved the vid drone over. She'd seen the animal prints when she'd been there, but she hadn't noticed how the dirt around Christine's body had been manicured. It'd just looked like dirt.

"Evidence?" the other person asked. "Coroner said there were some bite marks. Perhaps an animal attack, what with all the re-wilding. She was wandering in the woods and caught unawares..." Janey recognized that voice. It belonged to the detective in charge, Detective Manoush Aziz, who was also in full protective gear. "I wonder what she was doing out here all by herself."

"Lured out here, maybe?" the man said, probably a crime scene technician. Detective Aziz hadn't worked with a partner. "Then made to look like an animal attack and covered up by whoever lured her out her."

"Any evidence of that?" Detective Aziz said.

"Not yet," he said. "Still waiting on the odorometer and the non-organics to come in. Drones reporting in shortly on the area scan."

"Good job, Howard." The detective nodded and bent over a bush a few feet from the shallow grave.

"What you got, Manoush?" Howard asked.

"A partial shoe print, hidden by this bush. Missed by the visual drone sweep."

"Great! There's your evidence." Howard came over, scanned it with his evidence collector, and waved a pocket drone over to take footage. The screen showed the drone camera zooming in on a near-complete shoe print. Janey could easily make out the top half of a print and much of the bottom. Horizontal lines top and bottom with a break in the middle where the arch was. "Running it through the database." Howard peered up at the detective. "Visual sweeps are only 99.5% accurate in most cases."

"I know, Howard. You so love to tell me the limits of your job."

"Only so you can do yours so well, Manoush." He grinned under his hood.

His device pinged, and he frowned. "No match."

Margie grinned, looking at the shoe print image.

"What?" Howard said.

"That's a Doc Marten standard issue boot. The kind used by corporate para-military units."

"They shouldn't be operating on Granton lands."

"Exactly."

Janey paused the replay and sat down at the table. She used the table screen to scan the report, looking for more details about the para-military unit. The detective had followed up through her contacts, not named in the report, to the Modesto area, inland ninety miles, which led her to a secretive medical facility in the region. The address and contact information was listed in the report. Then after months of working the PR department to arrange a visit to the facility, the detective notes stopped with a cryptic list of words. "Monaco. Coffee. Corp. Arabica. Station. Lab."

What did that mean? Detective Manoush hadn't included the medical examiner's report. What had been Christine's cause of death? Why was the detective's case file so lacking?

There had been a funeral in Sonoma sub-Granton, forty-five miles north of San Francisco, so the body must have been released back to Christine's parents there. Janey had even said a few words at the funeral full of friends and family, though she couldn't remember what they were. The grief had pressed on her on that spring day, the hillside tree cemetery full of the bright orange poppies and dark green oak trees lording it over the sloping hills.

She sent a note to Detective Verde, asking her to

track down the medical examiner's report on Christine. She also asked Verde to see if she could track down Detective Manoush Aziz. While she waited for a reply back, she ran a search on Manoush Aziz in the Granton worldwide registry. No current listing, only a record that she'd lived and worked in Granton San Francisco up until four years ago. Hopefully, Verde would be able to dig deeper than she could.

Next, she turned her attention to the string of words Aziz had listed in the file—"Monaco. Coffee. Corp. Arabica. Station. Lab"—and ran a search for the entire list. Altogether they netted nothing, so she researched them one at a time. Monaco was a tiny principality in Europe, one of the wealthiest regions in the Sol, a tax haven still ruled by a monarch. Arabica could refer to "coffee arabica," a coffee tree species and the first known cultivated kind of coffee. It could also refer to the Bosnian Arabic alphabet, the Belarusian Arabic Alphabet, an old journal of Arabic and Islamic studies, or a preparation sold in the 18th century as a diet for ill people. That last usage was a fancy name for a dish of lentils. Coffee, station, and lab were so general as to be of no help.

Janey went back to Christine's files and clicked on some audio-only notes. Detective Aziz had dictated her report notes. The audio files were a backup of the originals, if she'd had them transcribed. Except for the last audio. In it she mentioned Janey's role in the investigation with a reminder to ask Janey again how she'd found Christine's body. But the detective never had. Shoddy police work or had someone shut down the detective's investigation?

Janey's private video comm rang with Mom's jaunty chime. She'd forgotten her scheduled daily call. Except it wasn't eight yet. Mom was calling fifteen minutes early.

She straightened her hair in the ponytail, brushed off her cheeks, and opened the vid, her adrenaline spiking and heart thumping like a rocket trying to escape gravity.

"Hi Mom. Are you okay?"

"Of course. What's wrong, Janey dear?"

EIGHT

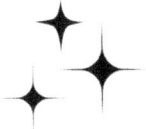

"You're calling early." Janey sidestepped the direct question.

The vid showed Mom sitting with the aunties at the square table that doubled as their Pinochle table out on the front porch of the small Las Cruces home Janey had grown up in. These five ladies were inseparable. Since Mom had become ill, one of them or someone from the greater community of aunties and uncles was always around. They looked after their own.

"We finished an early lunch, and I wanted to talk to you." Dana yawned. "Now tell me, sweetie."

The aunties chorused 'Hellos'.

Janey waved at them.

"Nothing. Just a case, Mom. How are you? How are you feeling today?" She tried to brighten but wasn't sure if her smile reached her eyes.

"Oh, sweetie—" Then her mom said something quietly to the others and shooed them off. There was rustling on her end as the others left the porch. "Tell me." Dana gave her a compassionate look that crashed through all of Janey's walls, 22,000 miles away.

Janey broke down, shook her head a lot, then finally wiped her face and cleared her eyes. She told her mom about getting Christine's case files and reviewing them for a related case. Dana didn't need to know details about the former, and Janey never talked about her ongoing cases with her mom.

"Oh, sweetie, I can't imagine how hard that is." Mom's deep gaze of understanding almost unleashed another round of tears, but Janey didn't want to spend their time together like this. So she gave her face a good scrub and took a deep breath.

"How are things, Mom?" She had to get Dana talking about her last twenty-four hours.

At first, Mom resisted, then Janey said, "It will help me, Mom." Dana was one tough woman, never complaining, always wanting to help others, and she never passed up a chance to laugh.

So Dana took a few minutes to share the shenanigans of the neighbors' kids and relayed jokes the aunties brought to her daily. Despite the laughter, Janey didn't miss Dana's pale almost translucent skin that seemed paler than yesterday, and the way her mom's hands tremored when she lifted her coffee cup. The symptoms were the same. She wasn't getting any better. And she appeared more tired than even the day before.

"What did the doctor say, Mom?" Janey asked when there was a lull in the jokes.

Dana shrugged.

"What about the fatigue?"

"Same as last week. Side effect of these meds," Dana said. "They only make me sleepier than usual, and that's okay with me. Better than the nausea the last round of drugs gave me. I never want that again. There really should be a ban on that kind of side effect."

"Totally. I mean who let that side effect slip in anyways?" Janey joked, and her mother riffed on all the horrible side effects she'd had to endure in the last four years. All with a glint of mischief in her eyes. At least her mom had her gift of gab and a way of making everyone around her smile and feel good.

As the conversation wrapped up, Dana asked, "Are you going to be okay, sweetie?"

"I should be asking that of you, Mom."

"Once per day is quite enough," Dana said. "Love you to the stars and back."

"And around the galaxy." Janey finished their standard send-off and closed the comm. She considered pinging her mom's doctors about getting the weekly check-in notes early, but no. Being a pest in this instance would not yield results. Unlike the pest she'd been to Detective Manoush Aziz about finding Christine, sending in her scenarios of what could have happened to her friend.

Detective Aziz had been polite but firm and even a little suspicious of Janey. Pestering the police hadn't worked. So Janey had hacked into her friend's private files, something the police hadn't or couldn't since it was only considered a missing person's case. A week after Christine's disappearance, Janey followed up on a passing comment in Christine's diary that led her to an out-of-the-way bar at the edge of the city in Bayview, where women were dressed to party and men dressed to impress. The damp, fetid stench of the reclaimed marsh-lands at the south end of the seawall had overpowered the heated front courtyard where people mingled, danced, and smoked.

Janey asked them clumsy, earnest questions. Their

flippant answers led her to the woods by the ocean late that night, which was where she'd stumbled upon Christine's body. She'd immediately called the detective, then had been hustled away, driven home by an officer, and left in the dark about the investigation. Detective Aziz had visited her the next day in the apartment Janey had shared with her boyfriend and gone over in painstaking detail what led Janey to Christine's body. Shivering, though she was wrapped in a blanket, Janey told the detective the people at the bar had mentioned a clandestine sexy meet by the old Stern Grove amphitheater. When Janey had arrived, she'd heard some growling and yipping at the tree line and went to investigate. She hadn't seen any animals, but she had stumbled upon Christine's body.

"I must have scared away the wolves," Janey had said.

"What possessed you to go toward wild animals?" Detective Aziz had asked.

"I had to know. What if Christine was hurt?" Janey said.

The detective had her go through the story one more time, then left, never contacting her again. Christine's disappearance had been Janey's first investigative experience in things that weren't engineering problems. And had completely changed the trajectory of her life.

Janey rolled her neck and shoulders. She needed to focus on the here and now. She called up both Amelia's Granton San Francisco photo ID and Christine's.

She shifted in her chair. Right. It wasn't just a passing resemblance. It wasn't just a first impression. The two women looked like they could be sisters—long, narrow face, big round eyes—though Christine had been twenty-eight years old and Amelia was twenty-three. Even the jaw was the same, narrow and elfin. Both had brown-hazel eyes. The same slim pixie build, though the image wasn't of their whole body. And their initial disappearance occurred at the same month four years ago.

Her comm buzzed against her wrist, and she waved open a channel. It was the security switchboard.

"Kim, oh! Right, the staff meeting," Janey said.

"Actually, I'm patching a call through to you from a guest."

"Can you handle it? I should get to the meeting."

"She asked specifically for you."

"Who is it?"

"She wouldn't let her ident show, but she's calling from a guest room. Want me to track it down?"

"No, that's fine. Thanks, Kim," Janey said. "I'll find out soon enough."

Kim made the comm switch, and Janey said, "Investigator McCallister here."

"Hello, Investigator. Am I calling at a bad time?" An unfamiliar woman spoke slowly, each word enunciated, her voice rich and melodious.

"Yes, ma'am. I mean, no, ma'am. How can I help you?" Occasionally, guests called the security staff main office, but this was the first time she'd been asked for directly.

"I request the honor of your presence for tea at ten o'clock in the Library Suite above the SkyBar."

So formal. That was in two hours.

"To whom am I speaking, and what is this regarding, please?"

"Oh, yes, right, dear. I am Mrs. Malina Bakaj, though my friends call me Lina."

The widow of the late Dima Bakaj. He'd been a guest on board three months ago. Her first question was, what did the widow want? Then, what was she doing on board

L'Étoile? And, why did she want to speak to Janey? Chief Milano was the one to handle clients.

"Mrs. Bakaj, yes, I can meet you at ten hundred—I mean, at ten o'clock." She eyed her wrist comm, time-piece, and microcomputer. It was eight-oh-three.

"You probably have a lot of questions for me, Investigator."

"I do." Like, why now? And what did she want with Janey? Though Janey had been the one to investigate her husband's death.

"I look forward to doing my best to answer them. Ta ta!" The comm went silent.

"Well," Janey said to the empty room, "what could Bakaj's widow want after all this time?"

She had to go to the meeting. Her husband had been killed on her watch.

Janey left her quarters, headed to the staff meeting in the conference room, and handed out the day's assignments. The team was gelling together nicely after a bit of a rocky start. When she'd arrived over three months ago, they hadn't trusted her, and she'd stumbled on a few cases at the start. But then they'd solved some high profile cases together, with a bit of danger, and they had bonded over both the successes and the dangers.

To Meilani Shawhan and Antonia Lane, she gave the casino positions, both undercover as players. Shawhan was five foot three and had been a gymnast in high school. Lane was five foot nine and a former college basketball player. They'd both arrived at L'Étoile over a year ago and were good friends. They nodded and eyed each other, holding back their grins. They both liked that kind of work and were good at spotting irregularities. A robust AI vid system would notify them of most gambling irregularities, but you needed the human touch to really diagnose what was going on.

She gave Ed Kou rounds in the below staff areas including quarters, engineering, farming, and housekeeping, to give him a break from doing the casino floor repairs. She handed Mandlenkosi Dube rounds in the guest corridors and the recreation areas in the upper levels. She didn't anticipate any problems, but it paid to be ready for anything.

"Nice change of pace," Mandlenkosi said, and Ed agreed.

The two men preferred to work together and would be in touch all day long. As long as they kept their eyes open and did their jobs, Janey was fine with their ongoing communication.

That left Larissa Ferreira. The sixth and seventh team members, Natalia Goldberg and Clark Alexander Bernard, were on leave Earthside.

Ferreira looked at her expectantly from across the table.

"I have a job for you," Janey said. "Meet me in my office after the meeting."

"Yes, boss," Ferreira said.

"She doesn't like to be called boss," Shawhan said.

"I know." Ferreira raised her hands in mock surrender.

"Chief Milano is our boss," Lane said.

"One more thing," Janey said and glanced around the table. Everyone looked alert. "Advance to the next module in your training manuals. Firearms tests coming soon—I'll announce that day-of—and I'll be recommending you all for field combat training."

Lane pursed her lips.

"Something to say, Lane?" Janey asked.

Lane shrugged, then met Janey's gaze. "Chief Milano never saw the need for so much training."

"But I do." She looked around the table, slowly, at each of her team members. "You were all here for the Bakaj case. We all need to be ready for that kind of crazy. Okay?"

"Yes, ma'am." Lane straightened in her chair. As did the others.

Janey stood, and the meeting adjourned. She refilled her coffee cup and took it across the corridor to her boxy office. It was small, but it was hers. Ferreira trailed her and stood without speaking while Janey settled behind her desk, sipped her coffee, then stood and came back around her desk. She was jumpy and needed to pace. But the office was too small for that with one other person in it, so she perched on her desk.

Larissa Ferreira was Brazilian and Filipina, and she was happy doing a little of everything in the security department. At eighteen-years-old and straight out of Basic Space Wing training and a six-month tour on the Space Wing Space Station in medium Earth orbit, she was eager to learn. Space Wing discharged her honorably, and with her enthusiasm and attention to detail manifested in her reports, she'd make a good investigator one day if she wanted to specialize in that direction.

"I need you to do a personal security shift here." Janey waved her the staff quarters number.

Ferreira glanced at her comm for the location. "Yes, ma'am."

"Make sure no one comes in unless they know the passcode," Janey said. "Mai Chen is there now. You'll be relieving her. I'll be there soon to talk to her. No one comes in except me or Kim, or another security officer, but only after you've gotten the approval from me."

"Who are we guarding?"

Janey stood and moved to the wall screen and opened Amelia's hotel guest record that included her photo. "A guest who needs our protection." She turned to face Ferreira. "She's asked for sanctuary. Amelia Gain."

"Oh." Ferreira nodded, eyes down and to the left, indicating talking to oneself.

"What do you know?" Janey narrowed her eyes at the young security officer.

"Just rumors, really."

"And you didn't report them to me or Chief Milano?"

"Like I said—rumors. Nothing substantial. I know you prefer evidence. A good investigator needs evidence...clues."

"We do, but we also sometimes need to follow our hunches. What are these rumors?" Janey crossed her arms over her chest and peered down at Ferreira.

And why hadn't she heard them before now?

Ferreira lifted her chin, not intimidated by Janey's attitude or one-foot advantage over her. Good for her. Ferreira had grown up fast in the rough and tumble region of the northeastern Brazilian Empire, in Sao Paolo, and she could stare down the meanest drunks from her petite height. Janey had seen Ferreira do that both in the commissary and at the SkyBar.

"Rumors of young women passing through with much older men."

"Here on L'Étoile?"

Ferreira nodded.

"When?"

"A few weeks back. It was one of those things overheard in the commissary, I think, from some kitchen staff doing room service. They get around."

"They do," Janey said. "Do you remember who said this? Any other details?"

Ferreira blushed. "Just that they envied the young women all their luxuries."

"Who said this?"

"I'm sorry to say, Investigator McCallister, I honestly don't remember." Ferreira held her gaze.

Janey nodded. "Here's what I need you to do. Look through personnel records and see if you can identify who. I'm assuming that the one who spoke was a woman."

"I'm pretty sure it was," Ferreira said and opened up her holo screen on her wrist comm.

"And, Ferreira, I'd like you to start documenting all rumors and hearsay like this. All right?"

"Yes, ma'am." Ferreira stood at attention.

"At ease." Janey smiled and shook her head. "I had no idea when I took this job that I'd be in a trainer's role."

"You're good at it. It certainly wasn't happening before you got here."

Ferreira had started six months before Janey had arrived.

"If Amelia wakes up before I get there, tell her who you are and that you're there on my authority. I prefer she not leave the room, but if she insists, go with her. Keep her out of the casino."

"I'm her bodyguard, acting as a protector?"

"Yes."

"Okay." Ferreira grinned.

NINE

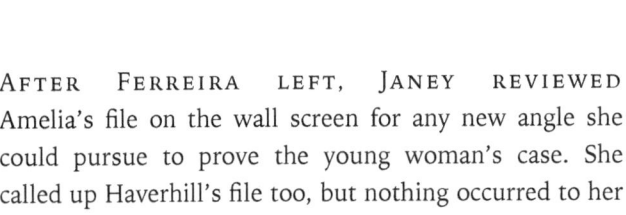

AFTER FERREIRA LEFT, JANEY REVIEWED Amelia's file on the wall screen for any new angle she could pursue to prove the young woman's case. She called up Haverhill's file too, but nothing occurred to her other than the obvious: she would need to interview Amelia again. Maybe after a night in a safe place, Amelia would feel more relaxed and open up.

She sped through the nightly reports from Kou, Dube, and Ferreira, approved them, and then she sent them onto Chief Milano.

Then came a knock at her door, and Kim entered with a plate of pastries.

"I snagged the last one for you," Kim said.

"You're the best."

"Thank Mai Chen," Kim said. "She must have known you caught a case and had a long night, so she made your favorite cream-filled buns."

"She's a gem."

Kim nodded, lost in thought for a moment. "And we

all benefitted. Didn't you see them in the conference room?"

"I've got a lot of my mind. Like you, my friend." Janey took the plate of pastries and set it on her desk. "You're a gem for bringing them in. What's up?"

Kim waved away the question. "What do *you* need?" She strode over to the wallscreen with Amelia and Haverhill's profiles up. "This Haverhill an untouchable?"

Kim was masterful at diverting the conversation away from herself. She hadn't said a word about her vacation leave, but something had happened to bring her down.

"You know you can talk to me," Janey said.

"I know," Kim said. "So Haverhill… What's his deal?"

"Other than Amelia's word against his, I have nothing. I need to talk to her." Janey called up Amelia's disappearance report from Granton San Francisco four years back. "Her disappearance report is the only red flag I have, but it's not much to go on."

"And?" Kim turned her big compassionate eyes on Janey and waited, the epitome of patience.

"You know me well." Janey sighed. "Amelia was reported missing around the same time as another woman was reported missing, and—" Janey brought Amelia and Christine's pictures front and center, over the other files.

"Are they related?" Kim asked softly.

"Not as far as I can tell."

"Who is the other woman?"

"My best friend, Christine Baptista."

"What happened to her?" Kim took in the images, subdued.

"She was found murdered at the edge of the forest."

Kim put a hand on Janey's arm. "I am so sorry, Janey."

"I was the one to find her." Janey blinked back the tears. "I wouldn't give up. I found clues. I spearheaded a search. I quit my teaching job. I was obsessed. I couldn't believe the authorities when they said she'd just run off to start a life elsewhere. She'd been engaged to be married. She was happy."

"What happened to her?"

Janey shook her head. "She'd been dumped in the woods." She forced in air past the heaviness in her chest. "Police said their thin leads led nowhere—if they said anything at all. But I found her."

Kim said nothing and just stood in solidarity with her.

"They closed the case because they didn't have any suspects. At least, that's what they told me. Her fiancé was cleared and then moved away. I left town soon after that. I needed a break. Then my mother fell sick. And—" She shrugged.

"You found your way to us."

"After four years in Space Wing. And now a young woman needs our help."

No way was Janey letting even one woman slip through the cracks on her watch.

Like she had with Christine.

Janey cleared her throat and blinked away the tears.

Kim gave Janey a steadying gaze and spoke gently. "I'll be at my post if you need me." She fussed with the hibiscus propped over one ear—an orange one today. "You look like you could use some time in the solar chamber. When was the last time you went?"

"Last week. I'm fine."

"I heard Valdez was on board," Kim said.

Janey made a face. "*Was* being the operative word."

Kim gave her a look like it was her fault Valdez was

such a mercurial presence in her life and left her office. But maybe it wasn't Valdez Kim was thinking of but someone in her life. Kim never spoke of her love life, come to think of it.

Although Valdez didn't actually say he was leaving. What was he up to? Where was he hiding? She could call up his hotel record under his fake ident, but why should she chase him down? Maybe she was giving the man mixed signals. Maybe she couldn't do relationships right now. It looked like neither could he. What a pair they made.

Janey cleared her wallscreen, locked her office, and headed down to speak to Amelia.

She ran her holo security badge at the door panel but got no response. Good.

"Passcode please," Ferreira called.

"Alpha-delta-niner-four-omega," Janey said. "It's Investigator McCallister."

Ferreira opened the door. "Can't be too careful, eh?" the petite security officer said and pointed to the covered tray on the table. "Mai Chen left some breakfast for Amelia thirty minutes ago."

"Has she gotten up?"

"No."

"Have you peeked in on her?"

"Just for a second to confirm her presence."

"Good."

The quarters were bigger than hers—a small one-bedroom instead of the studio she had. She and Ferreira were in the open-plan room that held a small couch, a table that seated four, and a kitchenette nook. The adjoining bedroom had a private bathroom and was where Amelia was sleeping.

Janey went to the bedroom door and it slid open.

Amelia was wrapped up in the covers, her knees to her chest, breathing deeply. She looked tiny in the queen-sized bed.

Janey bent over the young woman and said softly, "Amelia, it's time to wake up. It's nine."

Amelia moaned and said something in a foreign language that sounded like *"wo she dao la."* Mandarin for "I got it."

"What did you get, Amelia?" Janey touched her shoulder.

The woman sat with a start, her hair mashed on one side, fear in her wide eyes. "What? Where am I?"

"You're in quarters on the service level. Safe and away from…" The rich aroma of coffee wafted in. "Would you like some coffee? There's a breakfast tray for you too. I'm sure Mai Chen, one of our cooks, brought a nice assortment for you."

Amelia nodded and yawned.

"You said something. While you were asleep."

"What?" Amelia squeaked and darted her gaze around the room as if looking for something or someone.

"It's okay. You're okay here," Janey said.

"What did I say? No one knows I'm here, right?"

"Only Kim—the woman who brought you here last night. You remember her? Mai Chen, a member of the kitchen staff who was here earlier this morning. And now one of my security staff. You'll meet her when you get up."

Amelia slipped out of bed, not looking at Janey. "Kim said she had some clothes for me."

Janey glanced about and didn't see any. She called over her shoulder. "Ferreira, can you bring in the clothes? I think I saw them on the couch. Oh, and the coffee too."

"No, I'll get the coffee in a sec. I want to feel presentable." Amelia glanced at the bathroom. "Maybe take a quick shower, if that's okay."

"Of course." Janey patted her hand.

Amelia froze, her vitals spiking.

"I know you're scared."

"I sometimes talk nonsense in my sleep. Was it silly, what I said?"

"No, you said 'I got it,' in Mandarin. Pretty sure. I only know the basics. I didn't know you spoke Mandarin."

"We all learned it in school."

"I did too, but it didn't stick." Janey chuckled.

Amelia didn't smile. "If you don't mind, I'll take that shower now." Her voice was small, child-like again.

"I'll just be out there with Officer Ferreira if you need anything. I'm sure the bathroom is fully stocked. We'll leave the clothes on the bed."

Amelia sped for the bathroom, and Janey returned to the small sitting room.

Fifteen minutes later, Amelia came out of the bedroom looking fresh, dressed in black stretch pants and a black sweatshirt that Kim had provided. They were a little big on her. She'd availed herself of the makeup customizer and looked pretty in the soft eyeshadow and pink lipstick, but her eyes were haunted.

"I just have a few more questions for you," Janey said. "But first, you need to eat. Then we'll talk."

Amelia sat at the table and ate from a plate of breakfast options, from cereal and hardboiled eggs to croissants and even sticky rice and fish.

Ferreira placed a steamy mug beside Amelia and sat opposite her. "I warmed it up for you." She watched

Amelia eat toast spread with egg. "Hi, I'm Larissa Ferreira."

Amelia nodded. "Hi, Larissa." And then she continued to dig into the food with a big appetite.

Ferreira worked on her holo screen, probably doing the research Janey asked.

Janey let Amelia eat in peace and studied her holo screen of Amelia's file, as she had been doing while Amelia was in the shower. She'd developed a theory as to what might have happened to Amelia after she'd left Granton SF.

"You can ask me your questions." Amelia wiped her hands on a napkin and eyed the plate, nearly empty.

"Did you leave Granton SF of your own free will?" Janey asked.

Amelia nodded.

"Why?"

"I thought I was getting a great job opportunity I couldn't get anywhere else—at least, not at home." She made a face. "I needed something exciting. Doing sales at one of the biggest coffee conglomerates far away. Promise of training, advancement, and travel to exotic locales." Amelia fiddled with the tie strings on her sweatshirt neck and didn't make eye contact.

"Did you get that great job opportunity?"

Amelia shrugged. "At first."

"Tell me about it."

"In between and sometimes during the sales training and work, there was travel, nice clothes, great pay, and great guys who paid attention to me."

"But you were only nineteen."

"So? I wanted to see the world. This seemed like the way to do it. The Independent Empire of Ethiopia seemed so exotic." Amelia gulped her coffee and glanced away.

Her vitals had appeared normal until this moment, when her heart rate spiked. Janey's ocular screen went fuzzy for a millisecond and then adjusted back to normal.

Either something was wrong in her implant, again, or maybe it was something Amelia was doing. Something to keep an eye on.

"Then what happened, Amelia?"

Amelia shook her head and wrapped her arms around herself. After a moment, she finally spoke. "When I turned twenty-one, that's when it started. At first, I thought it was fun. Visiting a different part of the world with a different man. I felt special. Then I'd get dropped off at headquarters in Djibouti and told to get back to work. I had to pretend to my office mates that nothing was unusual. I was told to hide all my nice clothes and jewelry from them and act normal. I'd never know when I'd be called. It was fun for a few years." Her voice dropped to a whisper. "Then I started hating life."

"And Haverhill? How does he fit into all this? He said you were his girlfriend."

Amelia snapped her gaze to Janey's, wide-eyed, pale.

"It's okay, Amelia. Breathe. You're not breathing." Janey leaned forward and touched Amelia's arm.

Amelia sputtered. "He's—he's…" She shook her head. "I can't talk about it." She ran for the bedroom and locked the door behind her.

Janey could easily override the lock with her security clearance, but Amelia didn't need any more people invading her space.

"Amelia, I'm right here if you want to talk. I want to help you." Janey stood at the door.

"I need sanctuary. I need—" Amelia went quiet.

"What do you need, Amelia?"

"My life back."

"I'm here to help you do that. Why can't you just go back to Granton SF?"

"I forfeited my place. My parents—I wouldn't want to bring this kind of trouble to them. Besides, they'll—they'll come find me. They'll never let me leave."

"Who? Haverhill?"

"Y-Yes. A-And the others," Amelia choked out.

"What others? Who else, Amelia?"

"I don't know." Amelia's voice sounded sad, helpless.

"Come out, Amelia, and let me help you."

"I just want to sleep."

"Okay." Janey leaned against the door jamb. "I just have one more question for now."

Amelia said nothing.

"Were you a sex slave?"

TEN

AMELIA DIDN'T REPLY FOR A LONG MOMENT, then she finally said though the bedroom door, "Yes."

Every woman should have a choice on how she wanted to live her life and should receive the opportunities to act upon that choice. Every single person ought to have that choice. If you had education, luck, and connections, it seemed like you could have that choice.

"We're working on getting you sanctuary," Janey said to Amelia.

No sound from the bedroom.

"Amelia, I'm going now, so Officer Ferreira is here if you need anything."

"Thank you," Amelia said in a faint voice.

Janey repeated the security instructions to Ferreira, with the young security agent nodding and attentive. Then Janey checked for Haverhill's current location. He was in his suite on the seventh level. She exited the room and headed for the staff elevator bank that would take her to the front of the hotel-casino.

She needed to confront Haverhill again and find out

who he worked with or for. He'd already admitted to knowing Amelia. She was afraid of him and others. Janey needed confirmation that Amelia was in danger. She needed to confront Haverhill without creating an incident that would get her reported back to Milano and his boss. They'd probably put her back on probation, and she couldn't afford that. She couldn't put this job in jeopardy. Mom depended on Janey's salary for her experimental drug treatments and to pay the bills.

She was ruminating on an angle and waiting for the staff lift when Kim commed her.

"How is Amelia? Did you get her full story?" Kim asked.

Janey let the door open and close without getting in. "She's shaken up. She's had a rough couple of years, drawn out by adventure and riches before being coerced into prostitution."

"Oh, dear. As I suspected."

"How many other young women are out there like her?" Janey said, more to herself than Kim.

"I imagine too many," Kim said after a moment. "How are you holding up?"

"Fine. I'm fine. I just want to get to the bottom of this, and I am coming up with no clear leads, except talking to Haverhill again."

"Gotta go!" Kim clicked off without her cheery goodbye. Chief Milano had probably stepped into the squad room.

She hadn't checked in with Milano lately and wasn't about to now. Not without something solid to report.

A minute later, the doors to the service elevator opened again when her comm buzzed against her wrist. This time it was Chief Milano.

"McCallister here."

"In my office now."

"I'm on my way to do an interview."

"Office. Now."

"Yes, sir. On my way."

Three minutes later, Janey stood in front of Chief Milano's desk, his dancing lady figurines lining the front edge. He looked up from his large holo screen and peered at her over his fake glasses. He still wore those—part of his obsession with the past.

"What's this I hear about you investigating Jonas Haverhill?" Milano said.

"Another guest has reported a claim against him."

"I have seen no report."

"I'm still gathering evidence, hence the second interview."

"You've already spoken to him?"

"Yes, last night. Undercover. I wanted to speak to him again in an official capacity"

"You are not to speak to him again."

Janey blew out a breath. "Why? Did he complain?"

"No. The request came from Mr. Schoeneman."

"How did he hear about it?" She'd said nothing to the reclusive hotel-casino owner.

"That's none of our concern," Milano said. "It's his station. What he says goes."

She focused on keeping her breathing even. "How do you propose I follow up on this guest's report? That is my job, isn't it?"

"A paying guest?"

"Of course." What kind of question was that? "As per regulations, I need to follow up." Breathe in, breathe out. Don't clench hands. "Is there something else going on? What do you know?"

"Nothing, McCallister."

"Sir, you put me in a difficult position. What would you have me do if I can't interview my prime suspect?"

"What are this person's allegations?"

Janey firmed her lips. "Rape."

"Serious." He nodded. "Evidence?"

"Only her word against his. Medical says no evidence, but she was in a difficult situation of essentially being a sex slave. For years."

"Horrible." He shook his head, seeming genuinely sad about Amelia's situation.

"It is. That's why I don't understand why Schoeneman is halting my investigation."

Chief Milano sighed, took off his glasses, and rubbed the bridge of his nose. "I honestly don't understand either. Is there any other way you can go about getting what you need?"

"Not without getting Haverhill's explicit permission. I was on my way to ask him, but I don't think he's the big fish in this scenario. She's afraid to tell me who is. I'm not sure she even knows, but she's definitely holding something back." Giving up the fight for total self-restraint, she clenched and unclenched her hands behind her back. "Haverhill is my best lead for this."

Chief Milano put on his glasses. "I have to defer to Schoeneman."

"Tell him what I told you. He has to understand."

Milano shook his head. "Until you have evidence, you need to find another way, McCallister."

Janey frowned and turned to leave.

"Good job with the weekly reports, McCallister." He nodded at her.

"Did you read my recommendations?"

"Next level field training for the team? Yes."

"And?"

Chief Milano eyed his screen. "Not sure it's the right time."

"They're progressing well with the hand-to-hand and marksmanship. When is the right time?" Janey asked, keeping her voice light and curious, so as not to threaten Milano with the anger that wanted to thrash out.

"I'll let you know." He didn't look up from his holo screen.

That was her cue to leave.

Infuriating. At first, she liked how hands-off Chief Milano was, but now his actions bordered on negligence. He was motivated by his appetites and didn't want anything to agitate his cushy routine.

How was she going to get the evidence she needed against Haverhill or whoever was behind him?

For now, however, she had to put Haverhill and Milano musings on hold. If she didn't hurry, she would be late for her appointment with the mysterious Mrs. Bakaj.

ELEVEN

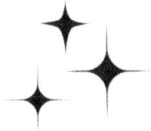

FOR THE TEA WITH MRS. BAKAJ, JANEY DRESSED in a grey wool pantsuit offset by a pink and teal scarf over the pearl choker her mother had given her and teardrop pearl earrings. Mom had given her the choker as a high school graduation gift, packed with photos and holos of her childhood. Janey was going into the front of the house and wanted to dress the part of the urbane sophisticate.

She'd done her due diligence on Mrs. Malina Bakaj. She'd come aboard L'Étoile alone four days ago. It was her image in the guest roster that gave Janey pause. She'd seen the woman already twice the night before— once at the bar right before Amelia appeared, and then again, a few hours later flirting with a dark-haired man.

Janey commed Ferreira, who said that Amelia was still asleep, and she'd just checked in on her. The young woman deserved justice. Yet there was nothing Janey could do until she found another way to substantiate Amelia's claim. She needed ideas. Maybe by the time she was done with tea with Mrs. Bakaj, something would occur to her.

From her quarters, Janey crossed into the front of the house. The stately lobby was not busy at this hour, only a few guests in conversation with the front desk personnel. She entered the casino. The slots flashed their strobes but jingled with one or two gamblers. The SkyBar was quiet, as were most of the gaming tables.

Twice in as many days, Janey hustled up the staircase beside the vibrant green living wall and took the mezzanine hall to one of the private suites. Her presence in front of the door alerted whoever was inside, and the door opened.

There she was, the elegant woman Janey had seen the night before. This time she was dressed in a black sequined pantsuit with a brooch on her lapel full of rubies, sapphires, and diamonds—no doubt costing Janey's yearly salary, if not more. Malina Bakaj, like her husband before her, didn't look a day over seventy. He'd been ninety. Malina could also be that age.

"Won't you come in?" Mrs. Bakaj gestured to the book-lined room with its royal blue plush couches, perfect for curling up on. "I took the liberty of ordering us afternoon tea, even though it's a little early. I hope you like tea, biscuits, and clotted cream. Oh, and finger sandwiches. They're so much fun."

A long, low real wood table fronted the couch, and there was an ornate silver tea service displayed on it.

Janey nodded and stepped in. No one else was in the spacious room.

"Please sit." The older woman sat and poured herself some tea. "How do you take your tea?"

"Black, please." Janey sat at the edge of the couch and folded her hands over her clutch with her small gun, handcuffs, and makeup kit in it. She wanted to be prepared for anything, though she didn't think Mrs. Bakaj was any kind of threat. She just didn't want to be caught unprepared again.

"Mrs. Bakaj, how can I help you?"

"Right to the point. Please call me Malina. Or Lina." She waved her hand as if it didn't matter, sipped her tea, and sighed. "Just the best. The chef is why I came, you know." She nodded. "In addition to meeting you that is."

"I see."

Mrs. Bakaj sipped more tea, gazed at the pastries, and sighed.

Janey waited for her to speak, but when she didn't, Janey asked, "Are you all right, Mrs. Bakaj? Malina?"

The older woman waved her hand as if in question, her bejeweled fingers sparkling in the room's soft lighting, and then she sighed again. "I'm fine."

But she didn't seem fine. Something was on her mind.

"So, the reason I'm here…" Janey prompted. "How can I help you?"

"I called you here because I wanted to get the story of Dima's last few days from the people around him." She folded her long fingers around her teacup. "And I heard you were the investigator who solved his theft and murder." She sipped again.

Her vitals were steady, her pulse was strong, and she wasn't pretending even a little to be the grieving widow. What was this woman's ulterior motive for this meeting?

"I'm not sure what I can tell you that isn't in the official record. What specifically would you like to know?"

"I don't want the official story. I want to know how he was. Was he happy? Did he seem happy?" She nibbled on a tiny tuna sandwich cut into a triangle.

"I suppose so. He was kind to me." Janey eyed her tea as it cooled in front of her.

Mrs. Bakaj finished the sandwich and reached for a scone with small dark fruit in it. "I heard he was sweet on you."

"Who did you hear that from? He wasn't inappropriate, if that's what you're implying. Only kind."

"Oh, nothing of the sort. I was referring to a young man who is also sweet on you."

"Who?"

"Doesn't matter, but what does matter is I'm curious about an item of value. It wasn't in my husband's possessions when they were returned to me. It was so kind of Mr. Schoeneman to ship them at his expense."

While reclusive from most staff, Mr. Schoeneman, the owner of the station, kept close tabs on what happened to his hotel-casino guests.

"Yes, nice of him. What item are you referring to?" Janey asked. Did she mean the gem or the little black book?

"Something that had lots of information in it." Malina smiled sweetly.

"I know of two such items. One is in Sol police custody, a gem, and the other we released back to you, with the rest of his belongings. A little black book."

"Do you know when the gem will be released back to me?"

"I don't. You'll need to take it up with Sol Police headquarters."

Malina nodded as if confirming something. "Thank you."

"You're welcome. Are you sure there's nothing else?" Janey picked up the saucer and teacup.

Malina nibbled a sandwich.

Janey waited and watched and let the silence extend. The way the woman scanned the room and wouldn't look at her was a classic sign of avoiding something.

"Mrs. Bakaj..." Janey prompted. "If there's nothing else, then I really must get back. I'm in the middle of a case." She settled the saucer and teacup on the table with a chink and stood.

Malina's heart rate spiked. "Are you in a rush?"

"I do have a case I'm working. I'm curious as to the real purpose of this meeting."

Malina sighed, glanced at the rug, and then held Janey's gaze. "A certain dark-haired young man, an admirer of yours, wanted to know if you were all right. I told him I'd check up on you."

"I see." Her cheeks heated, and she sat back on the couch.

Orlando Valdez.

Mrs. Bakaj had been flirting with him last night in the casino while Janey finished her nightcap, although she hadn't recognized him at the time. He'd done something different with his hair, and she'd only caught a glimpse of him from the back.

Why bring up Valdez? What was Malina's motive?

Malina shrugged an elegant shoulder. "You know him, I see. He gave an obviously false name, but he was so charming, I didn't mind." Her cheeks reddened, and she fanned herself.

"And the name was?"

"Ravel Bolero. He had on a red velvet close-cropped jacket. Oh, the musicality of his Catalonian accent... He was sweet."

How many roles was Valdez playing? He had been speaking in a French accent when she saw him at the pai gow table. Same jacket though.

"Curly dark hair, almond eyes, and broad-shoul-dered?" Janey asked. "You know, your husband tried to play matchmaker with us too."

"My husband was a romantic at heart. Which is why when Ravel Bolero, or whatever his name was, let slip that some things were left behind, I just needed to know what they were. My husband had many secrets, you know. Although how this Ravel Bolero knew, he wouldn't say. Most mysterious, don't you think?"

"Indeed. Nothing was left behind—as I explained. Did Ravel Bolero, or whatever his name was, say what they were?"

"Clammed right up when I asked." Malina lowered her voice over-dramatically. There was no one else in the room. "I think he said too much. So thrilling. I feel like I'm in the middle of a spy vid."

So unlike Valdez to spill. What game was that man playing? Why would he drop hints about one of his investigations to a civilian? Or maybe he was getting careless, and she didn't know him at all.

"What did you know about your husband's business dealings, Mrs. Bakaj?"

"I told you. It's Malina." She reached over and patted Janey's hand. "I know nothing. He told me nothing. We had separate lives for a long time."

"You were married for over fifty years. Five children, and thirteen grand and great-grandchildren. He told you nothing? You never wondered where his fortune came from?" Janey blurted out. What possessed her to ask that?

"Industry. Weapons. Chemicals." She peered at all her rings. "Like I said, he had secrets. I had mine."

"Hasn't his estate been settled?" Janey asked and clenched her purse tight. What was the purpose of this meeting? Impatience coursed through her. The desire to throw her clutch at the wall was strong, but her self-control was stronger.

"Yes, it has. He and I had been living our separate lives for over five years at the time of his death. I have my own fortune. My own life. My children are all set up, as are their families."

"Your former husband's fortune was made mostly with a drug called Felicitan," Janey said. Just to see what Malina would say or do. "He held the patent for it. No doubt his company still does."

Malina sat back against the couch, pale, her breathing shallow. "That is a dangerous drug," she said. "I had no idea. Is that why he was killed?"

"I think it's more complicated than that." Now that she'd flapped her mouth, she wasn't sure how much more to reveal, so she opted for caution. "Mrs. Bakaj, Malina, I can ask the Sol Police to send you the formal reports if you'd like?"

Malina waved her hand as if batting something away. "No, that won't be necessary. It's all probably watered down for public consumption." She set her tea down with a clatter, spilling the dark liquid onto the saucer. She apparently didn't trust the Sol government.

Janey stood again. "If there's nothing else..." to this odd conversation.

"I've probably kept you long enough from your duties. I just wanted to be sure Dima was happy in his final days. And everyone including you seems to say he was. Thank you for indulging an old woman's whims," Malina said, peering at her rings. Then she glanced at Janey, steel in her gaze. "Whatever it is you still have of my husband's, be sure to send his possessions to my quarters before I leave in three days."

"All case evidence was sent to Sol Police," Janey said.

Malina held her gaze.

Did this woman know Janey had made a copy of the little black book? Could that be what she was fishing for? Could she be searching for those who had a copy of the information? If so, to what end?

Janey headed for the door, which glided open silently on her approach.

The little black book... Dima's business connections might be Malina's connections too.

She needed to take another look at that little black book.

TWELVE

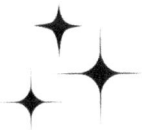

THE LITTLE BLACK BOOK WASN'T REALLY A BOOK. At least, not anymore. The actual book was in evidence at Sol Police headquarters in New York, where Valdez had no doubt filed it for his case a few months back after he'd helped her catch a murderer.

What she had was a translated list of names, as the original was in Cyrillic—names compiled by Dima Bakaj. Janey speculated the people on the list had been Dima's business partners in his drugs and weapons businesses and that Dima was going to turn over the list to the authorities. He never got the chance as he was killed before he could do that.

Settled back in her office, Janey stood at the wallscreen and stared at it. She wanted to search the black book but needed data to compare it to. So she started with the connections between Schoeneman and Haverhill. How connected were they? She input the query and immediately items scrolled down the screen. Lots and lots of business deals between the two men.

Not so unusual. Lots of the guests were business partners, clients, or customers of Schoeneman in his many
businesses of asteroid mining, cutting edge tech,
graphene construction, and all kinds of agriculture both
around the globe and above it. He was one of the richest
men in the world, if not the richest, and he was the only
one who could afford to build this space station hotel-
casino with the world's longest space elevator.

Then she cross-checked the list with the names in
Dima Bakaj's little black book.

Five minutes later, the database spat out a match: S.
M. Bertrand. Male or female? No clear first name, so she
couldn't tell. Bertrand was in Dima's book and was
connected to Haverhill Industrials via a partner company.
Bertrand was also listed as a board member in one of
Schoeneman's companies. If Bertrand was in Dima's
book, then maybe he had a criminal record.

Next, she ran a query for S. M. Bertrand in all known
criminal databases that her L'Étoile clearance would
allow her to search. Her clearance wasn't as broad as a
Sol Unified Planets investigative clearance, what Valdez
had, but it allowed for a fairly broad and deep sweep of
information. Alongside, she ran a media search. Media
popped up right away. However, no criminal records
were found.

Images of Bertrand stacked up on the screen—sometimes dressed in male clothing, and other times in quite
revealing gowns, heavily made up with lots of rouge,
mascara, and lipstick, showing plenty of cleavage. Lots of
articles quoted the flamboyant and outspoken S. M.
Bertrand. All the publications shared an anti-Granton
pro-corporate stance.

The Granton regions, where all citizens had universal
health, housing, and income, often had to fend off media

attacks like these, even though they had repeatedly won the right to self-govern. As did ever other corporate zone.

Across the North American Region, and all over the Sol, on planet and off, the Grantons were patchworked in between corporate city-states and agricultural zones, usually owned by their neighboring corporate city-state.

"GRANTONS MUST BE DISBANDED. THEY COST THE NATION-STATES TOO MUCH."

That argument hadn't held up in the Sol Unified Court the half-dozen times it had been challenged over the years. Not since the Right to Self-Governance laws went into effect fifty years previous as part of the formation of the inter-planetary wide Sol Unified Planets government.

"GRANTONS TAKE RESOURCES FROM PRIVATE CITIES."

Science and economics had proved that wrong time and time again. Every corporate nation-state region that had a Granton within five hundred kilometers benefitted from the trade and traffic.

"REGIONS MUST BAN NEW GRANTONS."

And still the corporate lobbyists insisted that Grantons were bad.

Janey sighed. Old arguments spewed by S. M. Bertrand—who wasn't a politician. What business did this person have attacking the Grantons?

Janey focused on the details. No good getting riled

up. He or she was an owner of a nondescript investment firm by the name of Skinner, Grossman, and Hunt. Janey tapped into the business data, but she only found investment jargon, couched in such generic terms as to be useless:

> "Double your annuity investment on the lunar exchange. We charge the lowest rates on Earth and Luna and can facilitate all of your investment needs in Mars Station and beyond."

Sounded like a front for an outfit that could get anything for anyone.

Just what were they supplying and to whom? What did she stumble into, and did it have anything to do with her case?

Janey blew out a breath and paced her office—a short walkabout. The rhetoric about Grantons was getting to her. Grantons helped so many people, allowing the possibility of a better life the for-profit areas never could. Company towns, all of them.

Her whole childhood had been about leaving the corporate zone she grew up in to move to a Granton. She was one of the lucky ones who'd been able to get into one.

She dug deeper into the media items and encountered generic speak again in a news report from NTT Agency, the Nippon Tech Times Agency, out of Japanese Shogunate.

> "Bertrand, Haverhill, and Schoeneman signed a business deal today that will bring one hundred million credits to their mining dealings on asteroid 2011 UW158."

The news item was posted seven days ago and told her little, except these three people knew each other and were in business together. One hundred million credits. That could feed the homeworld for years.

She couldn't interview Haverhill without Schoeneman's say so. To do so would surely be grounds for firing her.

And what was Haverhill's connection to Amelia Jones?

The young woman was too distraught to talk. She could push her, but the odds were small that she'd know S. M. Bertrand, and even if she'd met the person, then what? What could she do with that information? What was her angle? How could she prove Amelia's case? Or disprove it?

Stuck and frustrated, Janey cleared the board, headed for her quarters, and changed into her workout clothes for the second time that day. Luckily, she had a second blue sports bra, blue tank top, and blue long leggings, as the first set was in the auto wash. She slipped on her running shoes and stared at the wallscreen set to a view of a live weather feed of the Americas from high Earth orbit. If her ocular implant was a thousand times more powerful, that would be the view she would see from one of the viewing rooms at the top level of L'Étoile.

Where was an annoying, sexy, impetuous rogue Sol agent when you needed one? Valdez could probably dig up dirt on Bertrand, Jones, and for that matter Schoeneman. He could sneak into places she would never have access to—databases, locations, personas. Maybe he was still aboard. He didn't say he was leaving. She ran a search on Jacques Laval, his current alias. He'd booked a suite on the mid-level and was still registered at the hotel, though that could mean anything with him. Was it time to reach out to him? And ask him what?

Before leaving her quarters for the gym, she sent a request to the Sol Human Rights Office for the sanctuary request protocols. She'd handle this herself.

"When you got nothing, you got nothing."

That thought chased Janey all the way to the staff gym at the other end of the staff corridor. Nothing was still nothing.

She nodded to her fellow staffers—one involved with the free weights and another on the bike. She hopped on the stair climber and set it to warm-up mode. She needed something more intense than the treadmill.

When you got nothing, you got nothing.

Where did that leave her? She couldn't talk to the man Amelia accused of enslaving her for years for sex. She had no leverage—nothing on either Haverhill or Schoeneman she could take to the Sol Unified Planets Court at the Hague. She had no idea what she was up against, and she had no clues to go on.

When you got nothing, you got nothing.

From an investigative standpoint, empty-handed was how Janey felt about Amelia's case. Like many business connections of Schoeneman and guests of L'Étoile, Haverhill coveted his privacy and paid well for it. He hid behind this protection and safely avoided getting questioned by her. Maybe it was Schoeneman who was protecting Haverhill, or maybe Schoeneman was protecting his own interests. The reclusive hotel owner was even further off-limits than Haverhill. If she opened a search query on him beyond a public media search using hotel systems, he'd surely know immediately.

Valdez could maybe do some recon for her—maybe

come up with angles she wasn't seeing. Sneaky spy that he was.

Feeling boxed in, Janey pushed her workout hard on the stair climber, her shoulders and thighs aching, and she ended her twenty-minute workout drenched in sweat. Back in her quarters, she took a fast shower, changed into a sleek black pantsuit, and felt at loose ends. The intense workout hadn't cleared the heaviness she felt at Amelia's plight.

She wanted to do something—investigate and make things happen—but her hands were tied. There was something she could do—ask for help.

"Rhea," she said to her room AI.

"Yes, Janey. Are you all right? Your hormones are slightly elevated."

"I'm fine. Open audio message."

"Open."

"Orlando—" Janey sighed. She hadn't treated him well when he'd called last night. Maybe he wouldn't help. Maybe he would. "Please call me when you can."

"Is that all, Janey?" Rhea asked.

"Yes."

"Would you like me to file this one too?"

"No, send it."

"Done. Good job, Janey."

"Thanks, Rhea."

She felt better, but what if? … What if she worked elsewhere? Someplace with fewer constraints, more freedom, and more room for innovation?

Where had that thought come from?

Didn't matter right now. Even though her skills would be welcomed on any space station around the homeworld or Luna, she couldn't leave before her four-year contract was up. If she did, she'd have to forfeit the generous pay she was receiving to afford Dana's expensive medical treatments—and the price just went up because of the new experimental drugs. Nowhere else paid as well as Bijoux de L'Étoile Hotel-Casino.

Best to put the mad urge out of her mind.

Janey headed for the bullpen. At the front desk, Kim nodded a hello and pointed to her earpiece. She was listening in on a call and handed her a small picnic basket, daintily covered in white and red checkered cloth, like the kind her mother had in her kitchen. Someone had handwritten her full name in scrolling cursive letters on a tag tied with twine to the basket handle.

The bullpen behind Kim was vacant as staff members were working all over the station.

Janey lifted a corner of the cloth and inhaled. An aroma of roast beef and hot mustard wafted up. Her mouth watered at the delicious combination of traditional sourdough bread, spicy mustard, and still-warm roast beef, accompanied by a wrapped dark chocolate square and an orange. Her stomach grumbled. Lunchtime, it agreed. Mai Chen, bless her heart, had thought of her. She returned to her office across the corridor and ate half of the large sandwich and read the newsfeeds. Then she got to work.

In front of her curved, near-transparent vertical screen, she waved her hand to wake up the screen, then she palm-logged her security code on the table. She plowed through her backlog of reports to review and summarize for Chief Milano.

Thirty minutes later, she opened the basket for the other half of the sandwich. There was another note inside she'd missed in her haste to eat. She opened the folded note. It was typed.

"I had Mai Chen put this together. Some of your favorite foods. I feel really bad about how I treated you yesterday. Please accept my deepest apologies. You looked great. Best hostage ever. Xoxo OV"

Janey threw the note in the basket and growled. Orlando Valdez. His charming self. Working his wiles on her again.

At least he made an effort to apologize—for the second time in less than twenty-four hours.

Good for him. But no answer to her comm to him.

She peered into the basket at the huge other half of the sandwich. She sighed.

And good for her, she conceded. He had thought of her, after all. Maybe he'd been coordinating her lunch when she'd been recording her short request to him. It would be good to work with him again. They had their synergy, the way they sparked ideas off each other, and the way he surprised her with his warmth, humor, and intensity. Refreshing. Maddening.

She dug into the rest of her lunch with gusto, then hurried through the reports and reviews.

Amelia's case niggled at her, but she needed to come up with a different angle. She wasn't sure what that was yet. She reviewed Amelia's file yet again and didn't see anything that inspired a new line of research. Ferreira's report on the rumor documentation was in. Good job. Ferreira noted the name of the person who made the comment a few weeks ago—a young woman who worked in hydroponics. Janey would speak to her this afternoon, even though it was weak and an old lead.

Then she checked messages to see if Detective Juanita Verde had gotten back to her with the whereabouts of the detective on Christine's case and if she had been able to get her the medical examiner's report on the postmortem. Even though Janey had been in shock at the time, she'd seen visible marks of restraint on Christine's wrists and ankles as if she'd been held captive for a while. There was also some bruising as if she'd struggled. And then there was the unmistakable odd bend in her neck. Someone had snapped her spine. What had happened to the ME's report, and why was Christine's file so thin?

No one called her to a scene of a disturbance, so she worked on the backlog of old case files for Milano. No need to give him another reason to complain about her to Schoeneman. Every hour she checked her personal messages, but there was nothing from Detective Verde. After the third hour, she still didn't have a message from Verde, but she did have one from Kim: Speak to Paula about Amelia's case. I told her because Amelia needs out, and I know Sanctuary process can be iffy. Paula's plugged in. And safe.

Janey sat back in her chair, angry, a flush of heat flooding her chest. Then the intensity diminished. Kim cared, and if she vouched for Paula, then Paula was trustworthy. She needed to stretch her legs—she could do with the break—so closed out the reports, sent what was done to Milano, and then left her office. She nodded to colleagues and other staff as she tracked through the curved grey corridor to the front of the house—the lobby. All the corridors in L'Étoile curved as the hotel was built in a circle. The guest rooms and amenities were on the outer ring, and the hotel administration offices, the security center, and all the mechanics that ran the hotel and station resided in the inner ring. The hangar and other operations took up the entire bottom level.

As she took the arc that led to the lobby, corridor walls shimmered with shades of light aquamarine. Delicate plants dotted the wall alcoves—miniature fig and olive trees. The air smelled of the sea—salty and warm. She took in a deep breath and relaxed *everything* on the exhale. It was almost like being on the Greek Islands. When she had the time during her shift, she often strolled to the lobby and back to her office to reset her brain. Today, though, she wasn't just on a head-clearing ramble.

She turned into the round, spacious lobby. A brilliant chandelier dominated the high-ceilinged domed space, spilling out a warm sunlight-like effect of mid-afternoon. Olive trees with the small dark green leaves were interspersed along the edges of the lobby, and mosaics peeked through their branches, hints of yellow and green swirls revealed whenever the branches rustled in the breeze. There were no viewscreens of Earth or the stars, so the design made you think that beyond the walls you'd see the Mediterranean Sea. Piped in sounds of the waves lapping on the shore completed the illusion.

At the concierge main desk, Paula Redstone glanced up from her screen and nodded to Janey. Janey nodded back. Paula's brother and partner in concierge services, Peter, was nowhere in sight. While Peter always had a smile and a compliment for her, Paula seemed to endure her. Nevertheless, Paula wanted to help Amelia. That was Janey's opener.

She approached the counter. "Kim told me you could help Amelia."

"I can." Paula eyed her sympathetically, her face pale and lips pinched. She lowered her voice. "Is the young woman okay?"

"Yes, she's okay."

Paula let out a breath and held Janey's gaze. "Oh good." Color came back into Paula's cheeks. "Anything you need."

Paula was an unexpected ally. Janey had only one question.

"How come?"

Paula sighed and moved aside from her holo screen console. "Let's just say I've heard things, seen things. Janey, like you, I encounter all kinds in my line of work." She compressed her lips as if to hold back distaste. "I have to do what I can for them." She nodded with a sense of finality as if that explained it.

"Okay, good enough. I'm working the official channels, but in case that doesn't pan out, and provided I can confirm her story, I'd like her off the station with the next StarEl departure in two days. Can you get her a place in your...network?" A new batch of hotel staff and the next shift of asteroid miners that transited to the belt was due to arrive by then on the StarEl, the staff space elevator, with usually an equal number of staff and miners departing. StarEl was anchored at Earth Port in the central Pacific Ocean and provided a cheap way to shuttle staff back and forth. The five-day trip was a pleasant and relaxing way to transition from the planet to L'Étoile, perched far above Earth.

Paula moved back to her console, all business, and waved at the holo screen. "Yes. You just get her a new ID."

Janey knew someone who could help her with that. Someone with a lot of practice. Another reason to reach out to Valdez.

"Will do. Thanks, Paula. You're a gem."

Paula glanced up at her without smiling. "Make sure she's on the up and up, or we can't help her."

"Of course."

Paula glanced back at her console and sucked in a breath. "Janey, Schoeneman's jet is scheduled to arrive late tonight."

"That's outside the norm. Why wasn't I notified?" Janey leaned on the counter to get a look at Paula's screen. Space jets usually arrived at six a.m., not the middle of the night.

"Why wasn't I? It just popped up from the hangar chief. Looks like Chief Milano's been notified."

"He hasn't said anything to me."

"Me neither." Paula frowned.

"Who's coming?"

Paula scanned the information. "Looks like an investment group out of Guangdong Province is being flown in by one of Mr. Schoeneman's space jets."

"Do you have confirmation that Mr. Schoeneman is coming too?" Janey asked.

"Yes, he's on the passenger list."

"How many in the investment group?"

Paula looked at her oddly. Janey normally didn't ask such questions, but Paula didn't object. "I was asked to book five suites on the upper levels earlier today. Probably for these arrivals." The premium high roller suites.

"So five people?" Schoeneman's jet could hold up to two dozen people.

"Six, including Schoeneman, but I don't have anyone else's name."

Most unusual. She didn't like it.

"Thanks, Paula." Janey muttered under her breath, "All I need..." and headed for the staff area and her office, the mellow salty wind of the lobby lost on her.

Like she wanted Schoeneman here, questioning her every move, breathing down her neck. Her few encounters with him in her last big case had been uncomfortable, to say the least. She'd do her best to stay clear of the man, but it would a challenge. He owned the station. He would come and go as he pleased.

THIRTEEN

A FEW HOURS LATER, KIM STEPPED INTO HER office, humming and wishing her a good night. It was already five. Kim seemed cherry this evening. It was nice to see her feeling better.

Janey was in the middle of waving a message to Cho to relieve Ferreira for an hour or two. And then another message to Shawhan for the night shift. She was younger than Lane and might help Amelia to feel comfortable. Normally Cho only did security in the Machine Shop. Janey sat back in her chair and rubbed her temples. She was on call in a few hours. So was Ferreira, and they both needed a dinner break before their shifts started at midnight.

Kim gave her an inquiring look. "You okay? Want to talk about it?"

"About what?" Details of the security staff reports swirled before her eyes. She leaned back in her chair and massaged her neck.

"Valdez being here."

"What do you know about that?" Janey sat up

abruptly. She'd restrained herself from searching for him in the security feeds, but maybe Kim hadn't. Kim was fiercely protective of her friends.

"No, I haven't run a facial rec, if that's what you're thinking."

"I was." Janey sat back, disappointed, then berated herself. She'd reached out; she didn't need to stalk him too—or wish her friend would.

"Are you worried for him?" Kim asked.

Surprised, Janey barked a little laugh. "You know me well." She sighed. "A little. And there's nothing I can do. I left him a message." Maybe he could help with Amelia's situation.

"Good." Kim smiled and left the office.

Janey commed Ferreira.

"Yes, Investigator."

"Ferreira, Cho is on his way to relieve you. Did Amelia wake up?"

"A few times, but then she went back to sleep."

"Did she say anything to you?"

"No, ma'am."

"Okay, thanks, Ferreira. I did see the rumor report you sent me. Keep them coming."

"Yes, ma'am. May I ask a question?"

"Of course."

"Can I come with you tonight, undercover?"

"How did you know?" Janey chuckled. She needed another angle on Haverhill and needed to gather gossip to garner new information she hadn't found on the 'net.

"You don't give up. Like a dog with a bone."

Janey checked the time. "Meet me at the SkyBar at twenty-one hundred."

"Any particular costume?" Ferreira cleared her throat.

"You decide." Janey rubbed her eyes.

"Yes, ma'am. I'll make sure to have Kim say the passcode."

"You do that." Janey yawned.

"Oh, housekeeping came by, but I didn't let them in."

Janey shot to her feet. "Way to bury the lead, Ferreira."

"But I didn't let them in."

"Could you tell who it was?" Janey tracked around her desk and paced her office. "And when?"

"Male. Sounded young. At sixteen hundred hours."

"Did you get a name?"

"I asked, but he moved off after saying he was just checking that we had enough fresh food."

Odd.

She never got that request when she was in her quarters, though she wasn't there much.

"Okay, thanks," Janey said. "I'll research it. You go get dinner."

"I could research it."

"I got it, Ferreira."

"Sorry, Investigator."

"No, but now you know what to do next time."

"Yes, ma'am." Ferreira wouldn't end the call until she did.

"McCallister, out." She closed the comm and waved a new call to Mai Chen in the kitchen.

Mai Chen didn't answer. She was probably in the middle of something. Janey commed the chef.

"Valerie here." Not the chef, but the chef's right-hand. Shew was a chef in training and Gina's partner.

"Oh hi, Valerie. I need to check on a staff member's whereabouts at sixteen hundred hours, visiting the staff quarters in the D or E wing." Janey didn't want to be too specific and give away Amelia's location, which already may have been compromised.

"Sure, Janey. Let me check. Is everything okay?"

"Yes, just checking for a case, pulling on a thread. You know how it is."

"Sure." The comm crackled with faint sounds of the kitchen's hustle and bustle. Valerie was probably in Gina's office.

"Seale was on duty at the time for the staff side," Valerie finally said.

"Was he sent or called to one of those quarters?" Janey asked.

"He was asked to bring a birthday dinner to Room E2. You sure everything is okay?"

So not the wing where Amelia was stashed.

"Yes, it's fine. Thanks, Valerie."

"You're welcome."

Janey commed Peter Redstone next because whoever knocked on Amelia's door wasn't from the kitchen staff. Peter was in charge of Hotelier Reception and House-keeping with his sister.

"Redstone here."

Not his formal hotel greeting. He wasn't working.

"Am I disturbing you?"

"No, just about to go on duty. How can I help you, Investigator?"

"I'm tracking down one of yours, I think."

"Okay," he said with hesitation. "Last time you tracked down one of ours it didn't end well."

"For him," Janey said.

"True. What do you have?" Peter asked.

"I'm looking for someone, a man, who visited the staff quarters in the D or E wing at sixteen-hundred, offering to replenish the fresh food."

"I'm at my station now and checking."

Janey heard muted typing, like mice racing across a series of tiles.

"No. No one sent to staff quarters at that time."

"So not one of yours?"

"Thankfully not." Peter's disdain dripped from his voice. "And highly unlikely."

"How so?"

"We don't provide fresh food to staff. They have their own food-crafters and the commissary and kitchen credits. It's only guests we offer to replenish their fresh food as a courtesy. Mr. Schoeneman wishes them to want for nothing. It's part of the excellent service we pride ourselves on."

"Thank you, Peter. Appreciate it."

And thank you for quoting from the service manual.

Peter was too reserved to ask her about the case, but she'd seen him listening in on her stories in the commissary when he deigned to drop in. He was a sucker for gossip, like the rest. He was just great at keeping it to himself.

Whoever dropped by Amelia's room was not from housekeeping or the kitchen, even though the person seemed to have some knowledge of hotel operations. That meant Janey was probably looking for a guest. The maximum capacity was a thousand guests. Today the number was seven hundred and fifty-seven, according to the daily report. A doable search. Or she was looking for someone from a different staff department, who had no reason to do a food check for staff quarters.

She huffed a breath. Still doable, but a larger number of people to search through. At any given time, there were always two staff members to one guest—the mark of a high-end hotel. Two thousand staff, give or take, less the eighty people in the kitchen and housekeeping combined.

Next, she checked the security video feed for the wing.

On her widescreen, she watched a slight person in a white housekeeping jacket and long brown hair hustle toward Amelia's room, their head down and turned away from the ceiling cameras. When they stopped at Amelia's door and spoke, their back was angled toward the camera, shoulders hunched a little, chest protected— almost as if they knew exactly where the cameras were positioned.

Via the camera feed, she couldn't get a good read on the person's vitals or much of the body language. She wasn't getting any closer to answers.

But one thing was clear: Amelia's location had been compromised.

FOURTEEN

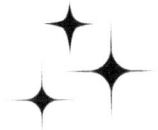

Janey commed Kim. When Kim answered, Janey said, "We have to move her."

"Okay. Why?" Her voice was calm.

"Ferreira told you about the housekeeping visit?"

"Yes."

"Well, I checked with the kitchen and with Peter. That person was not with either staff. I think he or she was a guest. I'd like to move her to another location. Ideas?"

"Ironically, the most secure rooms are the mezzanine suites above the casino."

"Too easy to find, and there's no way to get her there without passing through the casino," Janey said. "I don't want her out in the open like that."

"You're the map expert of the station these days."

"I haven't discovered a secret passageway there. We need a Plan B." Janey blew out a breath. This case was getting to her.

The hotel-casino had originally started as a service station and bare-bones lodging for asteroid miners on their way to the asteroid belt between Earth and Mars. It had all kinds of odd tunnels and shortcuts behind the manicured and polished walls of the L'Étoile. Janey had been sniffing them out in her odd hours.

"There is always an empty hotel suite," Kim said.

"But maybe someone wants us to move her," Janey mused aloud. Kim waited. She knew how Janey liked to talk things out. "So staying put is the safest course. Yes, that's easiest. Let me see who we can spare to help you out and give you a chance to have the evening off."

"Not necessary."

"You're not on call tonight. Necessary." Janey checked the work rotation. "I'm sending Shawhan to you. I just sent her a message to report to you with the evening's passcode."

"And what are you up to?"

"After dinner, around nine, Ferreira and I will see if we can catch some scuttlebutt about Haverhill at SkyBar and the poker tables," Janey said.

"Not many leads?" Kim asked.

"Nope, and Milano has shut me down on the direct approach."

"I meant to tell you he was in the office when you called earlier," Kim said.

"I thought so. That was careless of me. Can't believe I slipped up like that."

"The station is making you soft." Kim chuckled.

Jane smiled, but she couldn't muster a laugh. "I was warned by my Space Wing instructors that could happen. They looked down on civilian life." Janey rubbed her pounding temples and grimaced. "I have to fight against the softness. I need to stay sharp. Things happen up here."

"Unfortunately."

"And I need to be ready. Take charge."

"You go, girl."

Janey managed a little laugh this time and heard the door chime on Kim's end. "I'll let you handle that. That should be Shawhan. McCallister out."

Janey backed up all her day's work on her private and personal servers, shut down her screens, locked them, then locked the office. It was 6 p.m. Time enough to grab dinner in the commissary, shower, and change for her undercover rumor hunt at the SkyBar. Even time for a cat nap.

Three hours later, she sauntered into the casino and made a beeline for the bar. She wore a marine blue pantsuit with a low-cut back. Blue sparkly spinel teardrop gems hung from her ears, and she wore her pearl choker under the high-neck collar. With a black clutch containing her small gun and crime scene accouterment in hand, she strode up to the bar and nodded at Faizah.

Faizah winked at her and returned to her show of mixing a martini for the one guest leaning against the bar, a young jet setter with an iridescent pink and white low-cut gown and a bored look. Janey nodded at the guest and turned around to admire the view and take in the room, a bored look plastered on her face, she hoped. Part of the rich heiress wannabe look she wanted to pull off tonight.

SkyBar was her favorite part of the station. It got its name not only from its location on L'Étoile but also from the widescreen directly above the back wall of the bar and ceiling. Since the station was tethered to Earth by its elevator, StarEl, the starfield changed with the planet's rotation. Plus, the wall and ceiling screens could be tuned to anything, either from the station's powerful telescopes or cameras that faced outward to the cosmos, or from any recording the casino's entertainment director desired.

On the ceiling screen tonight she spotted the Pleiades, also known as the Seven Sisters, and the W of Cassiopeia, two of her favorite constellations. Good luck charms, hopefully, to finding some leads on Haverhill.

A cold glass touched her elbow. Janey turned, and Faizah winked at her. The bartender had made her usual —a fizzy water on the rocks. It was a Perrier with a twist of lime, and it was what she always drank when she was on duty. Faizah knew her cues. Fancy dress meant she was on duty. Leather jacket chic meant she was on her own time. And the little waitress uniform meant... well, that was easy.

Janey scanned the room. Ferreira was at a poker table, focused on Texas Hold 'Em. She'd spiked her short black hair, sprayed on blue sparkles on half her face like an ancient Pict, and was dressed in a strapless blue shimmery top and iridescent black wide-legged pants. That was one way to gather information.

Janey picked up her glass, lifted it in thanks to Faizah, and moved away from the bar. Time to work the room.

At the entrance, the loud jackpot machines would yield no chatter. People were too intent on playing them, praying to them, or yelling at them. Plus, the noise was crazy deafening. The pops, whirls, and dance ditties were designed to get people in the party mood rather than to encourage conversation.

She could stay at the bar, but there wasn't anybody sitting there at the moment, the young jet setter having melded into the crowd, mingling and watching gameplay. Maybe she'd come back when there were more bodies to flirt with.

She wandered to the high stakes poker tables set to

seven-card stud, near the enormously tall and thick floor-to-ceiling viewscreens displaying a direct feed of the nightly acrobatic show. She dropped in on the action for a few hands, using her department's betting fund for staff, cheering for the winners, and groaning with the losers. After an hour, she'd picked up some chatter about regulations coming in that would give some more tax breaks to emerging companies willing to mine the next layer of asteroids and lots of talk of sports.

After moving to the Baccarat *Chemin de fer* table and playing some hands there for about thirty minutes, she understood they were talking about the latest craze of space jetting in the far reaches of the asteroid belt—the very same area that would be open to mining soon.

None of that information was germane to her case. She tried a more direct approach, asking after Haverhill Industrials as if she wanted to possibly invest in it. She got nods of agreement but no juicy gossip. One more approach to try.

"I heard he was looking for—" She raised an eyebrow and smirked, hoping the finely dressed gentlemen and women would get the hint.

Men looked her up and down. One said, "I think he likes them younger."

"Yeah, way younger," another man said.

Janey looked at each of them, and they shrugged apologetically.

"Your sugar daddy not good enough for you?" one of the men asked.

Janey sniffed. "One could always do better. Am I right, ladies?"

The women, two around her age and one middle-aged, nodded and shrugged. One said, "Or get a new sugar momma." They shared a laugh.

"Absolutely," Janey said and laughed too. She hung around them an hour more, watching the game and making more small talk about the space jet races. Men loved to talk about their sports to anyone who would listen.

She wandered back to the bar to refresh her drink, passing by the lower stakes poker tables. Ferreira was at a new poker table, five-card draw, and she caught Janey's eye and shook her head. No news from her quarter.

After picking up her drink, Janey headed deeper into the casino toward the highest of the high-stakes tables. Another pai gow game was going on, this one as loud and well-attended as the one the night before. She checked. No Valdez. No one watched the viewscreen. The gamblers were a mix of men and women from all over the planet or from one of the space stations orbiting the planet. She was one of several people hovering and cheering. But after an hour and a half, she learned nothing of value there. She was debating where to go next when her comm pulsed against her skin. It was in silent mode while she worked the casino.

Janey stepped away from the table and found a quiet spot near the living wall, full of air plants mixed in with ferns, spider plants, and some pink, white, and orange orchids too. She was hidden from view from the casino floor and could see if anyone was coming up and down the stairs to the private suites on the mezzanine level.

"Yes?" she said softly.

"Madison here. Why didn't you pick up?" It was the security's night duty manager. Had she missed a call?

"I'm undercover in the casino. It's loud here. What is it?" She hadn't logged herself as working, though she was on call tonight.

"Report of a disturbance in one of the casino suites.

Shouting, they reported," Madison said, his New Englander accent pronounced.

"Which one? And when?"

"Kitchen staff reported it three minutes ago as they worked the mezzanine. They said it came from the Library Suite."

"Okay. Thanks. I'll check it out."

She hustled up the stairs and turned right down the hallway that looked out over the casino to the starfield beyond. No staff passed her on the stairs or on the mezzanine. Who had made the call? They could have exited using the staff elevator at the far end of the mezzanine hall—a passageway guests didn't know about.

At the Library Suite, where she'd had tea with Mrs. Bakaj, she knocked, announced herself as security, and waited for a beat. No answer. She used her security clearance to override the lock on the wall panel. The door opened silently.

The large room was quiet. Only the wall of books, the plush blue couches, the low table where earlier Mrs. Bakaj had offered her tea.

No one was there. She walked the perimeter but saw nothing amiss on any light spectrum she had her ocular implant scanned for. Her wrist comm set to biotag frequencies didn't pick up anything. No one had been in this room for at least an hour—time enough for the cleaning bots to pass through.

A faint thump came from the wall shared with the next suite over as if something had hit the shared wall hard. It must be quite big as the walls were supposed to be one hundred percent soundproof. She was in the wrong room.

Janey swore and rushed out of the Library Suite into the hallway overlooking the casino.

In that moment, a black-clad figure leapt over the short banister. She dashed to the banister and leaned over it. Twenty-five feet below in the Phoenix restaurant, there was no running figure, no one arrayed in all black, head to toe. Shrubbery dominated the restaurant, the diners cozily concealed from view. She commed Madison.

"Get the on-call security team to the casino *stat*. Black-clad person fled the scene via the restaurant and casino. Priority red."

"Yes, ma'am."

"And, Madison, start a video search for the—" She'd barely gotten a look at the person clothed all in black. She blinked and focused on the image on her ocular implant.

"For the suspect, Investigator?"

"Yes. Probably five foot six to five foot eight, dressed in all black, possibly. Male, I think."

Janey commed off and rushed into the adjacent suite. A horrific scene greeted her. The pungent coppery smell of blood overlay a faint lemony disinfectant from the last cleaning. The furniture was in disarray, a heavy cushioned chair overturned beside the shared wall.

Haverhill was sprawled on a blood-spattered couch, arms outstretched, eyes staring unseeing at the ceiling, his face and torso covered in blood, still crimson red and still wet. From her clutch, she grabbed crime scene gloves and slipped them on. She reached to feel his pulse, to verify what her ocular implant and comm readout told her. The man had no heartbeat. His body was still warm.

Stab wounds punctured his torso—at least ten. No chance of resuscitation. Too many vital organs damaged.

His white silk shirt was unbuttoned and open, revealing the wounds, blood dripping down the sides of his chest. Long knife cuts slashed both cheeks. He'd been stabbed in the face and in the torso while still alive. His arms and hands were clean, his nails manicured. No defensive cuts or bruising. He didn't even defend himself. A proud man like Haverhill would have defended himself to his last breath. Had someone over-powered the man? He wasn't small at five foot ten, and he had an athletic build as if he'd played midfield soccer, only a little soft around the middle.

Janey commed Soren. "I need you *now*. Mezzanine. Ten-ten." An incoming call pulsated as she commed off, but she needed to talk to Madison before anyone else.

"Set up lockdown," she said when Madison picked up. "No one in or out of the station. We have a ten-ten. Inform Milano." She commed off without waiting for confirmation. Confirmation would show up on her comm as soon as lockdown was implemented.

On land, they had hurricanes and tornados forcing people to shelter in place. At the Bijoux de L'Étoile Hotel-Casino space station, they had murders.

FIFTEEN

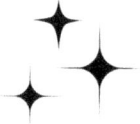

Janey checked the incoming call that she had missed. Lane had left a short message, breathless but clear.

"Attempted kidnapping but we prevented it. Meilani and me. We're okay. Amelia's okay. Good thing I came to hang out with Meilani." Meilani Shawhan was the one on shift. Antonia Lane sometimes hung out with her. The two were practically inseparable.

Janey turned away from the body and commed Lane. "What happened? You okay?"

"Yes. Three masked men jumped us."

"Inside the room?"

"Yes."

"Why?"

"We think they were trying to kidnap Amelia," Lane said. "But we fought them. Training's paying off, and they ran."

"You and Shawhan?"

"Two against three. Not bad, eh, boss? I don't think they were trained in street fighting."

Janey had recommended they prepare for their fight tests with all manner of street fighting, and Lane and Shawhan had been practicing takedown techniques with the other security agents.

"Good job, Antonia. Call the medics just the same. I want you all checked out."

"Yes, ma'am."

"Did you get a good look at the attackers?"

"No. They were dressed all in black, including balaclavas. Male, I'd say. Compact. Height no more than five foot six each of them."

"Okay, stay with Amelia. Document the scene and start your prelim reports. I can't spare anyone. We have a ten-ten in a mezzanine suite."

"Oh, dear. Who?"

"A guest. Jonas Haverhill. I need to make sure Amelia stays put. She knew him."

"Yes, boss. On it. Can I tell her?"

"Yes."

Lane closed the comm.

Janey took a breath to center herself, then she got to work, documenting the scene. Without touching anything, she'd scanned the couch, low table, and thrown chair in the light and trace spectrum, and she had found nothing out of the ordinary. No fingerprints, hair, or fibers either. She was about to work the rug and wet bar when Soren rushed in, a satchel slung across his chest. The tall, blond Nordic man wore a long black trench coat over a black tunic and slacks. He had sparkles in his spiked hair and blue swirls down one side of his face.

He gulped at the body sprawled on the couch. "We'll need to improvise to get the body out of here undetected."

Janey nodded. "Do you think Doc will come up here for a first-look?"

Doc was Doctor Wellesley Running Feather, the station's forensic pathologist and resident medical examiner, and she didn't like to leave her morgue. The owner planned for every eventuality, however rare, and Doc kept herself busy in the adjacent lab she shared with Soren.

Soren shook his head. "Unlikely. I'll document, take video and stills, get DNA and trace elements, and your data."

"Good man. Ping medical. They're used to handling bodies on stretchers."

Soren nodded, put in the call to medical, and then got to work working the scene and collecting evidence. The room had blood splatter on the rug where Haverhill lay but nowhere else. Most likely, it was where he was killed.

The suite wasn't the same one she'd met Haverhill in only the day before.

This chamber was done up in warm greens and browns with accents of warm reds and purples. There was a well-stocked wet bar in one corner. Perhaps Haverhill was meeting someone here for a private business meeting. It was not a room for seduction. But the force of the stab wounds, the number of them, and the slashes across the cheeks all spoke to an act of rage that seemed personal. Intimate. This was no cool and calculated murder.

Medical commed. "Horsely here. On our way," she said with calm efficiency.

"The body is a mess," Janey said. "I need it taken to Doc right away. Discreetly. That's imperative."

"Understood. We can handle it. Please do not worry, Investigator McCallister."

Janey commed off and turned to Soren, who was bent over something on the plush green rug.

"What is it?"

"Not sure," Soren said, without turning around. "Documenting it and will collect it for analysis."

Janey joined Soren at staring in the black paint or dirt granules nearly camouflaged against the dark green carpet. The wall-to-wall luxurious rug could hold more evidence.

"Soren, collect it and vacuum the whole rug."

"I'll need to go back for the equipment."

"I want you to stay here. Who can bring it up for you?"

"Doc is the only one besides me who can handle it."

"Get her up here then. She needs to leave that lab once in a blue moon and step away from her toys once in a while."

"On it." Soren made the call.

Janey moved into the mezzanine hallway and peered over the banister at the casino below. Gamblers at the tables—laughing, joking, or doing some serious drinking. Some watched the show on the viewscreen. Some flowed out to the exit and some strolled in. The wide space, as large as a football field, hummed and rumbled and roared with people partying and gambling and showing off their fine clothes and sparkling jewels to each other. She was itching to chase after whoever had jumped the railing and probably squirreled away to God knew where.

And there was Amelia. At least she was no longer in danger from Haverhill.

She commed Ferreira down on the casino floor. "Update?"

"Several eyewitnesses, or rather 'ear-witnesses,' said they heard a thump in the restaurant. But only a few people were in the restaurant, and they were hidden by their privacy shrubs, so nobody saw anyone leave the restaurant."

"Interview them anyway, Ferreira."

"Yes, boss."

"And, Ferreira?"

Janey checked her comm for verification. The lockdown was in effect. All the station's seven hundred and fifty-seven guests and over fifteen hundred staff couldn't leave. No space jets would be allowed to dock. As far as she could see in the manifest, none were currently docked. Then she remembered Schoeneman's jet. Venus hells.

Ferreira cleared her throat. "Boss? I mean Investigator McCallister. Are you there?"

"Yes. Who is there to help you?"

"Kou and Dube. They're doing interviews too. I'll get their updates and get back to you."

"Check also with any staff. Meet me back in staff room"—Janey checked the time. It was one thirty-five in the morning—"at 2:30 a.m. with everyone."

"Yes, ma'am."

"McCallister out."

She was about to comm the hangar security, when Doc approached, carrying a bulky black box. The statuesque woman looked very different out of her white lab coat. Her long, bead-fringed coat rattled with every stride. Her black hair was done in an elegant updo at least a foot high. Discreet she was not. Everyone would give this woman a wide berth.

Last time there'd been a murder on the station, Valdez had helped here. She missed his sharp gaze and his field know-how. That was all. *Yeah, right.*

"Doc." Janey nodded to the imposing medical examiner.

Doc grunted at her. Janey waved open the door, and Doc entered the crime scene. Impassive, she handed the equipment to Soren, who got to work, assembling the high-tech vacuum and scooping up trace.

Doc stood over the body.

Janey joined her.

For a moment no one spoke. Finally, Janey said, "What do you think?"

"He's dead." She pointed to each cut. "Heart, lungs, left ventricular artery, fourth rib, stomach, spleen, liver, and kidney."

Janey waited but Doc didn't continue.

"Cause of death?" she asked.

"When his spirit departed his body."

"And scientifically?"

Doc looked at her and lifted an eyebrow. "Not until I get him on my table."

"Can you tell me TOD at least? Ballpark?" Time of death. "He was still warm when I arrived. I spotted the killer leaving the scene and jumping over the banister."

"Table," Doc said.

"Thanks." Janey put a hand on the stalwart woman's arm. She really liked Doc despite her awkward social manner. The woman was probably the smartest woman in any room. Practical too.

Doc nodded, gave her a deep gaze, and left the suite, leaving medical to transport the body.

Janey commed Ferreira. "Status?"

"Conducting one more interview, but nothing new yet, ma'am."

"Send Kou and Dube to guard the crime scene until we're done."

"Yes, ma'am."

"And check with hangar security. Make sure all is secure. No one in or out."

"Yes, boss."

"And, Ferreira, get next of kin from housekeeping —discreetly."

"Of course, ma'am." Ferreira was a little breathless with excitement. Janey would need to give her more to do. Maybe she could sit in on her interviews of suspects, once she had some.

"Janey," Soren called. "I found something unusual."

Janey turned around to see him standing over the victim and putting a thread into an evidence bag. "What is it?"

"A red thread. Can't yet tell what kind of fabric."

In addition to his white silk shirt, Haverhill had on beige slacks, black socks, and black loafers. No visible red on him.

"Where did you find it?" She'd scanned his body at high-magnification. "I didn't spot it."

"Under a pant leg. And another thing." Soren cocked his head.

"Yes?"

"There's a tea set on the counter behind the wet bar."

Janey peered over the wet bar counter lower shelf. It was the same fine china tea set Mrs. Bakaj used. Could she somehow be involved?

"So there is."

What was up with that? Coincidence or something else? She didn't take Haverhill for a tea drinker—unless his guest was.

"You collected trace on it?" Janey asked Soren.

He gave her a look.

Of course, he had.

Janey nodded. "Bag and tag the whole thing."

"I'll need a few more hands." Soren had the big black vacuum, his satchel, and now the tea set.

The door chimed, and Janey unlocked it. Kou and Dube, the two older security guards, stood at the door.

"Thanks for helping out. I need you to make sure no one comes up to the suites," Janey said. "Have housekeeping put up 'closed for maintenance' signs at the bottom of the stairs. Top too, just to be safe. Only Soren, I, and medical get to come into the room. Understood?"

Both men nodded at her, serious, looking at each other as if assigning tasks. The wordless Kou headed toward the stairs, and Dube took up a post on the hallway beside the door.

A moment later, at the sight of two medical assistants in their white coats trundling down the hall with a stretcher folded between them, Janey breathed out in relief. Having a crime scene so close to the guests was a challenge. A folded black shroud was over one arm of a young man.

As they approached the door, Janey said, "Are you sure that won't be too conspicuous?"

The young medic said, "It will completely hide the body. We wrap them in it."

"Body bag." She frowned.

"No, it's actually a reflective cloak."

"So people don't actually see anything there." Janey nodded. "That's a good use of the tech."

"We think so, in situations like these," the young man said and held out his hand. "Medic Anthony James, ma'am. I don't think I've met you yet, though I heard you're one mean sharpshooter."

"That's what they say?" She shook his outstretched hand. "Investigator McCallister." She gestured toward the suite. "Soren is finishing up. When he's done, you can take the body." Janey nodded to the other medical assistant, Alison Horsely. Alison had helped at the last murder scene Janey had worked on L'Étoile.

"And we're taking it to Doc," Alison said.

"Thanks," Janey said and eyed the three other medics who she hadn't met yet. They nodded their hellos. Janey palmed open the door. She admired their quiet professionalism.

Soren slung his satchel across his body and lifted the vacuum box. He eyed the wet bar.

"Janey, can you take the tea set? I have the trace from it and already imaged for fingerprints. Wiped off by the looks of it."

"Right." Janey took off her gloves, lifted the tea service, and exited the suite. Too bad about the prints. She went down the stairs, wove through gamblers and revelers, passed the SkyBar, then the slot machines, and exited out the casino as if it was the most natural thing in the world for a well-dressed woman, a guest of the station, to be carrying her own tea service. Soren followed.

Behind the long lobby front desk, Peter Redstone and Paula Redstone, the housekeeping managers—and brother and sister—were helping several guests at the check-in desk. Usually, only one was on duty at a time, unless new guests were arriving. But no guests should be arriving. She had just put the station on lockdown. Peter lifted an eyebrow at her as if asking if she needed the secret door, as she had twice yesterday. She shook her head, no. A half-dozen guests crisscrossed the wide lobby. She didn't want to call any attention to the door if she didn't have to.

Chin held high, she took the main corridor leading to

the guest rooms and stepped into a guest elevator with Soren. Once inside and with the door shut, she flashed her wrist comm over a camouflaged security panel, and the doors opened on the other side to the service corridor. She didn't say anything until they moved into the service lift that would take them down to the security level.

"Anything else stand out?" she asked.

"I found more of the dirt or tiny leaves along the rug behind the wet bar and on the couch near the body," Soren said.

"Start with that."

"Sure thing." Soren glanced at her. "You're bringing that all the way to the lab?"

"You don't see anyone else here to do it, do you?"

"I just mean you should delegate things like that."

"Well, Ferreira is on interviews. Kou and Dube are guarding the scene. Medical has their job. Lane and Shawhan are busy. Who else is there?"

"You could pull Liberosa from Machinery."

"And leave that area unstaffed? No way. Plus, he's not rated for front of house," Janey said. "Milano wouldn't like that." She groaned. Liberosa regularly worked security for the machine shop, but she would maybe need him on this case. She'd know soon if she had to task him to do research for her. She'd already pulled Cho to watch Amelia. She'd called on him again before this case was over.

"I'm sure Milano received the station lockdown warning," Soren said as the elevator door opened on the lab level.

"I'm sure he has." And he wouldn't be pleased. He'd want to be briefed soon.

SIXTEEN

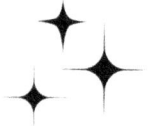

Soren unlocked the lab and tracked through the cavernous space past shelves of equipment. He led the way through the main aisle and deposited his vacuum and satchel on a long metal table. "You can put the tea set here."

Janey set it down carefully. Even so, liquid sloshed in the teapot. She used a glove on the table to lift the lid. A woodsy fruity fragrance wafted up. "Some kind of black tea. Orange maybe."

"I'll check the black trace from the rug, then the tea."

"Toxins. Poisons. Run the gamut."

"I know my job, Investigator McCallister."

"And I know mine is to be bossy."

He smiled at her tiredly. "Yep."

"I woke you up?"

"The case woke me up. Don't worry about it. I knew I was on call."

"Not worried. Just nosy."

"Understood." Soren unpacked his satchel.

"Comm me when you've got something."

Soren nodded but didn't look up from his unpacking. Janey checked the time. It was nearly two in the morning. She let herself out of the lab, strode down the grey corridor in her heels, took the lift up one level, and entered the conference room. She was early. Ferreira wasn't there yet.

Her comm beeped, and she glanced at it. Instead of a voice memo, Ferreira had left a transcribed message. Standing in the middle of the conference room, Janey glanced longingly at the quiet and empty coffee maker, then she waved open the voice message.

Ferreira started her message by saying that hangar security did have an incident in the previous hour, but it had been resolved positively, and they would report it directly to her.

Then she went on to say that she'd retrieved the details on Haverhill's next of kin, a wife, who was also on board, but she was under a different last name, a different suite, and under her own reservation. Ferreira added a note that there was a personal assistant by the name of Winston Wharton whom she was escorting down to the security level. She was asking in which interview room to put him. He was slightly suspicious because his bio tag showed him outside of his suite and not asleep at the time of the murder. The biotag and bio readings for the wife put her asleep in her suite around the time of her husband's murder.

Ferreira ended the message with: Did I make the right call? And do you want to do the notification to the wife?

Janey replied: Yes. And yes.

Then Janey instructed her to bring the assistant to Interrogation Room Alpha and to let her know when he was there, and she'd make an entrance. Interrogation

Room Alpha was down the corridor and more like a lounge than a true interrogation room—perfect for interviews of a more casual nature. She didn't want to scare the assistant just because he wasn't asleep at the time of the murder. He'd probably been in the casino or in one of the upper observation lounges. Maybe he was strolling in the arboretum or in the spa and Ferreira was being efficient.

A minute later, Ferreira sent her another message: `He's in. Need anything else?`

Janey dictated back: `Bring two glasses of water in ten minutes. Then do an evidence sweep of Haverhill's suite with Soren.`

Ferreira sent back: `Understood.`

Janey checked her internal sensors via her ocular implant. Most of her health levels were fine. All except the hunger hormones. They were low. Her stomach grumbled in response. Yeah, she was hungry. Dinner had been hours ago. Breakfast would be in a few hours, but she'd been working, burning energy. She checked the snack bin. Let Wharton stew for a few more minutes. There was a lone mini pizza. She heated in the cooker, ate it in three bites, and sipped some water.

She checked her comm for any messages from hangar security, but there wasn't anything. She pinged Scott Edward Ellias, the hangar security chief, for a sitrep, but he didn't pick up his comm. In the weekly department meetings, his reports were always thorough and concise and delivered with calm and enthusiasm. He ran a tight ship and was competent at his job, maintaining order at the hangar level for the arriving and departing guests. She'd also enjoyed his concerts in the commissary. Hopefully, he had the incident in hand. No news usually meant good news in her game.

Fortified from her snack and letting the incident at the hangar go, she hustled to the Interrogation Room and let herself in to the space, outfitted with a warm brown loveseat couch, several easy chairs of brown leather, and tall floor plants with large bright-green heart-shaped leaves. A cube table was nestled between the couch and chairs. "Hello, Mr. Wharton." She held out her hand. "I'm Investigator McCallister. Thank you for coming."

Winston Wharton stood and shook her hand. He was stoop-shouldered, thin, and willowy, and he dressed in a bright pink pinstriped tailored suit and pink striped shirt, plus a pink pocket square and pink thin tie. His light brown hair was cropped short on one side and trimmed long over an ear on the other. Pink sparkles covered the cropped side, as was the fashion. "What is this about?"

"Please take a seat." Janey gestured to the soft couch.

Wharton pinched his lips shut and eyed his holo screen hovering above his wrist and glanced at her, but he sat. In one hand, he clenched a crumpled pink silk handkerchief.

Janey took the adjoining plush chair and sat at the edge, her back straight.

"Where were you at 1 a.m.?"

Wharton gazed at her. "Why?"

"Please, answer the question."

"I was with some...friends. Why?"

"Can I get their names?"

"I actually don't know their real names."

"Then their fake names, please."

He opened his holo screen from his wrist comm,

waved, then read from it. "Blue Bear, Noodles, Humphreys, Rouge, Juniper, Mimi, and Niagara."

"What kinds of names are those?"

He shrugged. "It was a…costume party. Am I in some kind of trouble?"

"When did you arrive at the party?"

"Ten."

"In the evening?"

"Yes."

"Until what time?"

"Around 1:15. I just left and was heading back to my room when your agent flagged me down." He fidgeted and folded his handkerchief. "What is this all about? Please, tell me." He gazed at her with a dark certainty as if he knew what she would say and didn't want to hear, but he needed to hear the horrible news.

"I will. Just a few more questions. Was Mr. Haverhill at the party?"

"For a bit."

"When did he leave?"

"Around 11:30. Said he had a business meeting."

"Where?"

"The lower lounge."

The lower lounge was beside the casino and had couches and lounges chairs for the guests to lay back and admire a piped-in view of the stars or a show on the humongous casino viewscreens. There were plenty of discreet cameras all over the casino. They'd spot Haverhill and whoever he met with.

"Do you know who with? Don't you handle all his appointments?"

"I don't know." He sniffed. "I didn't handle this one."

"Is that unusual?"

"No." He didn't look fazed by that notion.

"Could he have been meeting a woman?"

"Perhaps. He did stress it was a business meeting."

"And do you have any idea what about?"

"None, Investigator." He yawned and covered his mouth with his hand holding the pink handkerchief.

"Was he in good spirits? Happy? Or something else? Sad perhaps?"

"He seemed fine. A little tipsy? Giddy maybe."

"Was that unusual?"

"No. He enjoys being here. L'Étoile is one of his very favorite hotels."

"Was he due back at a certain time?"

"No. Why? Is he okay? He tends to drink a bit too much. Sometimes I need to help him to his room." He squirmed in his seat.

"Mr. Wharton. I'm sorry to tell you this, but your boss, Jonas Haverhill, is dead."

Wharton stiffened, and he drew in a sharp intake of breath. His already pale skin blanched. "What?" He squeaked. "How did he die?"

"That's what we're trying to determine."

"Was he killed?"

"Why do you ask?"

"He was young." Wharton peered at her glassy-eyed. He seemed genuinely stunned. "Was he shot?" he whispered as if he had a morbid fascination with the idea.

"No, stabbed actually."

"Oh, goddess-mine." He slapped a hand over his mouth and looked green.

Just then Ferreira arrived with the water—perfect timing—and Wharton gulped the glass down.

"Have another," Janey said, and he gulped the second glass—this time, only halfway down. Janey signaled for

149

Ferreira to bring two more, and the young agent left the room quietly.

Wharton sat back in the couch, looking calmer, not green anymore, but he was still paler than when he'd arrived. He mopped his brow with his handkerchief and straightened his thin tie. "Will that be all?"

"No, I have more questions for you. I understand his wife is on board," Janey said.

Wharton nodded, and his breathing hitched. "Siobhan. She will be so—" He rushed a hand to his mouth again. "And the girls, too."

"He has daughters?" Haverhill with children was hard to imagine, let alone a wife, with the way he treated women. Plus, L'Étoile was not a place to bring one's family.

"Oh *non. Non.*" Wharton shook his head. His no sounded French, the nasally breath changing the words. "They're his—his—" He waved a hand.

"His women?" Janey said without heat.

"Yes, I guess you could call them that."

"So, I need to be blunt here, Mr. Wharton. Do you mean to tell me that Mr. Haverhill traveled with a harem?"

"Well, that is an old-fashioned term, but yes."

"Mmm." Janey sat back in her chair and crossed her legs, revealing her shapely calves. He didn't flicker a gaze to them. Her womanly ways were lost on Wharton—as she suspected. "Winston, do you know Amelia?"

"I do."

Ferreira returned with more water, set the glasses down on the small coffee table, and left.

"Is she one of Mr. Haverhill's women?" Janey asked.

"Yes."

"And this doesn't bother you," she stated instead of asked.

"They're all consenting adults. What they do together is their business." He was sweating and dabbed at his brow again.

"Are they all truly consenting?" She knew she was diverging from the murder case, but she needed to know.

"What do you mean? Of course."

"What if they weren't?"

"But they were. I have all the paperwork. Consent forms."

"They could have been signed under duress."

"*Non, non,* I was there. Lawyers, everyone. They were all happily in agreement."

"And his wife knew about this?"

"Of course. She was part of the contract signings. What does all this have to do with Haverhill's death?" He gulped, his sharp Adam's apple taut against his skin.

Janey eyed her wrist comm holo screen for the specifics of Haverhill's murder file so far, though she knew them. "Where were you at exactly one this morning?"

"I told you. I was at—that party."

Janey gave him a stern gaze.

"All right. I was in a private gambling game." He sniffed, folded and re-folded his handkerchief, yanked on his dress shirt collar, and reached for the water glass. He finished the rest of the water in two big swallows. "I have witnesses. In fact, Siobhan was there. She left early."

Private games were not allowed per L'Étoile's rules, but guests set them up all the time. Schoeneman didn't like that he didn't get any fees from the private games. Yet, he didn't ask security to shut them down.

"Who else? You mentioned 'the girls'."

"Yes. Sorry, not girls. Women. Cindy Kim and Chantal Lee. They were there too. I don't know where Amelia was. We haven't seen her in about a day."

"So the names you gave me…" She checked the table record on the cube. "The aliases." She rattled them off.

"Right." Wharton sighed as if defeated. "Juniper, Mimi, and Niagara are for Siobhan, Cindy, and Chantal."

"Was anyone else there?"

"I told you. Three other gentlemen were there, as well as two staff making drinks for us in the wet bar. I don't know their real names."

"Did Cindy and Chantal stay to the end as you did?"

"Yes, we were the last to leave, except for the staff." She asked for the staff names, so she could corroborate his statements, and waved them into her holo.

"When did Siobhan leave?"

"Around 11 p.m., I think."

"I need the location of the game."

"Of course." He gulped. "Was Jonas really murdered?" He whispered and panted, short of breath.

"Yes."

Wharton moaned and shook as if electrocuted, his body twitching, his hands rigid. Janey jumped to her feet. Was he having a stroke? A seizure? Wharton slumped sideways in the couch, dropping his handkerchief on the floor, barely breathing. His moans came in short bursts and sounded as if his breath was being squeezed out of him. The whites of his eyes shone, and his white face had turned grey. Oh no! He was suffocating.

Adrenaline pounded through her as she commed medical.

Wharton's breathing became louder, raspier, as if he

couldn't suck in enough oxygen, and his grey face veered even greyer.

She slipped a pillow under his head, loosened his tie, and made sure there was nothing obstructing his airway. Her first aid training taught her that much. "Mr. Wharton, are you okay?"

He didn't respond. From her ocular implant screen, she read his blood pressure as low, heart rate and respiration low too, but steady. He was breathing.

In two minutes, medical entered the room, using their medical emergency override codes. It had felt like twenty minutes. Two medics rushed over to examine Wharton. A third asked her what happened, and Janey recounted Wharton's reaction to the news of Haverhill's death.

The medics worked him over. One medic peered up at her. "He's had a grand mal seizure. He'll be fine." Wharton was still grey but breathing more normally.

"Glad he's all right. Was it triggered by shock?" Janey said.

"Not sure," the medic said. "When he comes to, we'll cover his history. We need to move him to medical."

"Of course," Janey said and got out of their way.

One medic unfolded the suitcase she was carrying into a stretcher. With her partner, they skillfully moved the assistant to the hover stretcher and guided it out of the room.

Janey returned to her office just as Ferreira commed.

"Soren and I finished the Haverhill sweep. Nothing disturbed. Multiple DNA collected that Soren said he'd run in the lab. He's returning there now. What do you need me to do next? Notify the wife?"

"Yes, with me. And the mistresses." Janey stared at the images of the three women, plus Amelia on the wallscreen-now-murder-board. Who had Haverhill met in the private suite?

"Mistresses?"

"Yes. Three of them." Cindy, Chantal, and Amelia. "We need to verify their alibis. For now, double-check their whereabouts and track down the private gambling room. Wharton said he was there with other guests and several staff. Check with housekeeping to track the staff down. Also, check on the whereabouts of Malina Bakaj."

"On it, boss," Ferreira said. "What about Haverhill's whereabouts before the murder?"

"I'll run that."

"I can do it."

"You have plenty for now, and I can set the facial rec to run. Wharton said he left the game around 11:30 because he had a meeting in the casino lower lounge."

Janey's stomach growled.

"And eat?" Ferreira said, a smile in her voice.

"Yes, Ferreira, and eat. We need our strength for the long day ahead. Then we interview Siobhan. I'll ping you when I'm on my way."

SEVENTEEN

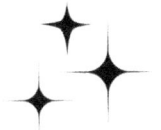

Last time Janey investigated a murder, Valdez was there and had helped, just by his very presence. He both excited her and pushed her to do better, be better. She called up his location on the security grid before she could talk herself out of it. There he was, under his alias, in the suite reserved under the name Jacques Laval. His biotag reading showed he was resting or asleep. It *was* nearly three in the morning. She had no good reason to comm him.

Before she left to meet Ferreira, she set up a search in the casino vid feeds for Haverhill's whereabouts to confirm Wharton's account. She waved a message to Shawhan and Lane to keep an eye on the search and review the results. She'd get a ping too, but in case she was in the middle of the next set of interviews, she wanted her team's eyes on it right away. Whoever Haverhill met with in the lounge could be his killer. And the sooner she caught the killer, the better. Preferably before Milano woke up or Schoeneman arrived.

Janey commed Soren.

"Tea," was the first thing he said.

"What about it?"

"That's what I found on the rug."

"Okay?" Janey said slowly. "And that's significant why?"

"The tea grounds in the rug are from the tea. Both the liquid left in the teapot and granules I found in the rug were laced with a chemical compound."

"What compound? And why didn't you call me sooner?"

"Because I haven't determined what kind of compound it is yet," Soren said. "Mass spec is still running. Give me another hour."

"Okay. Does Doc have something for me?"

"Chomping at the bit at this one, are you?" Soren teased.

"Of course. Always." Janey stifled a yawn. "It's a murder case."

"Right. Sorry," Soren said soberly. "Nothing yet from Doc. She's almost done. I can tell because her random humming stopped. Expect a comm soon. Maybe another thirty minutes. You need leads?"

"Yes. Things are pretty thin on my end." Janey stared at the lineup of photos: the assistant, Wharton, the wife, Siobhan, and the two other women. Then there was Amelia. And whoever was in the room with Haverhill. A figure clothed in black who'd disappeared. No word yet from Madison on any visual hits from the security vids. The suspect was probably in regular clothes by now, blending in with everyone else. "We're following up on alibis and conducting interviews with the victim's entourage."

"Entourage?"

"Yes. I'll share more later. Not over the comm."

"Understood." Soren clicked off.

In the still of Jonas Haverhill, he was sprawled on the couch. Perhaps he was drugged before he was stabbed—something strong enough to incapacitate him. That could explain how a robust man in the prime of his life was able to be overpowered and stabbed so many times without any defensive wounds on his hands or arms.

Janey commed Lane to check-in and yawned.

"Is it okay?" was the first thing Lane said.

"What?"

"We sent you our prelim on the attempted kidnapping."

"Right." Janey waved at her screen to call up the report and then scanned it. "No identifiers from the attackers?" No fingerprints, hair, or fibers.

"Nope. They were well prepared in that regard." Lane sounded disappointed.

"How's Amelia?"

"She's still pretty shook up," Lane said. "Resting. I was going to get her statement later."

"And you and Shawhan?"

"Ribs taped up. I'll have some pretty bruises soon. We're fine. We added the medical report with ours. Page two."

Janey caught up with the facts. "Ah."

"What?"

"Each of you got some hits in, including some face shots. So we could look for people with facial bruising."

"Oh yes." There was excitement in Lane's voice. "I'll run facial scans for that."

"Good. And run a scan for who is unaccounted for at the time of the attack, guests and staff. That will help narrow down your attackers and the murderer. Report in as soon as you get a hit."

"If we do."

"Think positive, Lane."

"You think there was only one killer?"

"That's my working theory right now."

Lane commed off, and Janey checked messages for anything from Detective Juanita Verde of the cold cases department of the Granton San Francisco police officer regarding Christine's files. But there still wasn't anything. San Francisco was twenty-one hours behind. It was early morning there. Verde probably hadn't arrived at work yet.

Janey left her office and headed for the service elevator, comming Ferreira as she walked. "I'm on my way to you." The security feed showed Ferreira on the sixth level. Notifying next of kin was never easy.

"Okay. I found the private gambling room. It's actually a suite, but it's been auto-cleaned already," Ferreira said. "Also, Ms. Siobhan N'Soumer is in Suite seven-oh-three, seventh level." One level above the gambling room.

"I'll be there in five. Did you track down the staff yet?"

"Housekeeping didn't return my comm."

"That'll be next." Janey commed off and took the service lift up to the seventh level. Ferreira was already beside the suite door. "Go ahead. Request entry."

Ferreira waved at the door pad to signal her arrival, called out Siobhan's name a few times, and then called, "Security. Please open up."

No reply.

According to the security feed, Siobhan was still supposed to be in the suite—and awake by the looks of the biotag.

Janey pounded louder on the door and called out

Siobhan's name a few times too. After a few more minutes, the door skated open to reveal a petite woman with long shiny brown hair cascading over her shoulder. She was wearing a floor-length chiffon nightgown bathrobe in opalescent pink. For presumably having just been woken up, she looked alert and awake, with a fresh application of soft makeup, and not appearing a day over forty-five.

"May I help you?" Siobhan peered up at Janey with wide blue-green eyes outlined in kohl. She didn't seem surprised to be receiving a visit from L'Étoile security at three in the morning.

"Siobhan N'Soumer?"

"Yes?"

Janey flashed her holo badge. "We're with security. I'm Investigator Janey McCallister and this is Officer Larissa Ferreira. "May we come in?"

"Yes, of course." Siobhan waved them in with an elegant gesture. "Sit, please. May I get you anything?"

"No, thank you," Janey said and sat in one of the plush blue chairs around a circular low table. Ferreira took the chair beside her.

"Is this about Jonas? He drinks too much. Has he been uncouth again? Hitting on pretty young women like your officer, Ms. Ferreira, here? He likes them petite, just like her. Who do I need to send credits to this time? At every hotel…" She shook her head as if that explained it and gracefully flopped into the chair opposite Janey, crossing her legs and peering expectantly at Janey, then at Ferreira, and back again to Janey.

"I'm sorry to tell you, Ms. N'Soumer, that your husband is dead."

"What?" Siobhan shot to her feet, clutching her chiffon to her throat. She raced away toward the kitchenette, then spun to face them. "Bastard! It's the middle of the night. Couldn't he have waited 'til morning?" Her face contorted with disgust. Then it was as if she realized who she was speaking to, and she restored her face to a mask of calm, still breathing heavily. "How did he die?"

"He was stabbed."

Siobhan gasped. Then she waved over her wrist comm.

"What are you doing, Ms. N'Soumer?" Janey asked.

"Telling Cindy, Chantal, and Amelia."

"When was the last time you saw Amelia?" Janey asked.

"Yesterday some time. Why?"

Janey's comm buzzed against her skin. It was Doc, the medical examiner. Janey waved the "in the meeting" preset message to Doc and peered up at Siobhan. "She's fine. I need to ask you a few questions."

Just then the door chimed.

"Excuse me," Siobhan said. She rushed to the door and escorted in Cindy and Chantal. Both women were younger than Siobhan, though they appeared a little older than Amelia, probably in their late twenties, and they were petite pixies. Cindy had short straight black hair, and Chantal had red curls. Both were in long drapey robes like Siobhan's, silky and shimmery. The three women huddled and whispered.

After a moment, Janey said, "Please sit. I have some questions."

Siobhan introduced the younger women to Janey and Ferreira. Then Cindy and Chantal both sat in the remaining chair, cozied next to each with ease, arms around each other as if lending comfort.

"Where were you at one this morning?" Janey asked Siobhan.

"In bed, asleep."

"Can anyone confirm that?"

Siobhan glanced at Cindy and Chantal. "Our call records, I guess. I mean beforehand. I was chatting with Cindy right before I went to sleep. Around midnight?"

Cindy nodded. "We were probably on our way to our room at that time. Wharton can verify. We left him at the level below."

Chantal clasped Cindy's hands. "Is he really dead? Murdered?" She scowled. "How horrid."

"Did Mr. Haverhill have any enemies?" Ferreira asked.

"I wouldn't know," Siobhan said. "Jonas always kept his business and personal matters separate.

Janey thanked Siobhan, Chantal, and Cindy and asked them to stay available for questions. Then she and Ferreira left the suite and headed for the staff lift. Once inside and moving down the security wing, she commed Doc.

"I have TOD and COD, Janey," Doc said. TOD and COD were for time of death and cause of death, respectively. "Plus, I spotted a few things that may or may not help your case."

"On our way," Janey said.

"Actually, boss, I'd like to run down the other guests at the game and the staff too," Ferreira said, then she glanced at her wrist comm. "Go to Housekeeping directly, face to face, to get some answers."

"Yes, good initiative, but you'll need to face the morgue at some point. Part of the training."

Ferreira gave her a look, begging off.

"Fine. Not today. Go. Divide and conquer," Janey said.

"Oh—" Ferreira waved open her holo. "Malina Bakaj

was asleep in her room at the time of the murder. The hallway vids show her entering her suite at 10 p.m., and the biotag shows resting heart rate starting at 11 p.m. and continuing to the current moment."

"Thanks. She's cleared then." No other evidence tied Malina Bakaj to the crime.

Ferreira got off at the security level, and Janey took the lift down one more level to where the lab was. In the lab, Soren looked up from his work and nodded at her in greeting, his mind on whatever he was peering at in his scope. His mass spec was humming.

Janey stopped at his metal table. Petri dishes of different colored dust and dark dirt-like leaves were lined up in neat rows. "About the vacuum contents? And the weapon?"

Without looking up, Soren said, "Nothing out of the ordinary except for the tea leaves. Still analyzing those to get the specific kind of tea. And the database is analyzing the stab wounds. Nothing yet. I did check with the kitchen on the tea set. It's the only one of its kind on L'Étoile."

"Thanks." She headed for the cold pathology lab next. Before entering, she changed into scrubs in the ante-room. Doc's protocol. Doc wanted the autopsy room as clean as possible.

Last time she was here for a case, Valdez was with her, too. She could do her job solo, but it was more fun with a partner. But Valdez wasn't her partner. She didn't know what he was to her anymore, except a jolt to her system. That jolt, that intensity, aliveness... she wanted that. And she wanted more than that.

She shoved aside thoughts of Valdez and hit the buzzer announcing her entrance into Doc's domain.

Doc straightened. She'd been hunched over Haverhill's neck, examining it. The tall woman was in full scrubs and a face mask, leaving only her piercing eyes visible.

"COD was this stab wound through the heart," Doc said, pointing to the organ, currently exposed to the air. "All the other cuts came before the fatal stab. Soren is analyzing stomach contents, running a blood toxicology screen, and analyzing my 3-D scan of the wounds for the weapon."

"Thanks, Doc. And time of death."

"I'd say 12:30 to 1 a.m."

She'd arrived at the room at one-oh-five.

"Anything else unusual?"

"Yes, many of his organs have been replaced by lab-grown ones."

"Why? He's a young man. Forty-five, his records say," Janey said.

"I detect no traces of previous illness," Doc said. "I don't know why, yet,"

"It does seem a strange coincidence." In her first murder case on the station, the victim's organs had all been replaced with lab-grown ones, grown just for him, and they matched his genetics perfectly.

Janey eyed the victim's hands and forearms. Nothing unusual that she could see with her ocular implant. "I don't see any defensive wounds. Did you find anything along those lines?"

"No."

"The tea could have slowed him down, drugged him, or incapacitated him," Janey said. "Maybe paralyzed him."

"Possibly."

"Thanks, Doc. You're a gem."

Doc chuckled. "Now get out so I can get back to it."

Janey hustled to get out of the scrubs and reset her vision to normal, a buzz of excitement in her chest. The tea was a lead. She'd know the kind of weapon soon. She wasn't completely empty-handed. Now they were getting somewhere.

EIGHTEEN

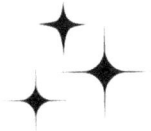

Traipsing around the station in high heels wasn't practical. Back in her quarters, Janey stripped down to her protective gear, tossed the nice clothes over a chair, hopped into her favorite jeans and boots, and added her weapons.

It was four in the morning. Before the day shift began, she needed to have one more conversation before reporting to Chief Milano at 8 a.m. If she didn't present him with some solid leads, she risked getting put on probation again.

She needed to get ahead of the situation and make an arrest.

She left her quarters and took the corridor to the other side of the staff circle. Lane guarded the door to Amelia's room. Shawhan had a purple shiner dominating one eye, glistening with the salve from medical. Magic goo. At least, that was what they called it in Space Wing. The sticky clear slime healed up surface bruises and minor cuts within an hour or two and was derived from a tiny bug discovered in the Rainforest Protectorate only twenty years ago.

"Boss," Shawhan said in greeting. "Amelia's asleep. Antonia is reviewing our suspect search."

"Thanks. I'm here to take Amelia's statement. Something in the preliminary report caught my eye."

"But we didn't get her statement."

"Exactly. Did anyone ask how the attackers gained entry into the room?"

"We did, but it's not in the prelim." Shawhan looked sheepish and had the professionalism not to shrug. "I don't know how to override these doors, and I forgot, I mean, I didn't ask the right questions."

"Yep. But you can redeem yourself by conducting the interview and asking the right questions this time."

"And leave the door unguarded?" Shawhan asked.

"Lane can stand watch," Janey said. "The likelihood of the attackers returning is low, but let's not take any chances."

Once inside the room, Janey sent Lane outside to guard the door and had Shawhan wake up Amelia, reminding her to be insistent.

While she waited, Janey reviewed the list Shawhan had compiled of people unaccounted for at the time of the murder. Shawhan's notes on the table screen listed several dozen people, including Janey, in the frame for the murder. Right. There were no cameras or biotag trackers in the mezzanine suites. Another name jumped out at her: Blue Bear—the assistant Wharton had mentioned as an alias for one of the gamblers in the private game.

The other names on the list included three people from the kitchen staff, five from housekeeping, a few from the spa, and two engineers from the machine shop.

Perhaps the staff were deep in the bowels of the hotel, in one of the service areas shielded from the biotag sweeps. There were some blind spots.

The list included five guests: two men from the Chinese Republic, maybe from the group around Valdez, and three more guests without idents attached, maybe from the new arrivals from Schoeneman's jet. Also, Siobhan N'Soumer, Cindy, Chantal, and Winston Wharton. Someone must have disabled the cameras and biotag sensors in the suite where the private game took place. That took a high level of skill.

At the bottom of the list was Amelia's name. What? Why was she on the list?

Another question for the young woman. Amelia did have motive, but did she have means or opportunity? How could she if she had been in the room with Shawhan and Lane?

On her holo screen, she switched to her personal messages. Still nothing from Detective Verde. She was giving up hope of ever getting to the bottom of Christine's murder. She jumped back into her business messages.

Ellias had sent her the incident report regarding the hangar entrance, specifically at the departures security gate. At 1:15 a.m., three men attempted to push past the security check and were turned back by him and his team. The three men had tried persuasion, then bribery, and then they'd attacked. At the first sign of push back from his team, the three men ran. He'd attached the footage from the incident. He apologized for the delay in getting her the report and for the problems with the footage. He'd had to make sure his crew got seen by medical and had had to confer with his direct boss, the hanger chief. Janey opened the vid, but just then

Shawhan exited the bedroom with Amelia and joined her around the table, Amelia sitting across from Janey and Shawhan.

Time to switch gears.

"Amelia, I'd like your account of the attack earlier tonight," Janey said. Shawhan glanced at her.

Amelia huddled in an Icelandic bright wool sweater too big for her and shook her head. "I—it was—I just…"

"Take your time," Shawhan said. "In your own words."

"I was drinking tea, here, at the table with you and Antonia," Amelia said in her little-girl voice. She cleared her throat and stared at the table.

"Do you need some water?" Shawhan asked.

Amelia shook her head, glanced at Janey, and then glanced away. "I'm fine."

"You know that Haverhill is dead," Janey said.

Amelia nodded, tears in her eyes.

"I thought that'd make you happy," Janey said.

Amelia snapped her gaze to Janey, shocked. "I didn't —no, not this. I just wanted to get away."

"Tell us what happened after you were drinking tea," Shawhan said.

"The door opened."

"Then?" Shawhan prompted.

"The attack. It was horrible. I didn't want that. I didn't want to go."

"Did you know them?" Janey asked.

"Why do you ask?" Amelia shrunk into the sweater, hiding her face in its wide cowl neck.

"I find it odd that the secured doors opened," Shawhan said.

"Without calling out a passcode, right?" Janey asked, glancing at Shawhan.

"That's right," Shawhan said.

"Well, either they had mad tech skills for a brute force attack and could override our double security system," Janey said, "or someone let them in." She knew of only one person who could override the doors on L'Étoile and that was Valdez. Was he somehow involved? Now she would *have* to talk to him.

"How could someone let them into a secure room?" Shawhan asked Amelia.

Amelia shrugged into her sweater.

"There are some anomalies with your biotag reading, Amelia, at the time of Haverhill's murder," Janey said. "Can you explain that? You were sitting right here with Antonia and Meilani. So why does the system show you as not being here?"

Amelia said nothing.

"Amelia, I'm arresting you as an accessory to murder," Janey said and put the handcuffs on the table.

"What? No!" Amelia shot out of her chair. "You can't —I didn't—"

"But you know who did."

For a moment, Amelia froze. The room's food crafter hummed a low frequency. Below that was the even lower, quieter drone of the laundries vibrating on the level below. A tinkle of Chopin piano music came from one of the holo wallscreens set to a French countryside, trees swaying in the breeze.

"Tell us what you know," Shawhan said, softly, as if she was a friend and not a menacing peace officer.

"I never met him," Amelia said quietly but in a deeper voice, not the high squeak she'd been using.

"Who? The killer?" Janey asked.

Amelia slipped into the chair, squared her hands in front of her on the table, and peered at Janey with a resigned gaze. "I didn't think it would go down like that. Please, he just wanted to talk."

"Talk to who?" Shawhan asked.

"Haverhill."

"I need a name," Janey said.

Amelia splayed her delicate long fingers on the smooth table surface. "I only knew him as Nancy's brother."

"Who is Nancy?"

"A girl, a woman, like me."

"An escort?"

"Yes."

"What did he want with Haverhill?"

"To talk, that was all. He wanted to find out where his sister was."

"Did you know Nancy?"

"No, but she's like me."

"In what way?" Shawhan asked.

Amelia shrugged. "He told me she'd left home young, like I did, and she had fallen in with rich men after a while, also like me, and then she stopped communicating with her family after a while."

"Like you?" Shawhan asked.

Amelia nodded and averted her gaze. Then she sighed and lifted her chin. She was facing the music.

"Where did he say home was?" Shawhan asked.

"He didn't," Amelia said. "He was careful to never leave specific details like that."

"When did he first contact you?"

"About three months ago."

"Have you met him? Can you describe him to me?"

Amelia frowned. "I've never actually seen him."

"Are you sure?" Janey pressed. They needed a name.

"You're both on L'Étoile," Shawhan said.

"If I did, I didn't know it."

"Amelia, how did this come about?" Janey sat back in the chair. "He approached you or was it the other way around?"

"He contacted me. By private message channels. He was smart. Somehow, he got the personal node I only used with friends, and he told me he was a friend of a friend and only wanted to chat."

"All your communications were by private node?" Shawhan asked.

"Yes, he didn't want anyone knowing."

"Knowing what?"

"He was always upfront about looking for his sister and thinking Haverhill knew where she was."

"Why did he think that?" Shawhan asked, and she glanced at Janey for confirmation that she'd asked a good question. Janey gave her a little nod.

Amelia sighed again and shrugged. "He'd never tell why, just insist he had proof that went way beyond."

"What did he mean 'way beyond'?"

"He didn't explain. He was good." She said that last bit to herself.

"Good how?" Janey asked.

"He knew how to manipulate me, get me to reveal things. Ugh." Amelia pushed back from the table, tracked around it to the tiny kitchenette, and got herself a glass of water from the cold box.

"Why you, Amelia?" Janey asked.

Amelia leaned against the counter next to the small sink, food crafter, and insta-coffee.

Janey's ocular readout flickered off and on again. It took about a millisecond, but Janey was waiting and grabbed the code with her wrist comm.

"Amelia, stop whatever you are doing," Janey said. The signals had to be coming from Amelia.

"I'm not doing anything."

"You are."

Amelia gulped her water.

"What is that?" Janey tapped her temple. "Your tech?"

Shawhan braced and said softly to Janey. "How did you know?"

Janey ignored Shawhan's question, watching, waiting, all the while scrutinizing her holo and her implant screens. How had she not seen this before? "You're transmitting something."

Soren would be able to better analyze this. She sent him the data with the note: SOS. Analyze now pls.

She kept her voice calm, steady, firm. "You have some kind of transmitter and receiver implant."

Amelia ducked her head and twisted her hands around the glass of water.

"Amelia, look at me," Janey commanded.

After a moment, the young woman gazed at her with scared rabbit wide eyes, her heart pounding fast to match.

"I know you're scared. I can see it on my ocular implant too," Janey spoke softly. "I got mine when I was thirteen. When did you get yours? It's an RF transmitter-receiver, right?"

"Yes," Amelia whispered. "But, no one is supposed to be able to detect it."

"Did Haverhill know?"

Amelia shook her head no.

"But Nancy's brother knew," Shawhan said, connecting the dots. "But how?"

"I don't know," Amelia said. "But he asked me to help him get close to Jonas."

"And the men who attacked us," Shawhan said, more a statement than a question. She put some steel into her voice.

"I—they—" Amelia blew out a breath. "I was supposed to go with them, leave the hotel."

"How?" Janey asked.

"A jet. But I didn't want to go. You were keeping me safe. And with sanctuary, I realized that would really accomplish what I wanted." Amelia looked miserable, maybe finally understanding she was in a heap of trouble.

Janey's comm vibrated against her skin. It was Soren's analysis of Amelia's interference. She studied his notes. They clarified a few things. Amelia's enhancements allowed her to send and receive signals, creating interference on some frequencies, as she suspected, and blocking specific communication channels. Soren had more technical language if and when she needed it. She waved a thanks and not now and added, block it now and peered at Amelia.

"I suspected." Janey kept her gaze on Amelia.

"How? You're the first to figure it out," Amelia said with awe in her voice.

"The little blips in my own implant when I was talking to you in the conference room last night. Then how the attackers got in. And the mix up around where the signals were coming from on the mezzanine." Janey sat back in the chair. "We've blocked it."

Amelia pressed her lips together as if holding back what she wanted to say. She wasn't denying anything, protesting anything.

"I need the enhancement specs to corroborate your story."

The young woman hugged herself and stared at the grey-beige recyclo flooring. Finally, she nodded.

"I don't know if the Sol will grant you sanctuary. You are an accessory to murder."

"I know." Amelia's expression was bleak. "But I didn't know he planned to kill Jonas. I really didn't," she whispered, covered her face with her hands as she slid down to the floor and curled up into a ball.

NINETEEN

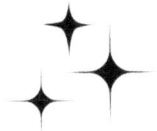

Ferreira commed, voice only, "Did you get it, boss?"

Janey was back in her quarters to catch a nap before the day shift and had changed into her pajamas, a soft buttery long sleeve shirt and pants combo.

"Did I get what?" She washed her face and brushed her hair.

"Details on Blue Bear—one of the staff I couldn't track down. I sent you what I gathered from the kitchen and spa staff. They're cleared, except for this Blue Bear. Still working on the engineers. Kou and Dube are working on clearing the five guests."

"Tell me."

"Valeric said that Blue Bear was working in the kitchen at the time, but no one could verify that. Their dossier doesn't say anything out of the ordinary about this person's work experience, but the personal information is sparse."

"Sparse how?"

"There's no gender, no photo, no emergency contact information. From the Seattle Granton."

No picture on file was unusual but not unheard of.

"The file said that the head chef had brought this person to L'Étoile two months previous. The person has experience in bars and restaurants, serving, and making drinks, but their special skill is horticulture."

That was odd.

"Thanks, Ferreira." She commed off. Just then her holo screen flicked up with an incoming vid call. It was Soren.

"I just sent you my analysis of the tea and tea water," he said. His sparkled hair was spiked every which way as if he'd been running his fingers through it.

"Can you give me the highlights?" Janey yawned, sat, and scanned his report on her table screen.

"Sure. The tea itself is a rare black tea, an *Assamica Kuntze* varietal," Soren said. "Only found in the Guangdong region of China and not grown on the station, nor is it imported. I checked."

"Thanks." She eyed the mini coffee maker. Could the tea have been brought in by Schoeneman's investment group? She needed to check the exact timing of their arrival. There was also the Chinese gamblers Valdez had played with two nights ago.

The Phoenix restaurant kept its own vertical gardens, and L'Étoile had an out-of-this-world class arboretum. If the tea wasn't cultivated here or imported, then someone brought it aboard intentionally.

Soren continued, "The substance found in the tea via mass spec is a clever combo of D-lysergic acid diethylamide and a derivative of tetrahydrocannabinol. And the blood tox screen confirms it."

"LSD mixed with the THC from marijuana, right?" Janey covered another yawn. "Strange." In her four years in Space Wing, she'd seen a lot of odd drug combinations, but clearly not everything.

"That's right. I've read reports in the crime lab trade journals on variations of these combined substances, usually in accidental or intentional overdoses," Soren said. "The combo tends to put people into a heavy, hallucinogenic sleep, resulting in seizures or injuries."

"Powerful and dangerous."

"Indeed," Soren said. "In this case, the chemical was synthesized to deliver seven hundred and fifty to one thousand micrograms per milliliter of the tea, all packed into a dissolvable capsule. The hot water released the concentrated form." He tapped on the outside of the teapot. "I found microsomal residue of the capsule in the pot and teacup. The dissolvable capsule was a sly touch because most people wouldn't analyze the inside surface of the teapot or cup so closely."

"Good job, Soren."

"Thanks." He frowned and then cocked his head like a parakeet examining a bug. "I personally have never seen this particular chemical coupling of these parent compounds."

"Enough for a COD?"

"Probably not enough to kill him, as far as I can tell," he said, "but it could do some damage. Mixing these two drugs can create unpredictable results."

"That speaks to planning. Lots of planning. And a willingness to take risks, what with the unpredictable drug mixture. Plus funding and connections." Janey paced her small room, from the food crafter and small sink to her bed and desk and back. She needed to stay awake to put the pieces together. Milano wanted a report. She wanted a suspect. He would want a suspect. They all wanted a suspect.

Where was he? Who was he? Most likely this Nancy's brother. There were a lot of places to hide on L'Étoile, especially in the lower levels.

"No professional lab would create this substance and risk its credentials and funding. It was most likely an underground lab," Soren said.

"Good point. I'll pass that information on to the Sol authorities when I arrest the killer," she said. That might be Valdez. He'd want to know about such a lab. This detail might tie into his case—a case tied to that gambling group from Guangdong, though she had no direct evidence to back up her supposition. Where were Kou and Dube with clearing the five Chinese guests? She suppressed a yawn in Soren's face. "Back to the substance in the tea. The two drugs you mentioned combine to create a Schedule One drug, right?"

Schedule One drugs were illegal because they had high abuse potential, no sanctioned medical use, and severe safety concerns. Could they have been stolen from Medical and mixed by a professional staying at L'Étoile? Unlikely given what Soren was sharing.

"It's beyond that. The Sol regulators can't even keep up with these cooks to give them a schedule. Bad business." He glanced at something outside the frame of the vid screen as if reading something. "A natural cannabinoid alone causes a mellow high or a panic attack at worst, but when altered like this, and in combination with the lysergic acid, it can oversaturate the victim's receptors. The victim could have suffered paralyzing and paranoid hallucinations or tremors—even psychoactive paralysis." Soren shook his head.

"These drugs could have softened him up before he was stabbed. Or maybe they were used to get him to talk. Good work." Janey tugged her hair up into a ponytail, her finger combing to relieve stress, and then she snagged a hairband from her tiny bathroom to secure her hair. Soren's face followed her on the continuous wallscreens lining every wall.

Maybe the assailant was smaller than the victim, so he felt he needed the drug to immobilize Haverhill, a taller, stronger man. Amelia had said Nancy's brother wanted to confront Haverhill about the location of his sister. Maybe he was the meeting at 11:30. Maybe the murder was an afterthought. They hadn't found the knife or another stabbing weapon yet.

"Thanks, Janey. Doc can give you more details on how it affected this victim."

"Anything else?" Janey hung up her dress in the closet, the one she'd tossed on the chair.

"I'm analyzing the stomach contents. A combination of factors could have made the drug more potent," Soren said.

"Good. I want to check all loose ends." Janey scanned her room as if the loose ends were amongst her tools, clothes, and the knickknacks from her mom. "Have you made a mold of the stab wounds? We still need to identify the murder weapon."

"In progress. I'll have the specs for you soon."

Janey closed the comm and got into bed under the covers. She started dictating the report for Milano, listing the chronology of the murder and a summary of her actions to date, but she was yawning so much, she was repeating herself to create coherent sentences. She had to stop, otherwise, she'd have to write the whole thing again. She could barely keep her eyes open.

"Rhea, wake me up at seven." That would give her a little under two hours of sleep. A decent nap.

"Sure thing, Janey. Block all messages?"

"Yes, but flag them top priority." They'd be the first messages she'd get when she awoke.

"Yes, Janey."

"Rhea, open voice message for Mom." She closed her eyes and slipped deeper into the covers.

"Ready for you, Janey," Rhea's soothing voice said.

Janey yawned and spoke softly. Rhea would be able to hear her just fine. Dana wouldn't care if her message was in a jumble.

"Mom, just checking in, sending this message early because I'm on a ten-ten and am going to catch some shut-eye. Love you to the stars and back. Send me the doc's report when you get it. It should be in by now. Oh, can you send me your cherry pie recipe too? Mai Chen wants to make it for Kim's birthday picnic. Oh yeah, we're not doing a surprise party for her. Faizah set me straight that Kim hates surprises in her personal life. Kim's been down. I want to cheer her up. I hope the party will do it. I want to do it in the arboretum. Darn, I forgot to call Madge. G'night, Mom!"

"Is that it, Janey?" Rhea said softly.

"Yes, send. And remind me to comm Madge after ten. A silent ping is fine."

"You got it, Janey. Sleep tight. Do you want your standard sleep protocol?"

"Yes."

Rhea turned off the lights, and the ceiling transformed into a smattering of clouds against a ribbon of night sky, stars winking through. Rhea turned on the sound of waves tumbling against the shore, and the scent of salty air circulated through the room. It was as if she was lying on her back in the park near the Pacific Ocean. Janey slipped into a dream where she ran along the coast trail, driving toward something or away from something, she wasn't sure. She only knew she had to keep going.

An insistent ping woke her, its high-pitched urgency sped up her heart rate and pounded in her temples.

"Rhea, time," she croaked. So thirsty.

"Seven thirty-eight," Rhea said.

"Venus hells." Janey bounded out of bed and filled a glass of water from the tiny sink. She had twenty-two minutes to draft the report and present herself to Milano. She had to shake off her fatigue and hop to it.

She dictated as she washed her face, brushed her teeth, and dressed in black slacks and a long blue over tunic with flowing sleeves. She stuffed her weapons in place.

Jonas Haverhill was killed between 12:45 and 1:15 am. Cause of death was a fatal stab through the heart by what could be a blade of some kind, but no weapon was found at the scene. The murder had no clear motive, though it looked like a crime of passion. Haverhill was supposed to have had a meeting prior to his death, but she didn't have the details on that either. Yet.

It appeared that the victim had been drugged with a rare and illegal combination disguised in a rare black tea from the Guangdong Province of the China Republic. She still didn't know who provided the rare tea, where the drugs in the tea came from, or where the red thread found on the scene originated.

The women in Haverhill's entourage and his assistant had been cleared. She was the only eyewitness to the black-clad person who fled the scene. She hesitated at how much of Amelia's story to put into the report. Ever since the young woman had asked for sanctuary, Janey wanted to protect her from all scrutiny, except hers. She left Amelia out. It was a preliminary report, after all.

She checked her appearance in the long mirror. Her hair was brushed and out of her face, and her clothes were decent and clean. Good enough. There were a lot of holes in the report she could have better filled if she'd stayed awake for what her team sent in. She waved over the mirror screen for updates from them. She had to be in Milano's office in ten minutes.

Soren had sent details on the mold for the object someone had used to stab Haverhill seven times and kill him. She waved open the 3-D rendering, and the holo image hovered and spun—a blade with a hilt. She read the text details. It was a six-inch double-edged blade with a two-inch hilt. The wounds had been deep, and the hilt had made marks into the skin. Soren noted that it took a lot of force to make those kinds of marks. That took upper body strength. And you'd have to know your way around a knife and basic anatomy, Soren noted. Doc had found minute traces around the wounds of a titanium alloy powder, specifically the Ti-3AI-V4 compound found in vehicle manufacturing, steel beams, nano satellite construction, and any kind of 3-D metal construction.

Like their machine shop used. Maybe someone in engineering had made this blade for Nancy's brother. Could he have had help on the inside or had he coerced someone?

Janey read on. Soren reported that the particulates did indeed originate from the L'Étoile machine shop.

Oh, Venus hells.

He was researching when the blade was made and

which engineer supervised it. Everything was recorded and cataloged in the machine shop. That was where most items that made up L'Étoile were fabricated, then recycled once they were worn out.

Soren went on to list the stomach contents and alcohol levels. Nothing remarkable about Haverhill's stomach contents, olives mostly, probably from his martinis. According to Haverhill's vitreous humor—the gel-like substance inside the eye—the blood alcohol content had been point-three-five. The man had been drunk when he died.

Her facial rec search of Haverhill in the hours or so leading up to his murder was done. She reviewed the footage at four times the speed and watched Haverhill enter the casino, flag down a server, and head to the lower lounge by the viewscreens. He sat on a plush leather chair. The server arrived with his drink—a martini of some kind, stacked with olives. Soon someone sat beside him. A smaller figure. A man, most likely. But his face was obscured as if by tech. She needed time to scrub the image and find out what was causing the blur. Had Amelia's tech caused that?

"Looking good, Janey," Rhea said. "Ready to send?"

Janey grunted. "Yes, send." She had five minutes, and she'd better be on time.

"Do you need a hug, Janey?"

"Rhea, I'm fine."

"You have a priority red message from Blue Bear."

"What?"

"They say to meet in the special place within the hour."

"They who...never mind. I have to go. Hold all personal messages."

Who the Venus hell was Blue Bear anyway? She had an idea. He could wait.

"Yes, Janey. Good luck."

Janey left her quarters to take the half-circle to Milano's office. Why had she trained her personal AI to be so cheerful? Sometimes she just wanted to be grumpy.

At Milano's office door, she waved in front of the door pad. The door slid open, and she entered.

"Schoeneman is not happy about the lockdown," Milano said by way of greeting and rubbed the bridge of his nose, where he rested the antique eyeglasses he fancied. He was dressed in his standard navy-blue suit with a crisp cream shirt.

"I'm sure, sir. Neither am I. We're following every lead."

"But you have no suspects. No one in custody."

She'd forgotten to attach the list. "Sorry about that, sir. One moment." She waved it over to him. "We do have a list of suspects we've been clearing. It's in progress. And I have someone, in particular, to run down."

Milano studied his wide translucent screen. She did the same on her holo screen floating above her wrist. There were only seven people on the list of names Kou, Dube, Ferreira, and Shawhan had been working to clear —five guests and two engineers from the machine shop. What was taking her team so long? Maybe they'd napped, like she had—collapsed, was more like it.

"Who is in the frame?" Milano asked. "Because we need an arrest—and soon. Schoeneman is here." Milano scanned his translucent screen, distracted. He chewed his bottom lip and looked pained. He waved a message over his comm.

"Sir? Is something wrong?"

"No." But he still looked pained as if he had heartburn.

"Why is Schoeneman here?"

"Not our business. He comes and goes as he pleases. And what's this I hear about a guest accused of cheating at pai gow?"

TWENTY

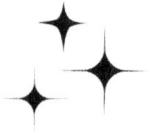

Janey blew out a breath. Time to get in front of this.

"The accused is Orlando Valdez, Sol Investigative—"

"I know who he is. *Dio santo!*" Milano clenched his jaw.

"You knew he was here?"

"Yes. I want you to arrest him."

"Why? On what grounds?"

For a moment, the chief said nothing. He clasped his hands over his rotund middle and leaned back in his chair.

"Chief?"

"I don't have an answer to your question as it was an anonymous report."

"How do you know it's him?"

"I saw the footage."

"What footage? Can I see it?"

"Sure, but don't you have a murder to solve?" Milano sidestepped her question.

Which was it? Why was he ping-ponging? Was he

hiding something? Or was he covering for someone? Was something else going on?

"If you want me to arrest Valdez, I'd like to see proof he committed a crime." If he had committed a crime, it would have probably been pre-arranged—and not by him. She hadn't seen any evidence of him cheating. She clasped her hands behind her back to keep from tugging on her clothes and took a breath. There had to be some mistake. "It's hard if not impossible to cheat at pai gow."

"Still..." Milano lowered his voice and put some bite into it. "Orlando Valdez is on board, and there's a warrant for his arrest. I need you to execute it and put him in holding." He peered at her over his old-fashioned glasses. "Just do it, McCallister. That's an order. I don't want him running around my station. Then get back to the priority case."

"I have to find him first." Why was he taking the report seriously? They needed to investigate the claim before arresting anyone, but she didn't want to question the chief's methods until she knew more. Maybe that's why the Chinese had been so quiet about the cheating. Instead of seeking their own justice by roughing up Orlando, they had filed a report with Milano.

"Do it, şimdi." Şimdi was "now" in Turkish. Milano liked to sprinkle his New Standard with words from his upbringing bouncing around the Mediterranean. "Use any and all resources. Call on kitchen security. Pull from engineering if you need too. Even from hangar security. Just do it."

"What's he accused of?" Janey asked, not budging from his tiny ten-feet-by-ten-feet office, the same size as hers. Today he had holos of blue lakes in snowy mountain valleys on his wallscreens.

"I told you. Theft from the Chinese betting group."

"You didn't. You only said that a guest was accused of cheating at pai gow. I know there was an incident, but it was probably a misunderstanding." The call of cheating had the sound of sore loser to it, maybe even a bit of manufactured drama.

"Why didn't you log it?"

When she didn't answer right away, Milano peered up at her from behind his wide translucent holo screen, where he'd been waving a message.

"Well?"

"I was there when he was accused of cheating, and I didn't see any evidence of it."

For a split-second Milano looked bleak as if the news wore on him, fatigued him, and yanked him down into a sticky morass.

"Investigator, go. Just go. Get it done. I don't have to tell you the consequences if you can't close this murder case."

"Sir?"

"Probation." He sighed, but he wasn't looking at her. He was gazing, sad, forlorn at the dancing figurines that always lined the edge of his desk.

"Understood."

When Milano didn't move from his fixed sadness, she left.

He hadn't asked her the identity of her prime suspect. The person with the Nancy's brother alias. The person she hadn't identified or found… yet.

Her office was next to Milano's. She went in, closed the door, and ignored the chair. She stared at one of her wallscreens set at a high-resolution hologram of the rotating Crab Nebula. The fast-moving pulsating neutron star lurking at the center of the nebula mesmerized her, soothed her, and reminded her she wanted to comm

Valdez. What could she say that would draw him out to her that she hadn't already conveyed?

She waved open a comm to him. "I need your help on my case. A murder case."

Personal matters aside, he'd helped her before. Maybe he'd help her again. They could both be professionals. Right.

Just before her meeting with Milano, Rhea had told her Blue Bear had left a message to meet him in their special place. That had to have been Valdez.

Why the need for subterfuge? She wasn't going to get any answers until she met with him face to face. For all his charm, he was very good at not sharing anything until he was ready.

Their special place... When he was on board a few months ago, they'd traipsed around to many locations in the hotel. But she knew the one he meant.

He was referring to the place where they'd first connected intimately: Star Watch—a star viewing room at the top of L'Étoile, designed as a cozy park. The location was private and not often frequented by guests, especially during the day.

She wasn't ready to go. She had to catch a killer. Valdez's arrest was not first priority—no matter what Milano wanted. No matter what the elusive Blue Bear wanted. She knew her job.

Janey stared at the list of suspects narrowed down to five guests and two engineers from the machine shop. One of them was the so-called Nancy's brother, but which one? She read each of their hotel records and found no mention of a Nancy, not that she thought she would.

Two of the guests, Zheng Lo and Jack Wang, had arrived three days previous with the morning arrivals.

Both men looked to be in their thirties and had hotel suites on the mid-levels. What was the hold up in tracking them down? They'd jetted to L'Étoile from another space station, Hong Kong Towers—a family-oriented mega hotel-casino, known for its immense water park and high staff turnover. Some of L'Étoile's staff had come from there.

The other three guests had arrived that night on Schoeneman's jet. She saw what was probably causing her staff problems. Those three had no names or photos assigned to them, just a point of origin from the flight: the Macau Spaceport. It was understandable why those three would be challenging to track down.

Why hadn't Kou, Dube, or Ferreira come to her for help?

The two machine shop engineers were Joseph Casa and Laura Hidalgo. Her team hadn't left any notes on them in the case file.

She commed Ferreira, and when she didn't pick up, she left a message asking for the status on the remaining seven suspects. She did the same for Kou and Dube. Perhaps they were all asleep. She could go wake them up, but that wasn't a good use of her time. Better use of her time was to focus on the killer. She commed Kim to ask her to get her team up.

What if the killer was hiding in plain sight? How could someone disappear so completely on the station?

There were seven hundred and fifty-seven guests and over fifteen hundred staff aboard L'Étoile, with all the amenities of a small city. There were lots of places to hide, especially if you had access to the staff levels below the hotel and casino, which guests did not.

She reviewed again the records for Casa and Hidalgo. Their biotags didn't read during the window of the murder. They could have been in one of the mezzanine suites that were shielded, or had they been down in bowels of the station, in transit? Some of the hallways down there were little more than service shafts and lacked comm routers in the walls. Some were shielded on purpose, due to the sensitive machines in those areas. It was about seven hours since the murder, and she couldn't believe none of her team had tracked them down. She doubled-checked the tracking system and saw now that Casa was in his quarters and Hidalgo was in the commissary. Maybe one of her team had cleared them and hadn't added the notes to the file.

So that just left the whereabouts of the three who traveled with Schoeneman and the two from the Hong Kong Towers. She checked the biotags for the latter but got nothing. She had no idents for the former. Great. Just great.

The hangar was locked down, with no space jets or planes in or out. Yet there was Schoeneman's jet parked in the hangar. Ellias hadn't reported any more incidents. That reminded her of the footage of the diverted attack at the hangar entrance he'd sent her.

She opened the footage and clenched her jaw. The attackers' faces were obscured and fuzzy. For each of the three men, their eyes, nose, and mouth seemed blurred as if paint-brushed with a child's hand. She froze an image and stared at it, using her own optical implant to zoom in.

Venus hells.

The image became more pixelated. She zoomed in again and got another layer of pixels. It was as if she was looking at a mask made out of a Mandelbrot set design. The deeper she went with her scan, the more the dots morphed in an infinite fractal swirl pattern. These men were wearing a sophisticated kind of clear-skinned bala-clava or facekini. Current optical and facial recognition tools were useless against this kind of tech.

For comparison, she called up the image of the man Haverhill met with in the hour or so before he died. Was it the same kind of blurred effect? She zoomed in with her optical implant. She was able to discern features, but they were bent and out of place as if distorted by the artistic hand of Picasso or Dali. Even the biotag was masked. His heart and respiration combo in his hotel record would have IDed him. The distortion effect on his face and the obscuring of his biomedical data might have been caused by Amelia's tech. She sent the image to Kim to render into the correct order—Kim was handy with tools like that—but there was no way to unscramble the block on his biotag.

Was this man Haverhill met with the murderer or a diversion? Was he the so-called Nancy's brother?

Then she pulled up the video footage of the person who'd fled the murder scene. Even by breaking the video down frame by frame at one-two-hundred-twentieths of a second, and then examining it at high magnification, she spotted no discernible identifying marks. The person was a blur of black. The face was masked, and the clothing absorbed light like a black hole. Stealth clothing.

Whoever was behind the murder—if she was indeed looking at the murderer, and she most likely was given the timing—was a tech genius, and beyond her and her teams' skills.

Valdez knew way more than she did about stealth clothing. He was a spy after all and a damn good one. He knew all about hiding in plain sight.

She was about to comm Valdez again when her wrist band buzzed against her skin, making her jump. Three short buzzes, then a pause, then three more short buzzes. A military distress signal from someone on the station, calling in stealth mode, and operating outside normal comm channels.

She opened her comm. It had to be Valdez. "Go."

"I'm in a jam. Come to our spot. Now." The male voice was urgent and low.

"Valdez? Is that you? What's going on? Where are you?"

But the comm was closed already.

Her heart sped up. What if he was hurt? What if...

With a deep and cleansing exhalation, she stopped the what-ifs and paced the length of her tiny office. The caller said, "Come to our spot." The Star Watch park.

He was in the station-top park where they first... her body heated at the intimate memory. Traitorous body. But she'd missed that connection.

At the wallscreen, heartbeat in overdrive, she tapped into the biotag locator system. It showed Jacques Laval, Valdez's alias, in his suite. So he'd been snooping around doing stars knew what for the last two days and leaving a false biotag behind in his room. She should have guessed as much. Damn him to Pluto.

She sprinted out of her office, took the service elevators up, exited into a grey service corridor, and headed for the park.

She let herself into the round atrium. The skylight was closed, blocking all sunlight. The last time they'd been here they'd admired the Orion Constellation, and he'd recited the Arabic names of its most famous belt stars.

Though it was morning, discreet lit wall sconces gave the space a dusk-like ambiance and elongated the shadows of the ferns and other bushes. The space was empty of guests.

"Valdez?"

No answer. Not even a rustle of clothing.

She adjusted her ocular implant to let in more light and scanned the room. There he was leaning against the wall, arms crossed, eyes closed, breathing slow and deep as if he were napping. Though he was in a shadow beside a bush, he showed up clear as day to her now, his face distorted from how she remembered him by makeup and prosthetics to change his nose—rounder, less pointed—and cheekbone structure—muted and molded to be like apples, instead of his sharp square cheekbones. His eyes were painted to look round with drawn lines splayed on his forehead where his eyebrows should be.

In two seconds, she'd matched his face to the one she had on file and matched his resting heart rate and respiration—as unique as a fingerprint. It was Valdez.

With a puffy jacket and pants in a bright sky blue, his face painted blue to match, with a blue poofy wig in a darker shade, he resembled a cartoonish bear out of children's immersive games. Although Valdez should have looked ridiculous in the outlandish costume, he didn't. His innate virility and commanding bearing shone through the costume like a trademark.

The only part of him not blue was his hands. Blue gloves stuck out of a fluffy jacket pocket. Staff and guests did dress up often when they played private games in their suites—one of the ways they liked to party.

"Valdez, you hurt?" She navigated around benches and bushes and stopped two feet in front of him. She scanned him from head to toe. No heat loss. Not a scratch on him. She blew out a breath. "You don't look hurt. You look ridiculous."

"You look great too, babe." He straightened and held her gaze. At least he had the decency not to give her a once over. She'd have decked him if he had.

"I am not your babe." She glared at him. "You scared me with your fake distress call."

"Not a fake. I am in a jam."

"What is it?"

"Can we sit and talk?" Valdez nodded to the bench. Their bench.

She waved him forward. In smooth athletic moves, he peeled off the blue bulky top and pants, stripping down to a white T-shirt and skin-tight long exercise shorts, showing off his broad and muscled chest and strong legs. Her body heated all over.

From inside the bulky blue top, he pulled out a pair of rolled-up blue jeans and a black leather jacket. Before her eyes, he'd transformed himself into a cool cat. He even slicked back his dark curly hair with a comb from his coat pocket. In no hurry to get to the point.

Venus hells.

"What are you up to, Valdez?" Janey asked. "What's with the cartoonish disguise? What are you working on? Answers. Now. Please."

He sat on the bench, extricated a small round case from his jacket pocket, and dabbed the blue makeup off his face. He plucked the prosthetics off and inspected himself in the compact's mirror to make sure he didn't miss any. He winked at her—she was staring.

Relationships were more than animal magnetism, she reminded herself.

"Are you trying to piss me off?" She sat at the far end of the bench.

Valdez slid toward her. She slid away toward the far end, ready to fall off the bench, then she held up her hand in a stop gesture. Her body flared again with heat, but she was having none of it. Her body and her heart could just hold on.

He stopped, watching her impassively.

"We're not doing that again, Valdez." She couldn't hide from the warmth in her cheeks, in her core, in her limbs. "Just no."

For a moment, neither of them spoke, they only held each other's gaze. He broke it off first. "There's something you need to know," he said at a whisper, even though there was no one around them.

She crossed her arms. "What?"

"I'm in trouble, and I wanted you to hear it from me first."

"What kind of trouble?"

"The kind Milano wants to arrest me for."

"How do you know about that?"

He gave her a look. Could there be more to it than the cheating at gambling?

Venus hells and all of Saturn's rings. Did Valdez kill Haverhill?

She was almost afraid to ask, but if she didn't, she wouldn't be doing her job. She steeled herself. Valdez was great at lying.

"Where were you between 12:45 a.m. and 1:15 a.m.?"

"Working." He shoved his hands into his pockets, his vitals calm, cool even. She hated how he could do that, turning his body so still and leveling his vital signs so she couldn't read him. It made her crazy.

"On what, Valdez?" she snapped.

"I'm on a case." He blew out a breath, taking his time and gazing at her. No pretense. Vulnerable even. His vitals were fluctuating normally, not muted. He was telling the truth. "I have a witness who can corroborate. I am not your murderer, Janey."

"How do you know about my murder investigation?"

"People talk."

"You mean you intercept comms. How do you do that anyway? We have secure channels—" Could his case have something to do with hers? Is that why he was listening in? She glared at him, hard.

He tensed. His heart rate and respiration slowed again. Skin pale, his expression went to neutral again, and a man she didn't recognize gazed back at her. It was as if she was watching an approaching ice age. Really?

"You called me for help. How can I help you when you get like that?" she blurted.

"Like what?" he said, but his shoulders relaxed on his exhale.

"Valdez..." She inched closer to him. "This hot and cold thing you do... I hate it... It makes it hard to trust you."

She wanted to trust him.

"I work undercover so much... It's my way."

"You're still working for the Sol Unified Planets Special Police Force?"

He nodded once. More color came into his cheeks.

"What do you need? What's going on? Are the pai gow gamblers really after you?"

He reached inside his jacket.

Janey went for her laser-sighted pistol under her jacket. Instinct.

"Whoa! You're wound tighter than a space elevator cable," Valdez said.

Her cheeks heated.

"Just reaching for my wrist comm—slowly." He slipped it on his wrist, turned it on by waving over it, and called up the holo screen. Then he held it out for her to see.

"You *are* acting pretty weird right now. My reaction is justified." But she let go of her gun's grip and scooted toward him to study the screen. A ledger of amounts scrolled in front of her. "What's this?"

"My bank balance. Notice anything unusual?"

"Besides the deposit of one hundred million credits?" She lifted an eyebrow.

"Yes. Look at the timestamp."

Janey looked. "What about it?"

"It's before the game even finished."

Two nights ago, when she'd arrived at the pai gow table in her waitress get-up, the game had been in full swing.

"By how much?" Janey asked.

"By a full five minutes."

"Oh. Jupiter's balls." Janey sat back.

"Yes, Jupiter's balls is right. I've been set up. My account was hacked. I didn't steal this money, but this account transfer makes it look like I did. I did win the game fair and square though. But not one hundred mill. I only won fifty mill, and that transaction doesn't show up."

"Why would they set you up? Who specifically? All of them—a coordinated group—or one individual in particular?" She glared at him. "Who did you piss off?"

"All good questions. Except that last one. Why did you have to go there?" Valdez frowned, showing a bit of an overblown pout.

"Who are you in trouble with this time?" Janey snorted, inelegantly. "Are you going to answer my questions?"

Valdez eyed the far wall. "I don't know why someone

or a bunch of someones would set me up, except that I'm getting too close to the truth. I don't know who specifically, though I have a guess. But I have no evidence, except this bank transfer I haven't been able to trace. The person is damn good. Better than me."

"Okay," Janey said. "Wait. Where are these gamblers from?"

"Guangdong Province mostly, China. Why?" His eyes widened.

"Our cases might be connected." Her heart quickened at the threads of the case coming together. "And I can see that you think so too."

"Any idea what the connection is?"

"Guangdong Province. We found traces of a rare tea that comes from there."

"Could be coincidence." He stood.

"I don't like coincidences," She stood too, certainty flooding her. Working together was the right move.

"Me neither." Valdez grinned. "Let's go get the bad guys!"

TWENTY-ONE

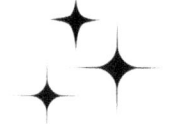

THEY SLIPPED OUT OF THE STAR WATCH PARK and headed down the quiet corridor to the service elevator. Jane waved in the command to descend to the security level. The service lift opened, and they stepped in without speaking.

When the door closed, Valdez spoke and peered at her with his intense brown eyes, like she was all there was. "Are you okay?"

"Why do you ask?" Janey crossed her arms over her chest at the way he scrutinized her.

"You look tired."

"I am." She gazed at him, cataloging the way his dark curls fell over his ears and nestled against the nape of his neck.

"Hard to give it your best that way," he said in a gentle tone. "There's no shortcut for a good night's sleep."

"It's my day shift. What are you now, my doctor?" She gave him a half-smile.

"Just someone who cares."

"Funny way of showing it. Holding me hostage." And not replying to her vid calls. Ghosting her. But her voice held no bite. He cared for her. Her burdens weren't only her own.

"I am sorry." He stepped into her personal space, notched up his full attention, full-spectrum light, baking her, and tingling all the way to her marrow. The flood of sensations was like a crackling blaze rushing through her body. Enjoyable, giddy, and provocative.

"Thank you. Even so, I want an explanation." Janey lifted her chin, refusing to lean into the waves of energy that had her inwardly trembling and tingly.

"I will, but not here. Where can we work?" Valdez eyed her lips.

"My office."

He reached out and squeezed her hand. She didn't pull away. He lifted his other hand to her cheek. She was tempted to lean into his warmth, but the elevator stopped on the security level, and the door glided open. Grateful for the interruption, Janey pulled away and strode into the grey corridor toward her office.

They were outside her office when her comm beeped twice—an urgent call from Milano. She ignored it, unlocked the door, and went in.

"Aren't you going to answer that?" Valdez followed her in and the door slid closed.

She blew out a breath and answered the comm. "Sir?"

"You have Valdez?"

How could he know?

"I'm not sure he did steal from them," Janey said by way of a reply.

"Why do you say that?"

"Well, sir, for one thing, I was there, and for another,

he told me he didn't steal the money, that he was set up."

Valdez opened his mouth to speak.

Janey shook her head and put a finger to her lips.

"Find Valdez and bring him to Interrogation One. I want to talk to him myself."

Valdez held her gaze, impassive.

She finally spoke. "Yes, sir."

Valdez frowned and shook his head.

"McCallister, think you can find him within thirty minutes?"

Janey eyed Valdez, who shook his head more vigorously.

She sighed again. "Yes, sir."

Valdez frowned and paced.

"Good," Milano said and closed the comm.

"You can't bring me to interrogation. We have cases to solve—yours and mine." Valdez rubbed the back of his neck. "Milano is slowing us down."

"I know." She reached out to comfort him but stopped short and drew her hand back. "I can't afford to cross him. You're going to have to tell me what you're working on. And now. Clock is ticking. Can't you have your superior officer clear you with Milano and read us into your case?"

Why were they going through this again? Same song and dance as the last case.

"Do you trust me?" He studied her.

"I want to, but I need facts." She turned toward her main wallscreen. Instead of notes for the murder case, holo images of mountain peaks scrolled past. Right now, the screen showcased the caldera of Haleakala on Maui, black rock stark against bright blue sky.

"But you like me." His voice was close, his body heat at her side. "Without facts. Right?"

"Now's not the time, Valdez." She didn't glance at him or sway toward him, as much as she wanted to lean him. Just for a moment… to not always be so alone.

"But you do like me." There was a smile in his voice.

"And that's relevant to the case, how?" Kilimanjaro filled the screen, as viewed from across the savanna, its massive snow-capped flat peak tinted red and angry by the setting sun.

"I just want to hear you say it," he said softly.

"You are an ego-monger, Valdez." She eyed him. "It's a wonder you've managed this long without falling into the mirror."

"Listen, Janey." Valdez edged closer to her until their shoulders nearly touched.

"I'm listening." She had to put some distance between them, so she tracked around her desk, sat, and crossed and uncrossed her arms. Then she waved open her desk's translucent widescreen. The murder case notes were all there.

Valdez leaned over her desk. He was staring at her. She glanced up.

"What?"

"Guangdong Province, our coincidence, your tea at the murder scene, my case—my gamblers." He waved his arms about—at the wallscreen, her, him, the station.

"What about it?"

Could one of the Chinese gambling group be behind the murder? Two of them were on her suspect list, and they hadn't been cleared. She called up their hotel records. Their bio tags showed them as being asleep in their quarters. Weird. They hadn't shown up there earlier.

"Someone in the Guangdong gambling group isn't who he says he is," Valdez said, pensive.

"Really? Which one? Maybe he's on my suspect list and—"

Valdez leaned over to get a look at her screen.

She shaded the screen. "What are you doing?"

"Let me see your suspect list. At least for the Guangdong group."

"Then what?"

"I may be able to help you catch a killer. We have thirty minutes before you have to bring me to Interrogation. So, let's get busy."

Janey considered for a half a second, then she waved the two names of Zheng Lo and Jack Wang to the wallscreen. Kilimanjaro disappeared, and the hotel records for the two suspects were displayed. Valdez reviewed the records and pursed his lips.

"What?" Janey asked.

"I need to call my boss. Read you in."

"That's what I said. One of them is your man?" Janey popped out of her chair. "Which one? I need to know what you know."

"I know." Valdez huffed. "Making the call." He moved to the other side of her small ten by ten foot office by a wallscreen streaming a live feed of the sunlight, and he turned his back to her. He then raised his privacy screen from his wrist comm. She could see him through a hazy film but couldn't hear him as he spoke to his superior officer. Warm, bright morning sun rays streamed in at an angle from the wallscreen, highlighting his profile and strong chest.

She had to remember to ask him about the fake ID for Amelia. Just in case the official request fell through.

With all the excitement of the murder case, she hadn't finished the application for Amelia's sanctuary request.

While she waited for Valdez to finish his call, she commed medical and asked for a status on Winston Wharton, Haverhill's assistant. The medical staff on duty told her that Wharton was sleeping but recovered.

"Has he said anything?" Janey asked.

"No," she said.

"When can I talk to him?"

"Not at least for a few hours yet. He's groggy and not coherent."

"He said something then?"

"Nothing of consequence."

"Let me be the judge of that," Janey said.

"Well, he said he couldn't believe it, and something about needing to find a new job," the nurse said.

"That's it?"

"At least while I've been on duty."

"How long has that been?" Janey asked.

"For the last three hours."

"Call me the minute he wakes up," Janey said and commed off.

"Winston Wharton is sick?" Valdez asked.

She hadn't used her privacy screen, not used to doing so when she worked in her office alone.

"You know him?"

"I met him."

"And?" Janey asked.

"And nothing." Valdez waved closed his holo screen and stuck his hands into his leather jacket.

Janey stood and glared at him. "Read me into your case, dammit. You color outside the lines all the time. Why not now?"

"I will—as soon as I get approval. I was only able to leave a message."

"I'm about to send an updated report to Milano about our joint Guangdong link. Do you have anything else to share? I thought you wanted my help. You have to give a little to get a little." She was also sending Milano the footage from the attempted attack at the hangar entrance. Ellias may have sent it, but she wanted it to be part of her murder file.

"I don't trust Milano. Do you?"

Janey considered how she was shielding Amelia from Milano—and therefore Schoeneman. "No, not entirely. Though I can't say exactly why."

Valdez said, "What are you going to do?"

"I'm sending this update to Milano"—she hit the send command—"and I'm taking you to Interrogation One. Though I don't want to."

He planted himself in front of her desk. "What? Wait. You're wasting time. Yours and mine."

"You need to give me something useful, and now. I have a killer to catch."

Valdez looked pained and shook his head. "I need to have this cleared. I—I'm waiting on him."

Janey stood, and with a flick of her wrist, she cleared and masked her wallscreens. "Fine. Okay, come on, then. Let's get this over with."

Valdez didn't put up any resistance as she brought him to interrogation, an empty room save for a wide comm table and two recyclo-metal chairs. He sat, plunked his legs on the table, leaned back on his chair, and shut his eyes. The epitome of a relaxed man taking a nap, not a care in the world, but she could plainly see the minute stress lines around his eyes and mouth. He may have other people fooled, but she was learning his signs and signals.

She commed Milano. "He's in, sir."

"I'll be right there. You'll assist."

"I have a murderer to catch, sir. Suspects to run down. My team needs a break; they've been working through the night."

"That's an order, McCallister. We have our primary suspect."

"We do? Valdez isn't—"

Milano closed the comm, cutting her off.

Venus hells.

Janey leaned against the gray wall by the door and watched Valdez sleep or pretend to sleep, the picture of nonchalance. He was not their primary suspect. Milano was mistaken or playing some game and obstructing her investigation. Dealing with Milano was not what they should be doing with their time.

A moment later, Chief Milano entered the interrogation room. He was without the old-fashioned glasses he always wore in his office.

He sat at the table. "McCallister, get us some coffee."

She straightened from the wall. "Um, is that the assistance you wanted from me?" she asked as sweetly as she could—so not her job.

"Right. No, it's not. Order us some then, would you? It's time for that second cup. You know how it is."

"I do, sir." It wouldn't do to antagonize her boss. She waved on her wrist comm for Kim to bring coffee for Milano to Interrogation Room One. Janey glanced up at the chief. "Coffee coming soon, sir." She leaned against the wall again, alert, impatient.

Without preamble, Milano slammed his palm on the

grey table and yelled, "Valdez, what are you doing back on the station? I don't see a badge this time."

Valdez opened one eye and then closed it again.

Milano shoved Valdez's legs off the table. "Wake up, man. You are in big trouble."

Valdez righted himself with easy grace. "Don't you have a murderer to catch?"

"Not anymore." Milano leaned in. "I think you did it."

"And my motive?" Valdez raised a brow.

Milano leaned back, hands clasped on his rotund belly, and said with a satisfied tone, "Because I have you for theft from the Chinese gambling group."

"Haverhill's murder has nothing to do with the Chinese. Plus, it only *looks* like I stole from them."

"You have no alibi for the time of the murder," Milano said.

How could Milano know that? What proof did he have? Unless he was grasping, bluffing his way.

"I was undercover nowhere near the scene of the crime."

"Details, Valdez."

"I can't."

"You get me that alibi or..." Milano let his voice trail off.

Valdez said nothing. He raised an eyebrow at her as if saying *back me up here*.

"Don't look at her. Look at me," Milano growled. "You didn't steal from the Guangdong group. Is that what you're trying to say?"

"I'm not trying to say that. I *am* saying it."

Janey opened her wrist comm's holo screen and waved up Valdez's bank transactions she'd scooped in Star Watch, sure that was what Valdez had wanted her to do, even though he hadn't said so. "Sir?" She showed her holo screen to the chief. "There *is* a discrepancy. The money was transferred to Valdez's account before the game ended by at least five minutes. He was still playing and wouldn't have had time to transfer the winnings that quickly. You know you need a passcode and double identity authentication to claim winnings. I can verify his actions on the casino video logs if you want."

"Where did you get that?" Milano glared at the bank data on her holo screen and then at her.

"From Valdez," Janey said.

"The document could be a forgery," Milano said.

"I don't think so. Very hard to do that," Valdez said, and he leaned back, crossed his arms across his chest, and feigned sleep again.

Kim let herself in, carrying Milano's coffee on a tray—a French press and a small espresso cup and saucer. She deposited it on the table beside him. "Sir, your coffee."

"Thank you, Ms. Iona." Milano poured himself a cup of the pungent brew and sipped it. He set the cup down with a quiet sigh.

Janey nodded her thanks. Kim raised an eyebrow at her, then glanced at Valdez and gave a little smirk for only Janey to see. Kim then left the room, smiling more broadly at Janey's frown.

Milano took another sip and set his small espresso cup down with a clink. He went quiet for a moment.

"Sir?" Janey said.

Milano straightened his tie over his rotund belly. "I didn't want to see it… but the signs were there…"

"See what?" Janey asked.

"Just that… someone is jerking me around. Jerking us around," Milano said quietly. "Didn't want to see it."

"What signs, sir? And who would do that? To what end?"

TWENTY-TWO

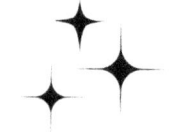

Milano waved a hand. "Above your pay grade. But it's time to do something about it."

"Do you mean how the case is being made against Valdez for the gambling theft?"

"Among other things."

"If it pertains to this case, then I'm grateful," Janey said, back in her position holding up the wall. She was glad Milano was finally seeing the light on this case. The other stuff, she didn't need to know to get her job done. For now.

"Who filed the report against me?" Valdez asked, his voice even and non-threatening.

"Isn't it strange that they wouldn't file it right away?" Janey added. "Why did they wait over a day?"

Milano glanced over his shoulder at her. "It was an anonymous tip. But when that much money is stolen, I take it seriously. Schoeneman wants no cheating in the casino."

"Has he been notified of the cheating?" Janey asked.

Communicating with the owner about station security issues was Chief Milano's main job. Maybe that communication was what he was referring to. Above her pay grade, indeed.

"Of course." Milano waved into his comm and said without looking up, "The recording is off."

Janey uncurled from the wall. "Sir?"

Why would he do that unless he was trying to help, not hinder, the investigation?

"Thank you, Chief Milano." Valdez straightened in his chair. "Going off the record works for me."

"You're not entirely off the hook, Investigator Valdez. I do not like how you slip on and off my station willy-nilly. I want your boss to notify me when you're here and clear you to reveal your aliases. Sol's Security Office should be cooperating better with us corporate city security. Especially Sol's special investigations unit."

"So you do trust that I'm working undercover?" Valdez relaxed his shoulders a notch.

"I've done some undercover in my day. No one takes the risks you do for fun."

"I used to." Valdez peered at the table with unseeing eyes, the stress lines back around his mouth and eyes. What risks did Valdez use to take for fun? He'd told her very little about his difficult childhood in the outskirts of agricultural Dallas Corporate Zone, but enough that she knew it'd been arduous and painful. He'd lost his parents to drug overdoses and his sister to the protective services system.

"But you're not sixteen and all alone anymore," Milano countered.

Valdez stiffened.

What was that exchange about? How would Milano know what happened to Valdez when he was a teen?

Milano stood, the chair grating against the eggshell-colored recyclo floor. "You're free to go."

"Thanks." Valdez stood too.

"As long as you get your undercover ass off this station today," Milano said. "By six pm station time."

"Because you don't like my charming face?" Valdez brushed some invisible lint off his leather jacket sleeve, his cool cat persona back in place.

"Because I need formal clearance from your unit superior for you to work here. Have them call me. *Pronto*." Milano pursed his lips. "Schoeneman could revoke Sol mining privileges to his interplanetary mining operations. Then how would your beloved Sol government cope?"

"Sol Unified Planets could then revoke the corporate city charter, but I'd rather skip the political debate, if you don't mind," Valdez said. "You'll clear my record of this ridiculous charge. Yes? It's horrible for my cover. I still have work to do."

"Like it never happened." Milano waved over his holo screen.

"Then it's a deal." Valdez shook Chief Milano's hand, serious and respectful, and he headed for the door. "I'll make sure you get my boss's call."

"You'd better, young man," Milano called.

Janey followed him to the door.

"Wait, McCallister. A word," Milano said.

"Sir?" Janey turned around. So did Valdez.

"What help do you need with the Haverhill case?" Chief Milano smoothed down his navy blue suit jacket and peered at her intently.

Janey hid her surprise. He never offered to help her before. He only ever asked for her reports, *pronto*. Another unexpected ally.

"Since you asked, can you get me the manifest for the private jet of passengers Schoeneman brought? It's above my clearance."

Milano frowned. "That's the one thing I can't do. It's a high rollers investment group, and Schoeneman's put them under his account."

"What level are they on?"

Milano shook his head.

"Can you at least tell me the story about this group?" Janey crossed her arms. "Why are they getting special treatment, and why now?"

"Is their arrival relevant to the case?" Milano sat on the table edge and sipped the remains of his espresso.

"Could be. The timing is suspicious. The jet arrived in the middle of the night, in the timeframe of the murder. Something doesn't sit right. Can't you tell me the specifics of the visit, or at least what their biotag idents are?"

"Schoeneman locked the travel manifest himself." Milano shifted his weight from one foot to the other. "Unless you have a lead."

"I do. I need to clear three from that group. They are on the suspect list."

"That wasn't in your report."

"I showed you the list at our briefing this morning." And you're wasting our time with accusations against Valdez, she thought but didn't say.

"Give me the rundown again." Milano could wave open the report on his wrist comm, but he liked verbal reports.

"At approximately 2:30 a.m., three unidentifiable males attempted to bypass hangar departures security. High-tech face masks. Even I couldn't see through them."

Milano frowned. "What could you see?"

"Fractals upon fractals."

"Mandelbrot sets," Valdez said. "I've heard rumors about the tech, but I haven't seen it. The masks are said to be made from some kind of new metamaterial."

"Resources. Funding. Secret labs," Milano said.

"Exactly. Other evidence, in this case, speaks to that as well," Janey said. "Will you please get me the manifest? Mr. Schoeneman wouldn't want to obstruct a murder investigation, would he? Bad for business."

"To say the least," Valdez said under his breath.

Milano ignored him. "I'll do what I can. Anything else? Other leads? I need a suspect in custody. Schoeneman wants business as usual with arrivals and departures by 6 p.m. tonight station time."

"So that's why you gave me that deadline," Valdez said.

"We're working on it." She glanced at Valdez and blew out a breath.

"We're doing our best." Valdez moved closer to her, and his hand brushed hers. She could feel his body heat, and more importantly, his support.

"If you cleared him to help me, Chief, even before he read us into his case," Janey said, "that would be a big help. Our cases overlap." She said that last statement confidently, even though the only connection was a loose one between the Guangdong tea and his Guangdong gamblers.

Chief Milano peered at each of them. To Valdez, he said, "I want a call from your people in the next ten minutes, or I'll have you confined to quarters until we have you escorted off L'Étoile."

"I have no quarters, sir," Valdez said with a straight face.

Milano gave him a look.

"I'll get right on it," Valdez added. "The call, I mean, not the quarters."

"See that you do." Milano left the interrogation room.

In the quiet small space, Valdez peered at her, jumping into an intimate gaze of desire, crossing the line. Crossing into her personal space.

"We have work to do, Valdez." She motioned for him to leave the room. "You need to call your boss again."

He eyed her lips. She slipped around him and exited first. "You're incorrigible."

He chuckled and followed her. "I'm a free man. I feel good. Just wanted my congratulatory kiss."

"Like I said, incorrigible." Janey led them back to her office and let them in. She marched to the wallscreen with her case notes and activated it. "What an annoying waste of time. I need to catch a murderer."

"*We* need to," Valdez said. "Wave me your files, anything and everything. I'll review it and see if anything pops. Also, I'm sending you the gambling group roster. Maybe you can help me see who doesn't fit." He sent his data to the wallscreen.

The list of over two dozen names scrolled.

"Fresh pair of eyes, Janey." Valdez waved open his privacy screen again for a second call to his boss.

"Fair enough." Janey sent him her preliminary report and all her notes, including all the evidence collected, a rundown on Haverhill, her research into his businesses and network, and the interviews with Wharton, Siobhan, and the two young women. She also sent her notes on Amelia, at the bottom of the list, but she kept those locked.

She started her scroll through the Guangdong gambling group. All men, all in their thirties and forties, and all seemingly independently wealthy. Each person's income source was listed unimaginatively as the Guangdong Group. Where did that money come from?

They all had backgrounds in engineering and manufacturing, though their domains varied widely from Zero-G space manufacturing and assembly to metamaterials and graphene additive construction—all high paying fields, and all related to the booming space exploration industry.

She opened Zheng Lo and Jack Wang's hotel records —the two on her suspect list. They were both thirty-four years old engineers, though what kind wasn't specified. Jack Wang had a wife on Hong Kong Station. There was a sister in Auckland for Zheng Lo. Her heart quickened. She'd have to tell Valdez about Nancy's brother.

She turned to him just as he asked, "Who is Madison Black? A business contact from Haverhill's files." Valdez waved the image to the wallscreen. Taken outdoors at a seaside sidewalk café, the image showed an elegant profile—medium nose, thick lips, strong chin and jawline, and a long column of a neck—eyes shadowed by a wide-brimmed straw hat, its brim encircled with a wide pink silky ribbon.

"Something familiar about that face," Janey said. "I've seen it and recently. Why did you flag it?" She searched for Madison's whereabouts on the station out of habit. While she was at it, she ran a public search for Madison Black in the Sol Unified data web.

He didn't answer.

"You cannot comment on an ongoing investigation. Is that it?" She glanced over her shoulder at him, sitting at her desk, working on his holo screen.

"Something like that." He'd set up a second screen on

the desk as was his working habit. She remembered that from the last time he'd worked with her.

"Is that case connected to this one?"

"Not as far as I know. But if it is, the good news is I'm not on it."

From her search, images popcorned across the wallscreen, showing off Madison in men and women's fashions, highlighting her masculine and feminine qualities in different parties and event premiers and runways. She was a handsome man and a stunningly beautiful woman. It didn't surprise her that a fashion trendsetter like this person would be all over Sol's media.

"Charismatic," Valdez said.

She sucked in a breath. She finally remembered where she'd seen the face before.

"What?"

"Remember Bakaj's black book?"

He perked up. "Of course. A list of Sol's worst industrial magnates."

"Before the murder, I did a public search on Haverhill, cross-referencing against Bakaj's little black book—"

"Why?"

"Why what?"

"Why were you researching him? And why cross-reference him with the list?" He asked as if the answer mattered a great deal to him.

"I'll get to that. What's important is I saw that face attached to a different name: S. M. Bertrand."

He frowned and waved into his second screen. "I need to…"

The location search pinged. "Uh, Orlando?"

He snapped his gaze to her, a guarded look on his face as if to steel against bad news.

"Madison Black is at the Phoenix."

"Why do we need to talk to Madison Black, evil industrialist, fashion broker, and trendsetter," Valdez said grimly. "How does this help us catch your killer?"

"You sound like Milano," she said. "Did you get a hold of your boss?"

"You're changing the subject."

"So are you." She lifted an eyebrow. "Okay, I need an excuse to stretch my legs and leave this tiny office. If Madison Black was in the casino before Haverhill died…"

"That would give you cause to question him or her."

On the wallscreen, Janey ran Black's biotag timeline for the window of the murder. "Per station logs, he or she was in her guest suite at the time of the murder. But before that, they were indeed in the casino, gambling by the looks of it. Good enough. Maybe they can identify who Haverhill was talking to before he went up to the mezzanine suite." She straightened her jacket.

"Before we go, what have you gleaned from my gamblers?"

"Zheng Lo has a sister in Auckland."

"I know. So?" Then he held up a hand in a wait gesture and spoke into his comm, his voice low and urgent, yet she could hear him recite a long string of unrelated words and numbers. He hadn't put up the privacy screen.

"What was that?" she asked when he was done and staring at one of her wallscreens, a holo of Pacific Ocean big waves breaking white foam on a Northern Californian beach and sighing back into the surf.

"Replying. Ident confirm." He glanced at her, but he was peering inward as if mulling over something. She gave him a hard look. He focused on her. "I want to tell you what I know. I do."

"What's taking so long?" She crossed her arms. "We're on the clock to catch a murderer here."

"I know. Boss man is probably in some urgent and critical briefing," Valdez said. "I can safely tell you this much... As Blue Bear, I was requested by one of Haverhill's entourage to attend a private meeting."

"By who?"

"Winston Wharton."

"What? Why didn't you say before? What about?"

Valdez shook his head. "Need to know."

"Why did he request you to attend? What can you share?"

"That's all."

"Venus hells."

"I know. I did have some thoughts in reviewing your case files... The murder looks personal as if someone really hated Haverhill. Who are his enemies? Who on your suspect list had a personal grudge against him?"

"Good questions—"

"But—" Valdez jumped in.

"But what if it was made to look that way?" Janey asked as Valdez did.

He smiled at her.

Janey sighed. She missed this. Working together.

"What was that sigh for?" Valdez moved toward her.

"Nothing. What if it was personal, but not in any obvious way?"

"Like what?"

She had to tell him.

"I left something out of my report." Surf pounded on the wallscreen. A string quartet warbled a soothing melody, the cellos haunting.

"What?"

"Amelia."

"Who is Amelia?" Valdez spoke softly.

"A young woman who three days ago accused Haverhill of rape and was a part of the 'agreement' with his other two mistresses and his wife. But she was really caught in a form of sexual slavery. I don't think she read the contract. She was attracted by the money and the lifestyle, but she didn't realize she was in until it was too late, and they had their hooks into her." She firmed her lips and unlocked Amelia's file on the screen. "You can't tell anyone about her. She's asked for sanctuary."

Valdez scrubbed his face. "Oh, Janey."

He paced the short length of her office, up and back a few times, and then he waved at his wrist comm but didn't speak into it. Instead, he mumbled to air and gestured as though he was in an argument with himself. Finally, he whirled to face her.

"You can't tell anyone what I'm about to tell you. No notes of any kind. Not even your private logs. Clear?"

"Clear," Janey said with no hesitation.

"No trace, understood?"

"Understood." She double-blinked and input a code into her wrist comm. "My personal recorder is off. Need me to double-pinky swear too?"

Valdez didn't smile. His gaze showed a seriousness he rarely revealed.

"This is what I came to L'Étoile to uncover."

"What? Amelia?"

"No, this human trafficking ring of young women."

"Oh." She sat, realization hitting her like a sudden increase in G-force. "That Haverhill is a part of. Why didn't you tell me sooner?"

"It's a sensitive case. A big one, and one that goes all the way to some very powerful people. Still uncorroborated though."

She let a beat go by. Then finally, she said what was on her mind. "Schoeneman?"

"I don't know." Valdez looked pained and sat in the chair behind her desk. "But all of Haverhill's party knows about the human trafficking. I'm sure of it. Wharton was about to tell me all when your agent pulled him out for that interview that landed him in medical."

"How do you know about that?" Janey waved a hand in a stop gesture. "No, don't tell me. Sources you can't reveal." She sighed. "Wharton collapsed at the shock of the news of Haverhill's murder. Maybe he knows something you don't. Hiding something."

Valdez shook his head and leaned back in her office chair. "He's a good guy."

"Other than working for a human trafficking ring."

"I think he only figured that out recently."

Janey scrunched up her face. "Unlikely. He worked with the man for years. He had to know what was going on."

"I believe him," Valdez said earnestly and waved at the murder board. "You mentioned Zheng Lo's sister in Auckland. Why?" His tone was cool, not giving anything away.

"Nancy's brother."

"Who is that?"

She blew out a breath, and it was her turn to pace her small box of an office. She spun to face him. "Amelia is an accessory to the murder—a murder I suspect was committed by a man known as Nancy's brother. Zheng Lo has a sister in Auckland."

Valdez popped out her chair. "Where is Zheng Lo now?"

"We haven't been able to find him."

"I mean where is he this very minute?"

"Why?"

He waved open a file on the wallscreen.

He'd circled one man's name: Zheng Lo, and drew an arrow to another name: Nancy Sinclair. That name was highlighted. He touched it and a photo appeared. A beautiful young Chinese woman with the name Shei Lo beneath it, and then in a handwritten note it said, "sister," followed by a question mark. A code was under the photo. Janey recognized it as a case file number.

"This young woman disappeared from Granton Auckland two years ago," Valdez said. "She was declared missing by the Granton. Then six months ago, she showed up in the corporate employee rolls of Gypsy Harvesters out of Columbia—an agriculture conglomerate. After that, there's no trace of her."

"Amelia said someone calling himself Nancy's brother convinced her to help him so he could get close to Haverhill. The man was convinced that Haverhill had something to do with his sister's disappearance."

"Help him how?"

"Targeted RF interference. Messed with our comms and facial rec," Janey said. "Do you recognize this person?" Janey brought to the front the blurred image of the man who had drinks with Haverhill in the hour before he died.

"No. Even the body resembles any number of the men in the gambling group. They all dress alike—black slacks and a black shirt, buttoned at the collar."

"Zheng Lo's sister, Nancy. Nancy's brother," Janey said. She ran a biotag search again for Zheng Lo, but she got nothing. "Where would he hide?"

"He's not in his quarters. He hasn't been for—come to think of it—since before the murder."

"You're tracking him."

"Not just him. All of the group."

"Are you going to tell me why them specifically?"

"Not without official clearance," Valdez said. "I wonder how Zheng connected the Gypsy Harvesters to Haverhill. I wasn't able to do that. It's not in Haverhill's list of companies."

"Would you know if Nancy was in Haverhill's entourage?"

"I'm not even sure if Nancy is Zheng Lo's sister."

"We need to find Zheng Lo. He's our best lead for a suspect."

"Can I have access to Amelia's records?" Valdez said. "I'd like to see if her story corresponds to the other women?"

"What other women?"

"The other women we've rescued."

"What?"

Janey's comm pinged. It was Chief Milano. She answered.

"Where's Valdez? He's in big trouble. I haven't heard from his boss." His voice was tight.

Janey shook her head at Valdez. "He's here, boss." Anger bubbled up from her gut. Milano and his bureaucratic needs. She waved the comm channel over to her desk and said to Valdez. "Milano, for you, at the desk comm."

Valdez sat at her desk again and listened to Milano drone on about rules and regs per the Sol Unified Planets Accords between Sol and corporate city security.

Her wallscreen flickered. She'd have missed it if she had glanced at it at right that second. Amelia's tech? Shouldn't be. Soren had blocked the young woman's frequencies. Something else was going on. She waved in the commands for a diagnostic to run in the background and checked the biotag tracker system again. For star's sake. There was Zheng Lo—at the Apex Promenade—a walkway above the casino with viewing screens show-casing the Apex Anchor, a pair of satellites actually 65,000 km above L'Étoile.

The Apex Anchor had been a part of the original asteroid mining station architecture that had enabled Schoeneman to make his vast fortune. With the Apex Anchor, Schoeneman had been able to transport space cargo jets daily to and from the asteroid belt, mining the ten percent of the asteroids that were rich with precious and rare Earth metals. Schoeneman liked to showcase the history of how L'Étoile came to be in a stunning setting—viewscreens made up the entire sloped ceiling.

According to the biotag tracker, Zheng Lo was stationary and alone up there. She tapped into the vids to verify, but she saw no one. Venus hells. She ran another biotag check and now Zheng Lo showed at the opposite end of the station—literally. No vids in that area.

When she focused back on the conversation, Valdez was lifting his hands, palm out, and insisting, "I sent the message, Chief Milano. Twice. I'll send it again. Are you sure nothing is jamming the transmissions from the station?"

Maybe Zheng Lo had another way besides Amelia to mess with the security system.

The chief harrumphed. "Better not be. I'll check. If so, we have a huge problem. Send me what you sent your boss. I need proof."

"Can't, Chief. Against policy," Valdez said.

"Who the hell are you working for?" the chief barked.

Valdez said nothing.

Janey jumped in. "Chief, we have a strong lead on the killer, and the clock is ticking. Our suspect may be on the Apex Promenade."

"Go, McCallister, and get us an arrest. Valdez, get your boss to call me. Milano out."

TWENTY-THREE

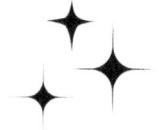

In the small round mirror in her office, Janey swept her hair up in a ponytail to get it out of the way. She checked her gun—the sights, the safety, and the battery charge. Good to go.

There was a ping on her comm. It was Kim letting her know that her team was up and available. Perfect timing. Janey waved a thanks and said to have her team be on stand-by for a stakeout and to have in-situ security clear the machine shop levels.

"Valdez, ready?"

He was settling something in his boot. She didn't get a good look at it, so didn't know whether it was a knife, a gun, or one of his high-tech tools. From the pouch that had once been his odd blue bear costume, he fished out a shoulder holster with gun. He slipped that on and then his jacket.

"Ready." He straightened.

"What do you know about this Zheng Lo?" Janey asked and left her office, Valdez striding beside her.

"There wasn't much about him in your file. You didn't even note what kind of engineer he is."

As they headed down the grey corridor, Valdez replied. "That's all I have. Even though I gambled with the group at various locations around the world and on stations for a few weeks, I haven't been able to gather more. He eats, drinks, sleeps, and even dresses like all the others. The bit about his sister was my only red flag about him that I recently uncovered." Frustration bit into his voice.

She passed the regular service elevator. Five feet beyond it, beside a solo tree fern, she palmed open a nondescript door, using the box beside the door, and slipped onto a square landing. Valdez followed, tight behind her, and the door slid shut behind them, A-1 painted in white on the door. A musty odor wafted up. The cleaning bots probably bypassed this part of the station. A winding narrow staircase spiraled up and below, square landings jutting off like tiny jetties at regular intervals. The railings and staircase were fabricated from sturdy recyclo metal and painted grey, like the walls and doors.

"What's that low hum?" Valdez asked from behind her as they descended the spiral stairs.

"I don't hear anything," Janey said, but a subtle rumble underfoot vibrated through her legs.

"Where are we going? Isn't the Apex Promenade above the casino."

"I'm taking us the back way to the machine shop."

"Why?" There was a smile in his voice.

"That's where Zheng Lo was last spotted by our vid system about five minutes ago."

"No, why didn't you tell Milano that?"

"Our communications systems may be compromised." They passed the door and the landing for sublevel A-2.

"Even though Milano may not be."

"But what he knows—"

"He relays," Valdez finished her sentence.

"Exactly."

He sighed. "The message to my boss didn't go through."

"Yes, and the weirdness with the money transfer. And Amelia's use of her RF receiver/transmitter."

"An illegal enhancement," Valdez said.

"It is now. Probably wasn't when she got it."

"Like yours."

"Yep."

"But why would Zheng Lo go to all this trouble? What is he doing down in the machine shop?" Valdez asked. "Does he want the engineers to make something for him?"

"Let's go ask him," Janey said, and she led them past sublevel B-1 and B-2, then stopped at sub-Level C-1. She approached the door and paused to glance down over the railing. They wouldn't be going there today, thank the stars.

Valdez also peered over the railing to the dim space below. "Where does this lead?"

"Weapons."

"I didn't know the station had armaments."

"Not many people do." Janey palmed open the service door with the keypad and led them down a grey corridor no more than six feet wide. The corridor was lit up by low energy phosphor-luminescent dots at three-foot intervals, good enough to see by but not bright enough to spot the dust on the grey-beige recyclo flooring. At five foot eight, she didn't have to stoop, but Valdez, at six feet, had to duck under the occasional pipes crisscrossing the ceiling.

"What kind of weapons?" Valdez asked.

"Laser cannons, rail guns, and a small complement of hand weapons."

Valdez whistled. "Prepared for attack from the outside *and* the inside."

"I wasn't even told about this place," Janey said. "It's not on the staff maps, like many things. I stumbled on it in my exploration of the station. Then Kim filled me in. I don't even know if Chief Milano knows it's there. He never mentioned it in his orientation."

"Who crews it?"

"Crew manages remotely from engineering, but it can be controlled from within. I recently got my hands on the schematics, buried deep in the station's archives. I haven't investigated yet." She stopped at a small grey door at the end of the corridor.

"Is that the machine shop?"

"Yes. This is the back way in."

He squeezed beside her, his body sideways, almost touching. "How do you want to play this?"

He was all business.

"Let me do the talking." She gave him a hard look. "Follow my lead."

Valdez held her gaze. "I can do that."

"Thank you."

She approached the grey door. There was no visible lockbox on the wall, like most of the doors on the station. At chest level, she placed her palm on the grey panel. The masked sensor read her heartbeat-respiration combination as well as her actual palm print.

The door clicked and slid open to reveal another long grey maintenance corridor. *What the regolith.*

"I thought you said—" Valdez said.

"This corridor wasn't in the schematics."

"You haven't explored this area."

"No."

She led them twenty feet to the next door and waved opened her holo on her wrist comm.

"Checking the vid feed?" Valdez asked.

"I need to see where Zheng Lo is and where all the engineers are. We also have our regular security there." So odd that she hadn't heard from them.

Venus hells.

"What?" Valdez said quietly.

"The vid feed is down. I have footage from fifteen minutes ago. Same with biotags. Some kind of jammer."

"Think Zheng Lo knows we're coming?" Valdez studied his holo screen humming above his wrist. The station vibrated a low bass sound, rattling her bones. It was not unpleasant. Soothing almost.

"Don't know. Could be."

"Maybe the engineers masked their biosignatures," Valdez said.

"I hadn't thought of that. Or it could be a hostage situation? Or he wants to hide? Or worse?" Janey leaned against the grey door—it was round this time, with no masked sensor that she could spot with her ocular implant. "He might have a weapon or be plotting an escape."

"He might be making a weapon."

"The knife used in the murder had been fabricated here in our machine shop."

Valdez clenched a hand. "What else could he make? Why?"

"I don't know."

He went back to studying his holo screen and was quiet for a long moment.

"Well?" Janey shifted.

"I don't recognize the signal, and I've jammed a lot of things in my days," Valdez finally said.

"I'll scoop it and send it to Soren for processing," Janey said.

"The machine shop is beyond this door?"

"Yep. But I can't open it."

"What's beyond this door, specifically? Maybe something is jamming the reader."

"Should be where they store scrap for recycling—if my schematics are accurate—but there is no sensor pad. I've scanned it."

Valdez reviewed his holo and shook his head. "No extra security measures on it. Not sure why it won't open." Then he chuckled. "What's this?" He tapped a grey circle about an inch in diameter at the edge of the door, where the seam met the grey wall. The circle had a vertical slit in it. "Some kind of keyhole. Old school."

Oh, stars. "I didn't see it."

Valdez had the grace not to tease her and dug into his boot. He came out holding two long thin files that looked like dental picks. He grinned at her and bent to work. "Old school. My school."

While she waited for Valdez to pick the lock, she opened an audio comm channel to her security team. "Bring everyone you can to the main entrance of the machine shop and wait for my signal."

"Ready for anything?" Valdez asked, bent over his task and wiggling the metal picks.

"Yep. And take Zheng alive."

"Understood, McCallister," Valdez said, and the door clicked and popped out an inch from the wall.

"Yes! Great job, old school."

"Gracias, señorita," he said soberly.

Valdez moved back and let her do the honors. She yanked the heavy thick door toward them and waited a half a second. No noise came from the darkness beyond. She glanced over her shoulder and nodded to Valdez. He nodded back, grim, his gun in hand.

Janey slipped out her gun and stepped over the raised door frame into a darkened space. She blinked to adjust her ocular implant's night vision. Valdez followed and pushed the door closed but not shut all the way. Even open a crack, the door was nearly flush with the wall and practically invisible, painted the color of the wall—a color-absorbing dull black. A sliver of light that only she could see peeked out. An egress if they needed it.

She moved forward and scanned the space. It was a large storage area, about seventy feet long and twenty feet wide, and it was full of rows of ten gallon-sized barrels, filled with colorful scraps of all shapes from the manufacturing process in the main factory floor, where the engineers made everything that built the station. The bins were sorted by kind of material—recyclo metals, plastics, fabrics, and wood. Valdez hadn't moved.

"Come on," she said.

"I can't see." His voice was calm, and he swung his head from side to side as if looking for her.

"Lift your arm directly out in front of you, palm down." Janey moved back a few feet so his palm bumped her shoulder. "Got me?"

"I got you." There was a smile in his voice.

"You're enjoying this."

"I'm always up for a challenge."

"We don't know what we're walking into," she said.

"I know. Lead the way." The excitement in his voice was strong. His solidness was at her back, encouraging her to forge ahead.

TWENTY-FOUR

THERE WAS AN ENTRANCE AHEAD OF THEM about fifty feet—if the maps of the machine shop layout were right. She was halfway to the entrance when Valdez squeezed her shoulder.

"What?" she whispered.

"I want to question Zheng Lo to see what he knows about the missing women." Valdez squeezed her shoulder again.

Janey picked up the pace. "I know."

"So don't shoot him, like the last guy."

"Not planning on it. Besides, that wasn't fatal. But no promises."

"I know," Valdez said, his voice at her ear.

Soon they were at a bulkhead door, separating the scraps storeroom from the massive warehouse. The round door, six feet in diameter, was part of the original construction from when L'Étoile was a mining station. It was made of reinforced steel, graphene, and carbon nanotubes—the strongest material humans had ever created.

Beside the door was a wide door panel. She opened it. Inside blinked yellow lights, indicating it was locked. With her wrist holo, she scanned on the other side of the thick door, but the room beyond was still being jammed. She had no idea who was on the other side of that door, nor was she getting any other kind of electrical signals. Normally, the machine shop was a buzz of every wavelength on the electromagnetic spectrum, due to all the ways they printed everything.

Valdez moved to the other side of the door. Janey palmed the door pad, and thank the stars it worked. With clinks and softs thuds, the thick door rolled left and receded into the wall.

Even from still inside the storeroom, glaring brightness had her clamping her eyes shut. Right. She dimmed her ocular implant for day lighting and blew out a breath.

She glanced at Valdez. He removed a hand from covering his eyes and nodded.

Time to go.

She waved her personal comm channel over to Valdez. He glanced at his wrist comm and nodded again and tapped his ear.

Janey pivoted, gun ahead of her, and tracked into the main machine shop. It was quiet. Too quiet. She didn't see anyone amongst the many big box additive machines, encased in clear thick plastic. Normally, the machines would be quietly humming, but nothing moved now.

Valdez was behind her. Though his footfalls were as quiet as hers, she could hear his clothing rustling. She raised her hand in a fist, the universal sign to stop. The rustling stopped. She crouched behind a box of supplies and pointed to the rows of eight-foot-tall machines ahead of them, lined up in rows. Valdez bent low and scurried to one. He glanced at her, waiting for her next signal.

Which way to go?

The huge machine shop spread out in either direction, with an area nearly the entire width and length of the round space station. They had a lot of area to cover—easily two football fields long. She saw no one.

Where would staff normally be at this hour? It was almost midday. Usually, one shift would be coming on duty while a handful went for lunch. But with the biotags jammed she had no clue who was down here. Could be all of them—the lunch-bound staff *and* the new crew. Could be no one, though that was highly unlikely.

Why would Zheng Lo go here? What was he up to? Did he want the engineers to fabricate a weapon?

Janey didn't know the layout like the guards on duty would. She swore. Kou and Dube and other security staff had done lots of rotations on duty guarding the machine shop. She had done none. She hadn't taken them with her because they weren't on duty yet.

To stay in quiet mode, she waved a message to Kou, asking him where the weapons manufacturing section was in the machine shop. Right away, he sent back the quadrant, which was to the right of where she presumed the main door was. He also asked for an update and let her know they were in position. She waved back Thanks. Stand-by. Wait for my signal.

She glanced at Valdez, and when she caught his eye, she made the hand motion to move forward and stay low. He gave her the okay sign. She headed toward the weapons area.

Beside each fabricator was a long table of completed items, all sorts of things needed by the station. Machine shop engineers would load the machines with the raw material, like recyclo metal, and then check the design code, make adjustments as needed, choose a quantity, and then set the machine to work. That way one engineer could oversee several dozen fabricators or more in one shift. She was passing silverware. Two aisles down Valdez was passing fabric—brocade from what she could surmise when she zoomed in.

She paused. Someone was speaking, maybe a few rows away. A male by the rumble of his tenor voice, but she was still too far away to make out what was being said. Valdez was behind her and a few rows back, near a pile of marine blue folded bedspreads. The tables near her were empty, and the replicators were still. She couldn't tell what this replicator had been used for recently. She hurried to get in line with Valdez and catch his eye. Once she did, she motioned for him to go wide to his left. She went further right. She wanted them to be on either side of whatever was happening and come upon the action from the front and the back.

As she approached closer, she heard angry commands from a man. "Faster. Hurry. No, not like that. Use the white."

Who was he speaking to? Perhaps a machine shop engineer who was making something for him under duress.

She crouched behind a stack of shiny recyclo wood, the kind used on the flooring in many guest suites. She peeked out and surveyed the scene.

A man matching Zheng Lo's image pointed a gun at a woman in an olive-green machine shop jumpsuit and a long black apron. The engineer's back was to her. Janey couldn't recognize her from the back. On her ocular implant screen, she checked the biotag system. No name appeared next to the data of the woman with a rapid heartbeat.

Zheng Lo frowned at the engineer and waved his powerful snub-nosed gun as he spoke, his heartbeat faster than resting rate too.

Janey straightened from her crouch, her gun pointed at Zheng Lo's center mass, and she shouted loud and slow, "Freeze, Zheng Lo. Put down the gun."

Zheng Lo swiveled toward her, gun aimed at her in a wobbly one-handed grip.

The engineer turned too. It was Laura Hidalgo—one of the engineers on the suspect list. Her ident file showed she was Chief Milano's wife. *Venus hells*.

How could Janey not know that Laura Hidalgo was Daniel Milano's partner? Seeing her name on the list was what probably had Milano depressed this morning. Why hadn't he said anything?

Could Hidalgo have made Zheng's knife?

"Laura, get down," Janey called out.

The engineer scurried behind the fabricator. The machine worked without a sound, layer upon layer, building something. The plastic covering must be sound-proof to be able to dampen all vibrations. Most objects took only a few minutes to make. Janey couldn't see what was being created.

What could possibly be so important that Zheng Lo had to take over the entire machine shop? Janey moved out of her cover and waved open a comm channel to her team, so they would get the signal.

She shouted at Zheng again. "Drop the gun, Zheng Lo. Now. I won't ask again."

He didn't drop the gun. "Don't take another step. I have a bomb in the strong room that will detonate in the next five minutes if I don't disarm it. And I won't disarm it until I get what I came for." The strong room was somewhere in the middle of the machine shop. She wasn't sure of its function, and she couldn't see it from where she stood. And what could Lo possibly need from the machine shop that would get him off the station?

"Mierda," Valdez swore.

"You wouldn't," Janey said but didn't advance.

"I would." Zheng shifted his gaze side to side as if searching for something or someone. "The rest of the engineers are in the strong room. If I don't get this tool done in the next five minutes…" He let the threat hang.

"Zheng, why do you want to blow this place up?" Janey said quietly, hoping to talk him down. Did he want to make a weapon or escape off the station? "Your sister wouldn't want you to do this. You're Nancy's brother, aren't you?"

"How would you know? You don't know anything about me or my sister." His voice broke. He was holding back a sob.

"I know Nancy disappeared from her Granton like lots of other women. I know she was most likely lured by a life of adventure and riches. And that she could still be alive."

Zheng Lo's face contorted into grief. "She's dead. He told me she died."

"Who told you?"

Zheng Lo shook his head.

The machine stopped humming.

Zheng Lo spun his gun toward the machine, toward Hidalgo, and screamed, "Turn it back on!"

"You don't want to do that, Zheng Lo," Janey said.

"I do." His voice came out as a sob, but he didn't turn back around.

"I know you're hurting. Your sister wouldn't want you to blow yourself up—and us along with it."

"She was a good and kind person. She just—she just wanted adventure. An out from the boring life in China." Zheng Lo swiveled back and glared at her.

"She wouldn't want this," Janey insisted.

"It's the only way I can make him pay."

"But Haverhill's dead."

Zheng Lo shook his head. "No, Schoeneman knew."

"Knew what?" Maybe if she could get him talking and disarm him, Valdez or Kou could disarm the bomb.

"He let Haverhill on the station with his women. He sanctioned the behavior. He must pay."

"By blowing up the station?"

The machine shop was on sublevel C and C-1, above the highly secured sublevels X and X-1: engineering that housed the generator that powered the entire station. A bomb going off in the machine shop, if powerful enough and directed enough, could blow the generator and destabilize the base of the station the hotel was built upon. That compromised the hangar, but more importantly, it could affect the connectors to the StarEl space elevator.

Worst case scenario, it would knock the station out of orbit.

Zheng Lo said nothing and waved his gun at Hidalgo to switch back on the printer.

Janey said in a whisper, "Kou, you got that?"

"Got it," he commed back.

"Free the engineers," she said quietly to Kou. "I'm on Zheng Lo, with Valdez."

"On it."

Zheng swiveled back to her, his gun hand wavering. "Who are you talking to?"

"Do you intend to kill someone with that gun today?" Janey said conversationally and moved forward, one step, then another. In her peripheral view, she saw Valdez scurrying wide toward Hidalgo.

"Stop!" Zheng clutched the gun two-handed now, right at her. His hands shook, but the gun was trained at her chest. Her protective gear under her clothes would soften the impact of a bullet. She could still land her on her back and have the wind knocked out of her, disabling her for a minute or two.

"I can't do that, Zheng Lo." She was five feet away from him, in an open area, unprotected by any of the tall, boxy fabricators. On her left, a silent fabricator was six feet away, too heavy to move or tip over. On her right, a long table with wooden lamp housings carved into curvaceous shapes. "But, hey, I can put my gun down." She lowered her gun to the cement floor beside the table.

Standing up, she knocked her shoulder into the table intentionally. The lamp housings jangled to the floor, rolling in all directions, some toward Zheng Lo. Distracted, he turned toward the clattering rolling pieces of furniture.

Janey scrambled toward him, gun still in hand.

"Stop!" he yelled again, waving his gun all around.

Janey lunged. She tackled his middle, pinning his gun arm at the elbow. His grip went slack, and he dropped the gun. A thin red bracelet peeked out from his black shirt. They both thudded to the floor, Janey on top of Zheng.

For half a breath, all was still. Then he elbowed her in the neck. She gasped and released her gun. He boxed her in the ear. She hissed out in pain as he bucked her off and rushed for the gun on all fours.

She grabbed his ankle before he got too far and yanked. He kicked backward, powerfully, toward her face.

Venus hells.

She dodged his foot and held on. Then she pulled one hand over the other, climbing his leg and sat on him. He was face down, kicking her back with his heels and yelling.

She ignored the thumps on her back and the yelling, cuffed him, jumped off his back, and hauled him to his feet.

"It's over, Zheng." Janey recited the rights warning.

His shoulders slumped, Zheng was silent, sullen, as if all his fire had been extinguished.

Panting, adrenaline coursing through her limbs, she glanced at Valdez. He'd gotten Hidalgo out of the way.

"Kou," she commed. "Report."

"Boss, confirmed. There's a bomb inside the strong room. Center quadrant. I've never seen anything like it."

Janey towed Zheng in the direction of the strong room, deeper into the cavernous area. Since he hadn't finished the fabricated tool, did that mean that the bomb wouldn't go off? She hoped so.

After four rows of replicators, tables, and tool stations, there it was—a room whose walls and ceiling were made from the same unbreakable thick glass that surrounded much of the station—about thirty feet long and twenty feet wide. Inside, about thirty men and women in lab coats were huddled off-center, some standing, some sitting, and some pacing.

Some of the engineers looked close to crying, some glared at anyone who would catch their eye, and some were praying. No one was looking at the case in the center of the room. The case was a brown faux leather attaché case, currently on its side. Peeking out of the case were thin black wires.

Kou was at the door, pantomiming to stay calm.

As they approached, some of the engineers rushed to the door, yelled, and shook their fists at Zheng. No sound escaped the room.

"What kind of bomb is that, Zheng?" Janey asked. "And why did you put it in a bomb-proof room?"

He shook his head, slumped against Janey, defeated.

The door to the strong room was shut. Beside it at chest level was a control box, somehow attached to the strong, thick glass. The panel face was cracked open and had been dislodged as if someone had detached it and then tried to replace it. All kinds of wires stuck out, like an uncombed porcupine. She peeked under the panel face without touching anything and zoomed in at a wide aperture to be able to see in even the dark crannies. Black and nearly hair-thin wires were attached to a small trigger device.

So the trigger device was in the panel box, connected to the bomb in a shatterproof room with thirty people who would die if she didn't disarm it. But it was possibly worse. There was no telling how powerful the bomb was. Its force could be projected downward and do some serious damage to the station's generator.

"Turn it off." Janey shook Zheng Lo.

He glanced about as if he couldn't believe his plan had failed.

"Zheng Lo, now," Janey said with steel in her voice.

He shook his head. "I can't. The key has to finish first."

"Why? How are they connected?" Janey asked.

"The RFID tag is built into the key," Zheng Lo said and shook his head. He knew he was beaten.

"What does that mean? Why did you need this key to detonate the bomb? How does the key disarm the bomb?"

Zheng said nothing.

"People's lives are at stake," Janey said. "They did nothing to you."

"The key is the only way."

It didn't make sense that a key would both arm and disarm a bomb.

Janey turned to Kou. "Twenty feet back. Hidalgo's machine. Can you turn it back on?"

Hidalgo spoke through her personal comm channel, the one she'd given Valdez. "You don't want to do that, Investigator." She was with Valdez, still beside the replicator.

"We just need the process to finish so the bomb will disconnect," Janey said.

"Right, sorry. Just don't give it to this man."

"Understood, Ms. Hidalgo. Kou, go. Hurry." Kou dashed away.

Zheng Lo grimaced. "You've wasted too much time. The bomb will go off anyway."

"Disarm it then." Janey dragged him to the front of the dismembered panel.

Zheng Lo shrugged. "I'm a dead man anyway. So is my sister. It doesn't matter anymore."

"You would let all these people die?" Janey shouted.

Valdez dashed to her side. "Can you disarm it, McCallister?"

"I can try."

"Do it. I'll watch Mr. Zheng Lo." Valdez grabbed Zheng by the cuffs and yanked him back a few steps.

Janey studied the panel. If she understood what

Zheng Lo had done, she had two minutes to disarm the bomb or thirty people would die.

The generator beneath engineering would be compromised, cutting power to the whole hotel-casino, possibly kicking the station out of orbit, and dangerously compromising the entire space elevator system.

TWENTY-FIVE

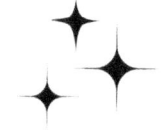

"Can you do it?" Kou asked at Janey's right shoulder.

"I got this." She firmed her mouth. "Go get the Chief, Soren, and medical. Everyone."

"You're an ace at this," Valdez said calmly at her left as if they were taking a stroll in the park.

She wasn't a bomb specialist, but she understood power mechanics.

Janey carefully tugged on the panel face and set her ocular implant to scan for every light frequency in the wire-strewn box. She identified the housing and the trigger in the mess of wire.

"Valdez, can I have your lock picks?"

Without a word, he handed her a slim case. She chose one pick and used it to pry more of the panel wiring from the housing, careful not to dislodge the trigger attached to the tangle.

In front of the door inside the strong room, two engineers shouted and waved their hands at her. She couldn't hear them through the clear soundproof walls.

"They're saying that will speed up the timer. And they're cussing you out for your stupidity and…other things you don't need to know," Valdez said softly. "I can read lips."

Of course, he could.

"They can't see what I can. I can turn off the trigger. Just need a few things." Janey gritted her teeth, blew out a breath, and glanced about. "Get me that cart, will you?"

In two seconds, Valdez dashed to a tool cart and hovered it back. She slowly set the panel face down on the cart and studied it.

Of all the stars. In the panel were set tiny, millimeter-sized jammers, like grains of rice. They were jammers blocking all the biotag and vid scans in the machine shop. Powerful buggers. Tiny wires a few hair-widths thick connected the jammers to the trigger—the trigger for the bomb inside the strong room. Zheng had used the tiny wires to connect seed-size devices into the control panel that most people would miss. She didn't miss them—not with her ocular implant.

A sophisticated jamming system. Zheng had skills.

If Janey and Valdez hadn't arrived when they had, the bomb would have gone off no matter what, and Janey and the rest of the security team would have only known about it after the fact as they scrambled to evacuate the hotel.

Zheng Lo was sabotaging the station by taking out the whole team of machine shop engineers—and him with it. And she still didn't know why he was on such a destructive suicide mission. He hadn't made any demands, as far as she knew.

Zheng Lo slouched, handcuffed to a center pole, far from anything, but near enough so that Janey could watch him out of the corner of her eye. However, she needed all her attention to deactivate the trigger. Her internal chronometer readout flashed seventy-five seconds left.

"Watch him," Janey said to Valdez. "He's a slippery one,"

"On it." He moved back out of her line of sight.

Soren rushed up to her. "What do you need?"

"I need to see the ionization trail better. I need something that can blow smoke."

Soren drew a gun from his waist holster. Before Janey could question his action, he hit a button and a spray of smoke jetted out, coating the front panel in a thin white film.

Janey blinked to adjust her implant. There it was—a stream of infrared light pointing into the power source of the panel still on the clear wall. "Do you have alkaline putty? To block the light. Just in case it still triggers from this angle."

"No, but will this scrap of plastic do?" Soren lifted a piece from the cart.

Janey scanned it for metals and found none. "Yes, that will do."

She pressed it hard against the source, cutting off the transmission.

"You did it," Soren said.

Janey breathed out, but her heart rate was still too high above normal.

"Not yet," Valdez said and pointed to the broken panel on the strong room outer wall, beside the door.

A red light flashed in the tangle of wires. She replayed the work she'd just done on the front panel. Venus hells. She'd missed something.

Another timer. The readout flashed one minute.

"This one is attached to an actual bomb," she said.

Her voice cracked. The red light flashed fast on the broken wall panel next to the door.

"How bad?" Valdez asked, his voice low and tight.

"Hard to tell what it's hooked into. I need to get it off the wall and secured. I think all these bombs had to work in coordination. If we can break the connection—"

"The strong room," Valdez said. "Get the people out and throw this bomb in. Take the other one out. You've dampened some of the bombs."

"Separate the devices," Janey said.

"That could work," Soren said.

"Maybe the bomb inside the strong room was a decoy." Janey eyed Soren. "If I unlock the door, we have—"

Soren got what she was asking. "We have fifty seconds to get them out and throw this in before it goes boom."

Janey grabbed the thin metal pick from Valdez's case and jammed it between the panel box and the glass, popping it off. The engineers shouted at her through the glass. Right.

The back of the box. There was a third bomb lodged against the grey back panel. This was designed to do the real damage of exploding into the strong room and probably setting off the larger bomb. She blinked to scan it and breathed out. It was much simpler to disarm. Thank the stars. She pulled her knife out of her boot and checked for which wire to cut.

"McCallister," Soren warned. "Thirty seconds."

She nodded and cut the blue wire. The bomb went dead, all light emitting from it shutting off. The door to the strong room automatically unlatched. She heaved the heavy glass door open.

For half a second, no one moved.

"Run! Come on! Out! Hustle!" Janey motioned for them to exit the strong room.

Soren waited at the threshold, panel box in hand. "Janey, something is ticking."

"It's not supposed to. I disarmed it."

"The panel of wires is awake again too," Valdez said.

Janey grabbed the mess of wires attached to the panel door. "Venus hells."

The last engineer dashed out of the strong room, carrying the attaché case with the first bomb. Wires stuck out every which way. He shoved it into a fabricator and shut the door. With the trigger bomb in the strong room, and the smaller bombs disabled, the main bomb shouldn't go off.

"Now!" Soren yelled, and Janey chucked the panel box as hard as she could into the center of the emptied glass structure. Soren tossed in the panel lid too. Janey shoved the door shut, but it didn't click shut. They needed to create an air-tight seal.

"Active bomb!" Janey shouted over her shoulder. "We need something to cover the door." An engineer nearby gasped at Janey's mess as she yelled for a caulking gun. Soren arrived first with one in hand. The engineer nodded his approval at Soren, and Soren ran foam from floor to ceiling. Another engineer did the other side of the door and the floor. Fast-acting sealant, thank the stars.

"We don't have time to do the top. Back up!" Janey yelled. When Soren tried to reach for the top with his foam gun, she yanked him back. "It'll have to be enough."

"It won't be." Soren frowned. "I can do it. We still have two seconds."

"Take cover!" Janey yelled, dragging Soren with her,

and she hustled behind the stacked wooden planks, ten feet away, Soren on one side of her, and Valdez on the other. The rescued engineers stashed themselves behind fabricators.

"Zheng Lo is still out there," Valdez said, and then he yelled to the prisoner, "Get behind the pillar."

Zheng Lo glared in their direction, defiant, but he complied just in time.

A low boom rattled the glass strong room, but the walls held. A crack splintered the door from top to bottom. Inside the strong room, the cement floor kicked up dust. It seeped out of the top of the door and through the vertical crack in the door.

Janey sneezed at the dust and its bitter smell. Behind her, engineers coughed and sneezed.

Medical personnel shouted, "Get back. Cover up!"

Janey stalked over to Zheng Lo cowering behind a pillar. "Let's go."

Her hands shook, but she still managed to undo his cuffs and quickly reattach them behind his back. She glanced about for Valdez. He was talking to Hidalgo.

Janey caught his eye and motioned to go. Chief Milano rushed into the muddle of engineers being checked out by medical personnel and hurried to Hidalgo. He examined his wife and then hugged her.

After a moment, he glared at Zheng Lo, then he turned to Janey. "This the one responsible for almost killing our entire engineering staff?" He rushed to Zheng Lo, a menacing grimace on his face.

Janey nodded and shoved Zheng Lo toward the exit. "And a suspect for murder, Chief. I'd like to interrogate him upstairs."

Medical herded the engineers toward the exit,

handing out oxygen masks and speaking in low tones to a few engineers who were still coughing a lot.

Without asking, Kou, Dube, Ferreira, Shawhan, and Lane parted the crowd for Janey.

Chief Milano followed with his arm around his wife, who was gesturing wildly and looked close to tears.

Janey led Zheng out the machine shop front entrance, down the corridor to the service elevator, and into the elevator.

"Why did you try to blow up engineering?" Did Zheng know something about the structure of the station that she didn't? Was that why he positioned the bombs the way he did?

Zheng said nothing, he just stared at the grey recyclo flooring.

"Who are you working for?"

Zheng shook his head. "No one."

That was a start.

"Did you kill Jonas Haverhill?"

Zheng sighed.

The service elevator opened, and she led him in. Zheng watched his feet as he walked, shoulders slouched. By the time she'd brought him into the interrogation room, post-adrenaline heaviness made her feel like she was walking through mud. Her throat was scratchy and parched from the dust kicked up by the explosion.

She shoved Zheng Lo into a chair, locked his cuffs to the center ring, and left the room. He shouted something after her. She stepped back in. "What's that?"

"I want my lawyer." He glared at her, then glanced away.

Oh shit. That meant she legally couldn't question him anymore.

She stepped back out of the room, and Valdez met her in the corridor.

"What's wrong?" He reached out to her but stopped just short of touching her cheek. He dropped his hand as the chief hustled up.

"The tool he wanted Laura to make. What was it?" the chief asked.

"Some kind of key. I didn't get a good look." Janey nodded at the interrogation room. "He's requesting his lawyer."

"That will take a day at least to arrange. Go in there and find out why the hell he intended to blow up my engineers. What did he hope to gain?" The chief glared at the closed door of the interrogation room. "And find out if he killed Haverhill. Your evidence is circumstantial at best. We need a confession."

"Violate his rights, boss?" Janey lifted an eyebrow.

"He nearly sabotaged the station." Milano frowned.

"He did say it was his intent," Janey said.

"Why?"

"To get back at Schoeneman."

"Find out why. Talk to him. He doesn't have to reply. Use your observation skills." He gave her a hard stare. "I'll set a guard rotation on the room. You recharge and be back here in thirty minutes." Chief Milano huffed. "I have a meeting with Schoeneman in five."

"At least you can tell him we have a murder suspect in custody." She yawned, an aftereffect of the adrenaline. No matter how exhausted she felt, she had to get answers.

TWENTY-SIX

Moments later, Janey was back in her office and had unlocked the Haverhill murder files on her main wallscreen. The surf pounded on the wallscreen from across the room as the details of Haverhill's case swam before her eyes. She wasn't fit to work. She needed a short break from everything. She slipped across the hall into the conference room's tiny private break room, kicked off her boots, and lay down, covering her eyes with her arm. Then she set her internal alarm for thirty minutes. She really should go to her quarters—she yawned—but the small bed was so soft. She relaxed, drifted, but at fifteen minutes, she heard muffled deep voices on the other side of the wall in the conference room, like Valdez and members of her team. She sighed and slipped out of bed, put on her boots, and washed her face again to wake up. She joined them. Time to put the pieces of her case together.

Kou and Dube were there, with Lane and Shawhan. So were Soren and Valdez. They were talking beside the coffee, pastries, and sandwiches. Her stomach grumbled. It was lunchtime. She served herself.

Amelia. The young woman's input could be helpful here. Janey commed Ferreira to bring Amelia to the conference room.

She bit into a pastrami sandwich and cleared the wallscreen, then she rearranged the information.

"What are you doing?" Kou asked.

Before she could reply, Valdez jumped in. "I think she's setting the scene."

Janey nodded and eyed her team. "Guys, take your food and sit at the far end of the table. I don't want to intimidate our guest." She turned to Valdez and assessed him. "I'm having Amelia brought here. You've been on this case longer than I have. How will she respond to you?"

"I haven't met Amelia, but I've interviewed plenty like her." Valdez sat and wrapped his hands around his coffee. "I'll only jump in if needed." He spoke in a quiet tone, showing her how he'd appear to Amelia—subdued and non-threatening.

Janey finished her sandwich and contemplated the wallscreen. If Amelia could help her connect the dots, then maybe Zheng would talk with the right information presented to him.

Ferreira commed her from the other side of the door and said softly, "We're here."

Janey let them into the conference room.

Amelia peered around with wide eyes, noticing the three men not paying any attention to her. "Ferreira said you needed my help."

"I do, Amelia. Please sit."

Amelia sat at the conference table, in the same seat she'd taken two and a half days ago. Ferreira sat beside her. Janey pointed to a square on the board, the live video feed of Zheng Lo in the interrogation room. "Do you recognize him?"

Amelia paled and nodded, her shoulders hunched.

"Please state your answer, Amelia," Janey said.

"Yes," Amelia said in her small voice. Then she cleared her throat and said louder, "Yes."

"Did he kill Haverhill?"

Amelia studied the feed for a long time.

"Amelia?" Janey pushed.

"I already told you what I know, what I did," Amelia said.

"We need to hear it again," Janey said.

Amelia straightened and turned to Janey. "If I tell you what I know, will I get immunity from prosecution?"

"That isn't up to me," Janey said.

"Will I, Investigator?" There was strength in Amelia's voice.

Janey turned to Valdez and raised an eyebrow.

Amelia glanced at Valdez but spoke to Janey. "Who is he?"

"Orlando Valdez, a special investigator for the Sol Unified Planets Police Investigative Services," Janey said. "He's here to help."

Amelia turned to him. "Can *you* get me what I want?"

"That depends," Valdez said.

Amelia said nothing.

"I know what you've been through." He held the young woman's gaze. "I can't speak for my bosses, but if it comes to that, I will do everything in my power to reduce any sentence you might get into time served."

"I am not going to prison. That monster had it coming." Amelia tightened her fists at her side.

"Who? Haverhill?" Janey asked.

Amelia scrunched up her face as if disgusted. She was shaking. "Haverhill, of course."

Valdez jumped in. "I mean counting the time you worked against your will."

"Oh." Amelia sagged against the table in relief. "All those years, lost, stuck…"

"You didn't know any better," Valdez said.

Amelia eyed him, a sadness weighing on her. She turned to Janey. "I want out. I want that immunity."

"We're working on it." Janey glanced at Valdez, and he nodded.

"Now tell us again how you helped Zheng," Janey said.

Amelia straightened and faced the wallscreen. She spoke to Valdez, telling him how she'd used her tech to allow a man she knew only as Nancy's brother to get close to Jonas Haverhill.

"But only to confront him about where his sister was. He was certain Haverhill had met her, but he didn't tell me how he knew."

Valdez nodded.

"I swear I didn't know he would kill him."

"Do you know where he got the tea?" Janey asked.

"What tea?" the young woman said.

"What about the knife? Do you know how he procured the knife?"

"I don't know anything about that. All I know is that not one more woman should suffer at that man's hands or influence."

Amelia nodded as if she'd decided and turned to Janey. "Not one more woman."

"Would you be willing to sign an affidavit to your story of how you helped him and why?" Janey asked.

Amelia blinked at her, thinking over Janey's request.

To give her time, Janey turned to Valdez. "Anything else?"

Valdez shook his head and turned to Amelia. "I'd like to speak to you about your experiences—how you met Haverhill, that sort of thing, if that's all right?"

"Do I need a lawyer?" Amelia collapsed against the back of the chair.

"I am not charging you with anything or arresting you," Valdez said. "You've been through enough."

"Okay," Amelia said. "I'll tell you everything I know in exchange for sanctuary. Investigator McCallister said she could help me. You can help me too, right? I saw that look you two exchanged."

"Together we can help you. I assure you." Valdez motioned to his wrist comm. "I'd like to record our conversation."

Ferreira said to Amelia. "Mind if I'm here?"

Amelia shook her head. "I'd like that." Then she glanced at Janey's team at the end of the table.

"We'll give you space," Janey said to Amelia and approached her team. "They'll be out of your way."

The two men and two women looked up from their work.

"Boss?" Kou said. "What can I do?"

"Did you clear all the suspects? I didn't see your notes on everyone."

"Weird." Kou waved up his holo screen. "We put them in."

"Give me the summary," Janey said.

"We cleared everyone," Ferreira said. "Except for Zheng Lo, Laura Hidalgo, and three more guests we had little details on." The three who'd arrived on Schoeneman's jet.

"Thanks, Ferreira," Janey said.

"Team effort," Ferreira said.

Kou and Dube nodded, and Lane and Shawhan lifted a hand in acknowledgment. Janey turned to Soren. "Look in Zheng Lo's quarters for evidence to tie him to Haverhill's murder."

"Murder weapon." Soren nodded.

They didn't need a warrant or even Zheng Lo's permission to search his place after his actions in the machine shop.

"Thanks, Soren," Janey said.

"I'd like to assist with evidence gathering," Shawhan said.

"Good," Janey said.

Shawhan and Soren left the conference room, and Janey turned to Kou.

"We have the bomb case to wrap up." He straightened in his chair and gathered his lunch. "Dube and I can go to medical and interview the engineers for their reports of what happened down there—see if the suspect said anything and try to find a motive."

Lane cleaned up their lunch and said, "I can talk to Engineer Hidalgo and get her report. She's probably in medical too. Ask her about her whereabouts during the window of the murder."

"Yes. Good idea," Janey said. The rest of her team left the conference room as she set up her holo screen to prepare her questions for Zheng Lo.

What did he hope to gain by attacking the engineers and potentially sabotaging the station?

Based on what Amelia shared, he killed Haverhill over grief at the death of his sister. But she needed more evidence than just Amelia's eye-witness testimony. They needed the murder weapon.

TWENTY-SEVEN

"MCCALLISTER, WE'RE DONE HERE, FOR NOW," Valdez said.

Amelia was wiping tears from her cheeks; Ferreira's hand rested on her shoulder.

"I'll escort her back to her room," Ferreira said.

Janey came around the table to join them. "Thank you, Amelia, for your help."

"Do you know when I'll get to start my new life?"

"Not exactly. But we're working on it." Janey glanced at Valdez, who nodded. She'd started the sanctuary application but because of Amelia's involvement in Haverhill's murder, the chances of her acceptance was low.

"Thank you," Amelia said and left the room with Ferreira.

"Are you coming with me to question Zheng Lo?" Janey asked Valdez.

"I don't need to, unless you want me there. I don't think he's behind the human trafficking ring. Amelia's story parallels other women's stories, but her information..." His voice trailed off. "I still don't have any firm leads on who is behind all this, though I have my suspicions. I really need to talk to Wharton to get what he knows. Do you mind if I do that without you?"

"No, I don't mind, but I would like to see your findings. The more I know about Haverhill and his dealings, the more I can understand Zheng Lo's motives." Janey headed for the door. She turned back to Valdez. "When will you be taking Zheng Lo away for booking?"

"Tomorrow, if my message gets through to my boss." Valdez frowned at his comm. "You'll lift the lockdown?"

"As soon as I finish my one-way conversation with Zheng. And I'll ask Kim for an update into the communications issues." Janey waved a quick message to the office manager.

"Trying to get rid of me so soon?" Valdez asked softly.

She held his gaze. "No. Then again, yes. Twice now when I see you on the station, you're a precursor to a murder."

"Perhaps I have a nose for trouble, or I'm a crime magnet." He moved toward her, eyeing her lips. "Or maybe you're the real magnet."

Janey approached him until they were less than a foot apart and put a hand on his muscled chest.

"My work…" he said apologetically.

"I know."

"I couldn't comm—the job."

"I know. It's complicated, you and me." She wanted to lean into his heat, so she did.

"I like the sound of the you and me part." He wrapped his arms around her, strong and fierce, and he bent his head to kiss her, soft, exploring. The door opened and someone entered. Janey deepened into the kiss.

"Get a room, you two," said Kim, a smile in her voice.

Janey broke off the kiss but didn't move out of the embrace. Valdez lifted an eyebrow at her as if asking if she wanted to get a room. She smirked, broke out of his warmth, and spun toward the door. "I have a case to wrap up."

Kim smiled knowingly and then dove into her reason for arriving, speaking fast, a little flushed. "Thought you'd like to know that the damage Zheng Lo's bomb did was minimal. The engineers who were well enough documented the scene for us. I heard you were a rock star, Janey. Grace under pressure. Cleaning bots and a repair team are on it. But if he'd gotten away with his scheme—" She finally paused for breath.

"Has Schoeneman been briefed?" Janey asked.

"The chief is with him now. All he has all the engineers' accounts and the footage of the aftermath," Kim said. "He wants you there."

"I was about to speak to the suspect."

"I heard he confessed," Kim said.

"Not to the murder. Just the attempted bombing."

"He can stew for a bit more," Kim said. "The chief and Mr. Schoeneman await."

"You came here to tell me this? You could have commed."

"Something is odd about the comms. Some kind of interference. Can't find the source yet."

"Valdez's messages to his boss aren't getting through, either." Janey frowned.

"I was wrong before. Messages are being sent, but I haven't gotten a response, so maybe return messages aren't getting through," Valdez said to Kim. "Strange."

"No one else has reported such a problem." Kim waved at her comm. "Yes, there is definitely something strange going on. I'll look into it." She headed for the door, waving into her comm, her fingers flitting like a hummingbird.

"Where am I to meet the chief and Schoeneman?" Janey called out.

"I assumed the chief's office." Kim examined her holo. "That's strange. The message doesn't say."

Janey commed the chief, but he didn't answer. "I'll check his office."

"I'll check the biotags." Kim frowned at her comm. "I'm not getting any readings. That's not good."

Janey dashed out the conference room to two doors down and across the corridor. She stood in front of Milano's office door, but it didn't automatically open. He usually didn't lock his office during work hours. She palmed the pad, and the door snicked open. No one was there. She entered and circled the small room to behind Milano's desk. His screen was off, his dancing ladies still. Nothing flared as out of place. She blinked through the visual spectrum. Nothing popped. Janey scanned with her comm to be sure there weren't any further bio-electric or electromagnetic anomalies.

Nothing.

She rushed back to the conference room. Kim and Valdez were concentrating on their individual holo screens.

Valdez glanced at her, a question in his eyes.

Janey shook her head, no.

Kim gazed up too, frowning. "Something's wrong. I can't tell from here. I need to go back to my office to run a diagnostic on the comm systems." She rushed out of the conference room.

"I'll make sure Zheng Lo is still guarded and then track down the chief and Mr. Schoeneman," Janey said.

"Where will you look?"

"The kitchen, of course. Mr. Schoeneman would not pass up a chance to eat some of Chef Gina's amazing Sol-class cuisine." Janey left the conference room and hustled to the interrogation room three doors down.

Cho stood guarding the door. He nodded at her. "Investigator."

"Anybody in or out?" she asked.

"No, ma'am."

"How long have you been at your post, and who did you relieve?"

"I've been here thirty minutes, and I relieved Chief Milano himself." He peered at her as if she was a bit bonkers, but then he went impassive under her glare.

Janey headed into the observation room. Zheng Lo had his head down on the table and was breathing deeply as though he was sleeping. He'd keep. Janey exited the room.

"Is everything all right, Investigator?" Cho asked.

"Yes, fine. Don't leave your post for anything and don't let anyone else in to question him, except for me or Chief Milano."

"Of course, Investigator McCallister."

Janey continued down the corridor toward the casino. She passed through the front lobby, the soothing Mediterranean air lost on her, and entered the casino. She rushed past the raucous slot machines and headed for the bar, filled with midday customers watching a live space jet race on the enhanced viewer above them.

Janey caught Faizah's eye and motioned to the bartender that she was passing through into the kitchen. Faizah nodded and didn't break her rhythm of making and serving drinks. Janey hustled through the large storeroom and pushed the swinging doors into the bustling kitchen. She tracked past counters and stoves for the quiet of the office and knocked to enter. She couldn't hear an answer, so pushed the door open and stepped in. Chef Gina clicked away on her table-flat keyboard. The staccato filled the elegant office. Then a walkie talkie from the standard emergency kit squawked a code Janey didn't know.

"Gina?"

Chef Gina peered up, her brow furrowed. "What is it, Janey?" She glared at the walkie-talkie. "The comm system seems to be down, and I'm having to manually handle room and restaurant orders with emergency handsets. Right at lunch. I haven't even had the time to let Kim know."

"She knows. That's why I'm here. I'm tracking down Chief Milano and Mr. Schoeneman. I'm supposed to meet them, but I don't know where. The message didn't say."

"Weird." Gina eyed her screen. "Makemba just delivered two specials of the day to the Modern Day Private Suite, on the mezzanine. Suite One, I believe. With the order was Frederick's favorite drink and Daniel's too. Safe bet that's where they are."

It didn't surprise her that Gina was on a first-name basis with Mr. Schoeneman and Chief Milano.

"Thanks, Gina. I had a feeling you'd know." She turned toward the door and then glanced over her shoulder. "What are their favorite drinks?"

"Two whiskies on the rocks. Actually, they've requested another round. The order just came in right before you got here. I was going to give it to the floor staff, but I'll give it to you instead."

"Good. I can then announce the successful closure of the case."

"Great. Just tell Faizah you're picking up their

265

orders." Gina nodded. "You'll have to tell me about the case when the chaos dies down."

"I'm sure Kim will get the comm system fixed pronto."

Gina looked worried. "And just as this new batch of guests arrives. And Frederick wanted everything super special for them."

"More than usual?" Janey asked.

"Yes, there's a special banquet tonight."

"Where? He's not closing down the casino, is he?"

"No, he wants to connect the two private suites on the mezzanine."

"But one of those rooms is a crime scene."

"He'll want you to clean that up. I thought you said the case was closed. I need access in two hours. I would have told you sooner, but—" She shrugged as the hand radio beeped. "I need to get back to managing these orders."

"Of course." Janey left Gina's office, crossed the loud kitchen, strode through the storeroom, and stopped at the bar. She caught Faizah's attention, telling her she was there to pick up Schoeneman's and Milano's drink orders and asked for a tray.

She carried the drinks up the stairs, beside the bright green living wall, and stopped at the first door on the mezzanine level. She commed the chief. Maybe proximity would make the comm system work. He didn't answer. She raised her hand to knock, but instead, the door slid open without a sound.

Chief Milano met her at the door, surprise in his eyes. "McCallister, what are you doing here?"

"You requested me." She stepped into the suite. "I have your drink order."

Milano blocked her from going further with his portly

frame and a hand on her shoulder. "I'm having a private meeting."

"With Mr. Schoeneman. I know. You told me so." She examined him. He had strain around his lips, and his respiration rate was a little low. His breathing was too shallow. He was under stress and hiding something.

"I called her here," a deep, charismatic voice said. "Approach, Investigator McCallister." It was Schoeneman. His voice was almost hypnotic in its power. She'd not forgotten it, even though she'd only met him in person once before, at the end of her first murder case on the station three months previously.

The chief stepped aside, letting her enter.

Janey put the tray on the low table without bobbling the drinks and remained standing.

"Sit, Investigator," Schoeneman said. He was in a tailor-made Italian grey silk shirt, grey slacks, and real leather shoes. "I hear you caught the murderer and would-be station saboteur."

Janey sat on a plush armchair in grey with silver threads and pushed aside the footrest stool. The image behind Mr. Schoeneman was an aerial holo view of the dazzling skyscrapers of Hong Kong.

"We have," Janey said, holding the older man's piercing gaze. "I was about to question him, but he requested his lawyer. I have a witness who confirms he's the killer. And, well, I was there in the machine shop. My team and I interrupted his sabotage."

"Well done. I'd like to give you a raise."

Janey blinked involuntarily, and Schoeneman appeared grey-green for a half a second. She'd accidentally switched to the infrared setting. She blinked again to switch to normal vision. "Thank you, sir."

"I just need you to get the suspect off the station

now. You'll personally escort him to the Sol Unified Planets Security Police. I have a bonus for you. I understand your family could really use it." He smiled, sat on the table, and leaned toward her as if taking her into his confidence, bringing her into his exclusive inner circle.

Janey peered at him and glanced at Milano, who peered back at her, pale, but he gave her no sign as to what Schoeneman was up to. Probably had something to do with the new guests and the special reception. "Most generous of you, sir. If I may ask, what's the rush? It is against protocol, sir. And there's a Sol agent on board now who can escort the suspect."

"You may not ask, Investigator. Please proceed as requested. I want him off this station within the hour. Use my jet. The pilot is on standby."

TWENTY-EIGHT

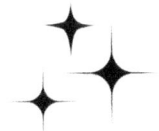

Janey eyed Schoeneman. He was calm, confident, and waiting as though his request was routine. Something was fishy, but she had to play along until she knew what was going on. "Yes, sir."

Standing behind Schoeneman, Milano had regained his color and nodded to her, and then he shook his head slightly. Was he disagreeing with Schoeneman's orders to release the suspect into Sol custody on the planet instead of to the agent on board? His disagreement, if it was that, surprised her. Her first instinct was to agree with the chief, but going against Schoeneman put her job at risk.

What should she do? Leave her post on L'Étoile and accompany the prisoner to Sol custody in New York? Or send him with Valdez? Did Schoeneman want her off L'Étoile for some reason?

If she did disobey his order, she could kiss the raise and the bonus good-bye, even though the extra money could help ease the exorbitant payments on her mom's next round of experimental drugs.

Milano had always followed Schoeneman's orders, yet in the space of less than a day, something had changed. Maybe it had something to do with the conversation she'd interrupted when she'd arrived at the door, but she had nothing to go on.

Still undecided, Janey turned on her heel and left the plush modern suite.

As she made her way down the stairs, past the SkyBar and the slot machines and into the lobby, busy with new arrivals, she decided that she had no intention of leaving the station.

Not yet.

She wanted to help Amelia. Plus, as the station's lead investigator, she didn't like the idea of leaving her post without having a suitable replacement, and there was no one who'd been trained for that yet. Schoeneman could keep his bonus.

She'd assign one or two of her team to go with Valdez and deliver the suspect into Sol custody. She would do as Schoeneman asked, partly, and make sure Zheng Lo was off the station within the hour.

First, she had to break the news to Valdez.

In the conference room, she expected to find him working. Then she remembered he'd gone to medical to speak to Wharton. Since the comms were down, she'd have to go there too and deliver the news in person that he didn't have until tomorrow to clean up his case.

She stopped by the operations office to check in with Kim. She was speaking into an emergency hand radio about checking the wiring in the wall ducts.

Janey passed the operations manager's front desk and made her way into the bullpen. Dube was typing at his workstation.

"Working on the report, ma'am, from the engineer interviews," he explained.

"Where's Kou?" Janey asked.

"Finishing up the Wharton interview in medical. He should be back soon. And Shawhan swung by on her way to Soren's lab to wrap up the evidence in the Haverhill case. That leaves Lane. She's still finishing up interviews with the engineers."

"Good job," Janey said. "I need to talk to you."

"What about?"

"I need you and Kou to deliver our suspect to Sol headquarters with Valdez and then get back here pronto."

"You need us to go?"

"Yes, extra security. The jet is ready to go within the hour."

"Overnight trip?"

"Only if you can file your reports before 4 p.m. station time. I need to wrap up all the reports for this case for the chief."

"Understood, boss."

She gave him a look.

"I mean, ma'am. But you are the one handing out assignments to us. Before you got here, Kim did it. But we never had to write reports." He sounded petulant. Then he glanced at her. "Sorry, ma'am." He straightened. "I can do better."

"I know you can." Janey didn't hear Kim talking anymore, so went to speak to her.

Kim looked exhausted. "I think I narrowed down the problem to the bomb you guys blew up in the strong room. It damaged some of the comm cables."

"And the receiving messages problem?" Janey asked.

"Your suspect probably did that when he planned to blow up engineering. This issue with comms took some planning. The station's receivers got knocked out of alignment. Engineers are outside on the station hull inspecting it and will fix it on-site—if they can. If not, they'll be taking another trip out there with the fixed parts."

The receivers were at the top of the station, connected to satellites in orbit.

"Pretty sophisticated. I wonder what Zheng Lo was really up to," Janey mused more to herself than Kim.

Then the hand radio squawked.

"That's your department."

Kim answered the radio. An engineer was reporting that the station's antennas had only been misaligned remotely, and they'd been able to fix the problem from inside the station. The visual inspection they did to be on the safe side had turned up no anomalies. She clicked off. "Well, that's good news. I'll run a test."

"Glad for it," Janey said. "I'll go talk to Zheng now, but he won't answer back. He lawyered up."

Kim said, "Good luck." She handled another hand radio call. Apparently, the comm system wasn't working yet.

Janey headed for the interrogation room.

"Anything to report, Cho?" Janey asked.

"No, ma'am."

Janey entered the room. Zheng Lo was still sleeping. She slammed the door shut.

He sat up with a start and glared at her. "Where's my lawyer?"

"He'll meet you at booking—at the New York Sol Police landing." She'd received the message on her comm just before leaving to find Milano and Schoeneman. At least one message had slipped in.

"When?"

"Soon."

Janey sat down and waved over her wrist comm and the tablescreen. "I'm recording." She stated her name and time.

"I'm not saying anything." Zheng Lo sat back.

"I know. I'm doing the talking, just so you know what you're up against."

Zheng Lo looked at her impassively.

"We're taking you shortly to the Sol Unified Police headquarters where you will be booked for one count of premeditated murder, thirty counts of attempted murder, two counts of tampering with private property, and one count of station sabotage."

Janey paused. He gazed back at her, showing no emotion. His vitals were steady, almost as if he were still sleeping. So different from the way he behaved in the machine shop.

"You're going to prison for a very long time," Janey said.

He said nothing.

She continued in a quieter tone. "I don't expect you to say anything. But know this—" She turned off her wrist comm recording.

He stiffened imperceptibly, but she saw it. His heart rate accelerated a notch.

"I will do what I can to find out what happened to your sister. Maybe she's still alive and was able to escape like Amelia did."

He shook his head. "I looked everywhere. Even I couldn't find her. And I have Level Ten programming and coding skills."

Another way of saying he was an excellent hacker, without actually admitting to anything.

"You disabled the station's antenna. Why? To prevent the Sol police from getting here? Muck up Earth-to-Station messages? What was the purpose?"

He firmed his mouth and glared at her but looked away as if he wanted to tell her but was preventing himself. It was common for people to want to confess. They wanted someone to know of their exploits. It gave them a sense of pride, sympathy, or relief. They often wanted to be known for their reasons or principles.

She gave him a moment, but he didn't say anything. Maybe he needed a nudge.

"I don't get it, Zheng. You don't have a criminal record. You're highly skilled, intelligent, and well paid for the work you do. What would push you over the edge like this? To murder someone? And to potentially kill over thirty more people—maybe even thousands more. You *did* damage property exceeding millions of credits in value."

Zheng Lo fiddled with his cuffs for a long moment, then he took a deep breath and lifted his chin. When he spoke, his voice was low as if he didn't have the energy to project. "My parents died last year. My sister was all I had. When I went to contact her about the news of our parents' death, she wasn't where she'd said she'd be. And then I questioned her friends and uncovered more lies. So, I tracked her around the world. She'd even been here on the Bijoux, six months ago. But her trail grew cold four months ago. Last I knew she'd been in the company of Jonas Haverhill. When I confronted him, he denied their relationship. I didn't believe it. Then I uncovered what he was really up to—trafficking women—and I tracked him here. Last night..." He stopped. "If my sister is gone, I have no more family. I am a lost soul." He lifted his chin. "I will say no more, Investigator."

"I understand, Zheng Lo. Family is important." She thought of her mother relying on Janey's salary to survive. But she also believed in doing what was right. That was sometimes at odds with following orders. "Sometimes we have to go to great lengths to defend our family. Even if that means doing what is wrong."

"So you understand—what I did?"

"I do, but that doesn't make it right. I honestly don't understand what you did in the machine shop."

"I told you. Schoeneman, that pompous ass, hides behind his money and power to do whatever he wants here. You work here. How can you not see it?"

"What people do in their private lives—"

"But he sanctions human trafficking—the trafficking of young women for sex. That is wrong."

"Yes, it is. I agree."

"And you do nothing? You still work for the bastard?"

Janey held his gaze. How could she work for such a man? Was Schoeneman really such a man?

He tapped the table. "Were you recording?"

"I wasn't. But this room is always being recorded."

Zheng Lo peered at her sadly, resigned.

There was a knock at the door. Janey opened it from her comm. Local connections were working. Kou and Dube were there, in formal uniforms.

Janey unlocked Zheng Lo's cuffs from the center hook and said to Kou, "Take him the back way to the jet."

"Understood, ma'am. And the Sol Investigator?"

"He'll meet you at the jet."

Kou grabbed Zheng Lo by the arm. Dube took his other arm and marched the suspect out of Interrogation Room One.

Her case was wrapped up. Valdez would be leaving soon too.

Janey's comm beeped. The system must be working again. "McCallister here."

"Meet me at Hanger Two," Valdez said and commed off before Janey could acknowledge or say anything else.

TWENTY-NINE

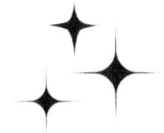

JANEY TOOK THE SERVICE ELEVATOR TO HANGER Two. Valdez wasn't in sight. Why did he want to meet her here when Schoeneman's space jet was parked at Hanger One?

The wide space was empty, except for a few technicians in jumpsuits punching buttons at standing workstations. One of them came toward her, grease and a grin on his face.

She puffed out a breath of recognition and called out. "Well, hiding in plain sight, I see."

Valdez grinned. "My specialty."

She pointed to her own forehead. "You have a smudge here."

"Sells the part, don't you think?"

Even with the grungy get-up, he was still the most attractive man she knew and wanted. She sighed. "So you're taking Zheng Lo back to New York?"

He nodded. "All we need is your final report and proper signatures by the time we land in two and a half hours." He moved toward her and peered hungrily at her lips and then at the crook of her neck. Then he took her in with a serious gaze, all business and something more. "A second ID and work pass to Mars will be waiting for Amelia."

"Thank you." Her chest heated, and she cleared her throat. "I'd better get to it." She turned to go, but Valdez stopped her with one soft word. "Janey…"

She turned back to him. His gaze magnetized, pulling her to him like a butterfly to the flower. She moved in for a kiss and didn't let him be gentle but pressed in to feel all of him, and she deepened the kiss into a wildfire.

He was the one to break it off, resting his forehead against hers. He panted. "We have to stop meeting like this."

"Where's a tool shed when you need one?" she joked.

"I want a bed and a week with you."

"Only a week?" Janey roamed with her hands on his back, his backside, and back up to run her fingers through his thick curly brown hair.

They heard voices in the distance.

"Duty calls," Janey whispered.

"I'll call you." Valdez caressed her cheek.

"I'll believe it when I see it." Janey moved out of their warmth.

Valdez nodded and turned away, a serious look on his face. He strode toward Hanger One, no promises on his lips, and no false hopes. Only wishes and passionate kisses left behind in his wake. If she'd had a quiet, stable life, if he had one too, then they'd have a clear chance. But they didn't have normal lives.

Ten minutes later, Janey was in her office writing up the report for both Milano and Valdez's offices. She was finalizing the report when she noticed a new message from Valdez. He'd sent it just before he departed. She opened it.

> Three new unhappy packages on the
> plane. Thank Milano for me.

Could Milano have gotten Schoeneman to give up three of his unknown guests—the three men who'd tried to abduct Amelia and then escape via the hangar? If so, thank the stars.

She waved a thank you back to Valdez. Then her comm pinged. It was Paula, head of hospitality, asking her to meet her at the StarEl lobby. Janey agreed and asked why, but Paula had already closed the comm.

Odd request. Janey hustled over to the sparse lobby for the space elevator where hotel and casino staff and asteroid miners regularly arrived and departed. Paula looked official in her all-black chic outfit, fine black heels, and iridescent teardrop earrings. Paula nodded at her as they stood shoulder-to-shoulder and waited for the space elevator to arrive.

Janey was about to ask for the purpose of her presence when the door opened and ten new faces strode out of the elevator, looking eager to get out of the place they'd spent five days in. Definitely, the slow way to get to the station, but it was the cheap way.

Paula greeted each one by name and shook their hands. One of them, a petite woman with a curved frame, handed Paula an envelope as they greeted. Paula handed that envelope to Janey while looking at the young woman. She finished greeting the group, and then she herded them toward the staff level.

In the emptiness of the StarEl small lobby, Janey opened the envelope and shook out the contents onto her palm. It was an ID bracelet and a small case that she knew contained an ID chip. A new identity for Amelia—good enough to get her through arrivals on the surface. One more thing was in the envelope. Amelia's contact on Mars. With these documents and the ID and pass Valdez provided, Amelia would be able to safely arrive at her new home.

She commed Ferreira to let her know she was on her way to see Amelia. The young woman would get her fresh start.

First, though, she checked the StarEl schedule. It'd be heading back down in two hours after it was cleaned and prepped for departure. Perfect. It was safest to get Amelia off the station through the staff exit.

———

LIKE CLOCKWORK, CHIEF MILANO COMMED HER at 5 p.m. for her report and her presence in his office. She'd already sent him and Valdez the report and was at his door as he commed. Not sure why she needed this face to face though. She was beat and ready to be off shift.

"I'm here, Chief."

He opened the door for her, and she stepped in and stood at attention before his desk.

"At ease, McCallister. Sit."

He glanced at his screen, scanning her report. She sat, waiting for the hammer to fall for the obvious reason that she was here and not on the space jet to New York, delivering Zheng Lo into custody.

Milano glanced at her through his old-fashioned spectacles. "I'll change the timestamp of the report to before the jet left."

"Sir?"

"Mr. Schoeneman knows a lot about a great many things, but nothing about how to run a security team." He tapped at his keyboard.

She didn't know what to say to Milano's admission that he was doctoring the report.

"Not my first time," he said while staring at the screen.

"Oh?"

Milano looked over the fake lenses at her. "You are doing a great job, McCallister. Keep it up. Dismissed."

"Yes, sir." Janey stood there for a moment, surprised at Milano's compliment.

"Anything else, McCallister?"

"No, sir."

Janey left his office. What was the point of the meeting? She'd never understand the need for administrators.

She headed to her quarters, took a shower, and sat at her work desk, fiddling on her holo screen with an upgrade to her comm-implant interface. Her comm pinged. It was Faizah wondering where she was.

"You're supposed to meet me for dinner to finalize plans for Kim's party," the bartender said.

"I am?" Janey eyed her schematics.

"Are you working in your downtime?"

"So?"

"Just get your butt down to the commissary and step away from your workshop."

"Fine." Janey closed her work and scanned her messy room. She'd deal with it later.

Five minutes later, she strode into the commissary. The room was dark, which was odd. Normally the room would be bustling with the dinnertime service.

The lights flashed on and her friends shouted, "Surprise!" Streamers dropped from the ceiling, balloons bounced off tables, and a disco ball drone hovered silently above them, casting rainbow sparkles throughout the room.

Kim came up to her and hugged her. "Well done, McCallister."

Ferreira shook her hand. So did Faizah, who hugged her too. The rest of the security staff was there, minus Kou and Dube. Mai Chen and her other friends from the kitchen were there, and many of the engineering staff were present, including Linda Hidalgo. And there was the chief, next to his wife, smug, a stein of beer in his hands. He raised it in salute to her and nodded.

Everyone was there, except for Valdez.

"How do you like your surprise party?" Faizah elbowed her.

"Well done, Faizah." Janey nodded and accepted the drink someone handed her.

Kim looped her arm around Janey's. "But he's missing."

"He has his job. I have mine." Janey sipped the cocktail, a Champagne Sparkler, to wet her tight throat. Her favorite drink—a little bitter and a little sweet. Like her life. She looked about at her friends and colleagues. She lifted a glass in salute to Chief Milano and then cleared her throat and passed the tears that lodged there.

Calls shouted out for a speech. She smiled.

"Thank you, everyone, for your help, support, and a job well done!"

Her friends cheered and saluted her with their drinks.

Janey threw back the remains of her drink in one gulp. "Let's party tonight, for tomorrow we work!"

Her friends laughed and shouted out their favorite hangover remedies.

Janey sat at a table. Her stomach growled. She was grateful for the plate of food Kim set in front of her.

"You have to stop forgetting to eat." Kim sat beside her.

Valdez would have booked Zheng Lo by now—and the three surprises. Amelia was on her way to a new life. And Janey had a whole new perspective on how this station was run. She didn't know if she liked the doctoring the reports part. But Milano was on her side, and so were her friends. She'd do all right.

But what about Christine's case? Why hadn't she heard back from Detective Verde? Were there more similarities about Christine's situation to Amelia's case, and what Valdez was working on? Had Christine stumbled across something that had gotten her killed? Why had Christine kept her true desires from Janey? Why hadn't she told Janey she wanted out of their good life in Granton SF?

Janey swallowed at the tears that wanted to flow.

Maybe Christine had been lured by light, lured by all that was out there in the wide Sol.

All anyone ever wanted was a good life. Why should she begrudge her friend from wanting something other than what she'd known?

One thing was for sure. She'd get to the truth of Christine's murder. She wouldn't give up. And she had her friends to lean on. She wasn't alone.

She smiled and wiped a tear at the corner of her eye.

"What?" Kim asked.

"Just that we make a good team," Janey said.

"It'd be better if Valdez was here too," Kim said.

"He's too distracting for anything longer than a day or two." Janey shook her head.

"You could use some more distraction, girl!" Kim nudged her in the shoulder.

"Oh stop." Janey dug into the roast beef, mashed potatoes, and salad. Perfect comfort food after an intense case. "What I need is to eat my dinner in peace."

Kim made to get up, but Janey stopped her with a hand on her arm and smiled. "And relax in the company of friends at the end of a successful case."

Kim smiled. "And talk about my birthday party tomorrow!"

Janey laughed.

―――

WOULD YOU PLEASE HELP OTHER READERS discover and enjoy Janey's adventures in *Lured By Light* by leaving a review on Goodreads or wherever you love buying books?

Then read on for a sneak peek of *Gone Green*, Book 3 in the Janey McCallister Mystery series, where Janey must discover who robbed the casino's vault, killed one security guard, and left another badly wounded.

GONE GREEN EXCERPT

CHAPTER ONE

INVESTIGATOR JANEY MCCALLISTER side-stepped the swirling cleaning bots in the staff quarters corridor and headed toward Chief Milano's office for the earlier-than-usual morning briefing. As she crossed to the security wing, a vibration rumbled up through the soles of her boots. Her heart fluttered. The space jet docking at this hour in the hangar shouldn't be felt three levels up in the security wing. What was going on? Something affecting the station's heavily protected generator?

She checked for incoming alerts on her ocular screen and wrist holo, but nothing beyond the night's security reports waited for her review. She also had the daily reminder to be back in her quarters in time to get her mother's morning vid call and check in on her mom's latest medical tests. The latest experimental treatment seemed to be working, for now. Thank the stars.

She commed Kim. "Did you feel that? Anything on sensors?"

"Checking..." Kim Iona was the security staff's office

and logistics manager, thankfully always at her post before anyone else in the department. A half a second later. "Nope. Nothing. Queried engineering. Will let you know if I hear anything." Kim took a breath, paused as if she wanted to say something. "You on the way to the briefing?"

"Yep. Know what it's about?"

"Nope. Sorry." A faint buzz in Kim's background. Probably another call coming in. "Gotta go."

Janey nodded, though the link was closed.

If it wasn't one thing, it was another. She didn't mind. That was the job. But still, she had to be on alert. Because the odd rumble could be anything, including the worst. That was why she'd amped up the investigator training for the security guards under her command. Ferreira was itching for the Level Five test at the shooting range in a few days, and at this hour, Lane would be training at the obstacle course in the gym. Both women had blossomed under her guidance.

In the last ten months stationed on Earth's preeminent space station hotel casino, Bijoux de L'Étoile, Janey had apprehended petty thieves, mediated staff squabbles, and caught two murderers. Anchored in geostationary orbit 22,000 miles above Earth, L'Étoile had many of the same problems of any small town. But because it was rated six out of six stars in the Xajak Review, thefts, squabbles, and murders cost everyone a lot more, including for the elusive and demanding owner.

As she approached the security chief's office, she checked her wrist comm reflexively for any last-minute update about the meeting, the odd rumbling, or anything else. The screen's messages hadn't change. Fine. Time to deal with what was right in front of her.

She entered the compact office and had several immediate reactions.

Irritation—what the hell was Orlando Valdez doing in her boss's office? The Sol Unified Planets special agent had no business on L'Étoile, that she knew of. Then intense desire exploded like a fire in her chest and lower—God, she still wanted the man like crazy, even though it was irrational, considering she hadn't seen him in person since their cases overlapped over half a year ago.

His wavy brown hair curled over his ears, a calculated carefree look. He lifted his chin at her, his intense gaze drinking her in, like a man too long in the desert.

But also anger heated her chest. Why hadn't he told her he'd be on the space station?

They talked on vid nearly every week, sometimes more. She commanded herself to take a cleansing breath and met his gaze with a bold one of her own.

He winked, cocky. He'd wanted to surprise her. Well, he'd succeeded. She clenched her teeth and ordered herself to relax.

The man was an itch she couldn't scratch away. Maybe she didn't want to. Maybe this time he'd stay for more than a few days.

"Good morning, McCallister." Chief Milano cleared his throat. "Agent Valdez is on indefinite loan from the Sol while he does work on his human trafficking case."

What? His case still wasn't closed? He'd been on it for over six months.

But she was getting her wish. He was on indefinite loan, here, on L'Étoile.

Then the next thing the chief said complicated things.

"He reports to you for all security matters. It's to your discretion on whether you need to clear any of his actions with me. Got that, Investigator?" Her boss gave her a hard look over his faux eyeglasses no one used anymore.

"Yes sir, Chief." Even though she felt Valdez peering at her, willing her to look at him, she kept her gaze on her boss. She'd officially be Valdez's direct report, his boss. They wouldn't be colleagues. She had to keep things professional between them then, if she was to follow regs. She had to follow regs, as always. This job was her mother's only financial lifeline.

"I'm sure you two will work well together, as you have in the past. Yes?" Milano lifted an eyebrow at her.

"We will, sir," Janey said.

"Chief Milano, it would be my utmost pleasure to work under the investigator," Valdez said smoothly, turning up the charm as he did so well.

Milano nodded at Valdez, then glanced over Janey's shoulder. "Good. Before we start the weekly briefing, Investigator McCallister and Detective Valdez, I'd like you to meet Ms. Veronica Ladipo, a journalist with *The Tell Papers*. She's here to cover next week's ten-year anniversary celebrations for the L'Étoile."

Janey spun around. A glamorous woman she hadn't noticed before was seated against the back wall. Valdez had filled her attention. She shouldn't let him do that. Not when she was on duty.

The journalist stood and reached out a hand to Janey. "Investigator McCallister, it's a pleasure to meet you." Ladipo held her gaze with striking green eyes, her dark brown hair, a halo around her head. "I'll stay out of your way as much as possible, though I would like an hour or so of your time this week to interview you and your team."

Janey shook her hand, at a loss for words. It was abnormal to have a working journalist on board. The space station hotel casino owner, Frederick D. Schoeneman, was a well-known recluse and never granted interviews to the press.

Valdez shook her hand. "A pleasure to meet you, Ms. Ladipo. I read your column regularly. I am one of your most ardent fans."

Ladipo gave Valdez a bright smile, pure joy, straightened the jacket of her bespoke black suit, and primped under his gaze. Most women did that around him. Jealousy flared in Janey's heart. She was helpless to the angry beast for a second, then recovered, and spoke.

"I'm surprised to see someone from *The Tell Papers* covering—" Janey waved her hand to indicate the surroundings.

"Social engagements and parties?" Ladipo said. "I know. Not my usual beat of writing exposés on despots, corporate greed, and industrial accident cover-ups. My editor thought it would be a good change of pace." She shrugged. "And I was curious to check out the Starry Jewel in the sky and hopefully meet Mr. Schoeneman himself."

"He knows you're here, I presume," Janey said.

Chief Milano cut in. "She's signed all the right paperwork, and Schoeneman let me know she and her camera crew were coming himself. He personally invited her."

"You have a crew with you?" Janey asked.

How Schoeneman ran his publicity was of no concern to her but bringing a nosy journalist and a crew on board could be a security risk. Why wasn't she briefed ahead of time or pulled in for the security screening?

"My film crew is waiting in the conference room to meet you," Ladipo said. "If you don't mind. Then we'll get out of your hair." Ladipo smiled, open and inviting.

Janey's hair was in a tight ponytail, but the journalist was nice enough.

"Thank you. The interviews will have to be later today." Janey glanced at Milano. "We have a briefing this morning and then staff training to continue. Perhaps after lunch."

"And we need to organize ourselves, our work arrangements." Valdez winked at her again.

Janey gave him a blank look, when she really wanted to glare at him. She tamped down on her anger that wanted to flare again. She didn't know if she wanted to kiss him because she missed him after not seeing him for seven months or smack him for keeping it a secret that he was coming to the station. Why hadn't he told her?

"I understand," the journalist said. "I'm here for the week. I look forward to speaking with you when you have the time."

"We will make sure you get your interviews, Ms. Ladipo," Milano said. "Please wait for us across the hall with your crew. Then I'll have someone give you a tour."

Ladipo stood. "I've already arranged that with house-keeping but would love the inside scoop for our B reel and—"

Whatever else Ladipo said was drowned out by a deafening high-pitched alarm that had the journalist slapping her hands over her ears, a wide-eyed look of shock on her face.

Through Janey's wrist comm, Milano's too, the high-pitched alarm blared off and on, blocking all thought for a split second. What tripped the alarm? Where?

Then the alarm stopped, but a red security code flashed on her wrist comm. She waved her hand over her wrist and the holo screen embedded in her wrist communicator flashed up. She stared at the screen, unbelieving.

Coming from a normally quiet part of the station, the red flashing code was unfamiliar at first. Then her ocular implant screen decoded it. Milano stared at his screen too, his normally ruddy complexion pale.

"We have to go. Now!" Janey bolted for the door. "We need all hands on this one."

Could be a false alarm, but she had to check it out.

"What is it?" Valdez asked, right behind her.

Milano swore under his breath.

"Ms. Ladipo, please excuse us," Chief Milano said, hustling his big frame around his desk. "Please wait for us in the conference room and stay there until I return."

"What is it?" the journalist said calmly.

"The conference room, please. And stay there," Milano insisted, stepped into the hallway, and turned to Janey. "McCallister, go. I'll call Soren and the others and meet you there."

"Yes, Chief." Janey burst into a run down the corridor to the staff elevator. Soren, the crime scene tech, and her security team would soon follow.

Valdez rushed into the elevator beside her. "Where are we going?"

Janey waited until the door closed and then glanced at him, fear tightening her chest. "The vault. It's a 10-33. An emergency. Needs immediate assistance. Officer down."

ACKNOWLEDGMENTS

So many people helped me create this book, the second in the Janey McCallister Mystery series. A huge thank you to all of you! It takes a village to create the world that lives and breathes in this book. Special thanks:

To my brother Sam Zoesch for his expert help in the pharmacological details.

To the experts in the Crime Scene Writers for their help in providing background technicalities, even if the world I have created is far from the realities they have lived.

To my Early Reader and Beta Reader teams: Beth Perry, Briana Burgess, Bob Morton, Carol Malone, Catriona Bain, Dodie Coe, Harland Monroe, Kay LaLone, Marilyn Lugner, Mary Van Everbroeck, Patricia Beaver, Sally Stackhouse, Shelly Small, Stephanie Thomas.

To my Patreon supporters: Chloe Adler, Elayne Griffith, Janet Patterson, and Lisa Boragine.

To F.S. for his support and interest and lending of his name for a character in this series.

To Leah Ellias, for asking me to do the honors of

naming a character after her husband who passed away in 2019. He would have loved it, she said. Thank you for the permission.

To my students for giving me feedback during our One Hundred-Word Critique classes.

To my first cover designer, the awesome Elayne Griffith, who helped me refine the cover concept and shape the book titles.

To my amazing, diligent, and patient critique partners, Patricia Simpson and Kay Keppler, for their support and encouragement and critical eye.

To my mastermind group, Leanne Regalla and Bonnie Johnston, for their moral support and cover feedback.

To my Blurb Babes, Lea Kirk and Tess Rider, for never ever tiring of refining my book blurbs.

To my proofreader, Paul Martin of Paul Martin Editorial, for his eagle eye.

To Dr. Peter Swan, International Space Elevator Consortium, who helped me with backstory on StarEl and encouraged me to insert the Apex Anchor, his creation.

A huge second thank you to Bonnie Johnston for her belief in me, amazing brainstorming sessions, and incredible tireless support.

And a universe-sized thanks to my husband and fellow creative nebula, Ezra Barany, for all the re-reads, edits, and more edits, geeking out on science right alongside me, and supporting my storytelling instincts every step of the way.

ABOUT THE AUTHOR

Award winning author, Beth Barany writes in several genres including young adult adventure fantasy, paranormal romance, and science fiction mysteries. Inspired by living abroad in France and Quebec, she loves creating magical tales of romance, mystery, and adventure that empower women and girls to be the heroes of their own lives.

For fun, Beth enjoys walking her neighborhood, gardening on her patio, and watching movies and traveling with her husband, author Ezra Barany. They live in Oakland, California with a piano, their cats, and too many books to count.

Sign up here for news on new releases and other goodies: http://bethb.net/lured.